MANMADE
CONSTELLATIONS

MANMADE CONSTELLATIONS

MISHA LAZZARA

BLACK STONE
PUBLISHING

Copyright © 2022 by Misha Lazzara
Published in 2022 by Blackstone Publishing
Cover and book design by Alenka Vdovič Linaschke

The characters and events in this book are fictitious.
Any similarity to real persons, living or dead, is coincidental
and not intended by the author.

Printed in the United States of America

First edition: 2022
ISBN 979-8-200-69675-8
Fiction / Women

Version 1

CIP data for this book is available
from the Library of Congress

Blackstone Publishing
31 Mistletoe Rd.
Ashland, OR 97520

www.BlackstonePublishing.com

"Well I know that human beings are unapproachable, that their souls are as far from each other as stars; only the remote radiance reaches to the other. I know that human beings are surrounded by dark, great seas, and thus they look across to one another, yearning but never reaching one another."

—**György Lukács**

"In that first stunning view it seemed as if the fireflies of a thousand summer nights had been gathered here, frozen forever in time and suspended among the stars."

—**Robert Burnham**

ELYSIAN, MINNESOTA

Lo pulled out the ad she had cut out of the newspaper, checking the address again. She fingered the paper's soft, jagged edges, the simple serif font, a small black box encasing the words: FREE CAR. 1333 FOREST STREET. PICK IT UP.

She breathed through her scarf, the inside wet with perspiration. The only sound, except her breathing, was ice crunching under her feet. All her attention was on the sidewalk, frozen and slick. One of the seams of her old boots had become unglued—her toes exposed to the frigid wind. Lo flexed her fingers in dirty white mittens and realized she could barely feel them at all.

As each year of her twenties passed, the cold permeated deeper and more permanently into her bones. She imagined herself freezing solid, enshrined forever on a barren sidewalk, never having left this town of eight hundred people situated squarely in the middle of nowhere.

So when Lo saw the ad in the paper, she decided that if she was going to survive another winter in Minnesota, she needed this car.

She had walked ten blocks from her duplex, one end of town to the other, and found herself on Forest Street with rows of rundown factory houses, long outlasting the factory itself. She was familiar with the street because it was impossible *not* to be familiar with every street in town, but she didn't know anyone who lived on it.

She stood under an unlit streetlight in the growing dark, staring at the house—1333 Forest Street. She wondered vaguely if she should be afraid. Is this what she had been warned about in elementary school? The free-candy-from-a-stranger scenario that mothers who bothered to stick around warned their daughters about? Single women on the street had been murdered in less suspicious circumstances than this, but nothing that exciting ever happened in Elysian.

A large porch spanned the left side of the house, and a single window with dark curtains framed the right. The screens on the porch had been haphazardly replaced with hard plastic sheets, cracked and mostly missing now. The storm door hung on its top hinge, and wind whistled through the gap.

She approached and knocked gently. Harder. Hardest. No one came. The door rattled. She pulled it open and walked onto the large front porch littered with garbage, mismatched mittens frozen solid in place, messy piles of junk mail. A thin orange carpet was burned away in spots. Cigarette butts lay frozen where they had singed small black circular holes. Lo felt the urge to clean up, to save what was useful and recycle what was not.

She raised her arm to knock when the front door flew open.

A woman in a red-and-green nightgown stood in the doorframe. She was old but not old enough to look as bent and brittle as she did. Her short hair was matted, gray at the roots and dark orange at the ends. She was pulling an oxygen tank beside her with a lit cigarette hanging out of her mouth. Lo looked at the tank, then the cigarette, then slowly backed away.

The woman read Lo's expression and laughed loudly, the sound tumbling out naturally at first but ending in a gag that turned into a wet, heavy cough. Lo backed against the broken storm door, and the woman's breath eventually calmed and somehow wheezed with a double frequency, a breathy sigh and a high-pitched whine.

"Don't worry, peach. It ain't as dangerous as folks believe. I can take the hoses out of my noses long enough to light up." She waved her hand dismissively.

"Okay, well, hello." Lo attempted to maintain some sense of decorum. "I'm Lois Gunderson. I live across town. I'm here about the ad in the paper." Lo suddenly felt the weight of this mistake—a stupid, pressurized, combustible mistake. If she blew up trying to get a free car from an old lady in the "bad part of town," her dad would never let her live it down. Even if she was dead, he'd find a way to ridicule her during her eulogy.

"*Mhm*, sure. Gunderson, you said—Jerry's daughter? Oh, I know Jerry, all right. I remember the day you showed up to town, as a matter of fact. Marcus and Jerry were friends." The woman bobbed her head as she turned around and walked into the dark house. Lo stood at the frame of the front door for a full minute until she had no choice but to follow the woman inside.

The walls of the dining room were lined with old newspapers, stacks of them pressed against each other. There were only two sources of light. One was from a TV she could hear around a far corner, the glow from an old game show emitting sepia shadows. The other came from a Christmas tree that she almost ran into when she turned the corner into the living room. Half of the lights were dimmed, some burned out. Several rows hung dark and cold, while others blinked in a melancholy tempo. The decorations were visibly collecting dust and matched the era of the game show. The plastic needles were paper-thin, threatening conflagration with each passing moment.

"Yes, I'm Jerry's daughter. I saw your ad. It sounds too good to be true, at least that's what my dad would say, but I thought I would just walk down and"—she paused for a minute, mindlessly brushing dust off an ornament with her finger—"check."

Lo felt like she should turn around and walk back out the door. But she didn't. She just stood there, warm in the cluttered house, transfixed by the old tree.

"You're here for the car? Why didn't you say so?"

Lo didn't respond. She glanced around the house for an answer. She noticed a few photos on the walls. School pictures of a single child, a boy. Suddenly she realized the old woman was shuffling outside with nothing on but her quilted muumuu and slippers. Lo hurried behind her and carefully shut the door.

The woman walked into the street, lugging her oxygen tank over the bumpy sheets of ice, and stood next to a giant pile of snow, smiling close-lipped, her eyes squinted in a mix of mischief and graciousness, as if she were the bearer of either great fortune or even greater misery. Lo noticed the woman's bloated belly as she walked beside her stretched shadow cast by a far-off streetlight.

"She won't start, but there's a shop down on the corner—Jeff's. Skip down there and tell one of them boys to come over here with some tools, and you'll have her running in no time. Pretty sure it's just a spark plug, maybe the starter." The woman attempted to brush snow off the windshield with the hand that wasn't clinging to the oxygen tank. "Hell if I know, but I'm sure it don't need to be sitting here uglying up the place. We'll discuss payment once we get her going."

"Payment?" Lo shook her head meekly.

She considered explaining to the woman that she was what some might call a *freegan* but doubted that word would mean much to the woman. It didn't mean that much to Lo either, except that it helped explain things. Things like: *I'm attempting to escape the oppressive capitalist system that creates mindless laborers out of living, feeling human animals*, and other things like: *I no longer want to live on my dad's dime, but there are very few meaningful work opportunities in Elysian.*

She tried a different approach. "Well, the ad said it was free. I don't have money to pay, and I don't—I prefer to find things for free, when available, because people throw so much away." She always felt a little ridiculous explaining things that she knew would sound crazy to people around town.

The old woman stopped brushing snow with her bare hand and looked at Lo inquisitively. She made a humming sound, hunched over and presumably freezing cold. "You sound like someone else I know— my son out in Idaho. Well, don't worry. It's free enough, if you're talking about money. I only need a favor. You would do a favor for a sick old lady, wouldn't you? I can tell that you would. They call me Blanche, by the way . . ." She stopped to take a breath. "Among other things."

TWIN FALLS, IDAHO

When the farm was quiet in the early morning, Jason and Alexis would make love. She would say something like, "*Mm*, let's make love, lover," and Jason would smirk because he knew *that she knew* that he would make fun of her for talking like a character in one of the romance novels that she read.

Her love of the genre had been passed down from her mom. Rows of them lined the shelves of the one-room yurt they shared on the farm outside of Twin Falls.

There were muddy boots and tennis shoes lined against the wall, coveralls hanging from hooks, some clean sneakers that he would never wear in the fields, and a pair of heels that put Alexis an inch above Jason. Two upholstered chairs and a coffee table faced a small TV. Behind the chairs was their bed, pushed against a lattice wall. Heat blew irregularly out of the electric furnace while the weather grew warmer as March rolled through.

This was all Jason needed. He'd worked on a lot of farms before this one, and so he knew that this yurt hidden in a stand of pines next to a cold, clear creek was enough, as long as Alexis was here with him.

Sometimes the old man with a thinning gray mohawk who worked with them—he told everyone to call him Giuseppe, even though literally no one believed that was his real name—knocked on the door and asked if they wanted some of his breakfast. Jason would yell, "Just a minute," and they would take their sweet time.

The past few weeks, Alexis had been suggesting that they look into getting their own land or finding more permanent work, so when she brought it up again that morning, Jason wasn't fazed. She was just getting the itch. This was the longest either of them had stayed on at any job.

She sighed. "I'm just saying, you have a degree you're not using. You could find a decent teaching job in the valley and help me do some farming on the side. They have a Black Farmers Market in the area, and we can get featured in those magazines that are finally starting to pay attention. My mom sends me screenshots of all the articles."

"Oh, wow, it only took a hundred years of destroying Black land management before people started to care—and I've told you repeatedly how much I hated teaching."

"I know." She was lying in bed on her back, waving her hands to keep him from getting sidetracked. "I know that, J. But I'm feeling motivated. I can fill out all those forms and find the right people. There is finally stuff going on—the Justice for Black Farmers Act, grants—all kinds of ways to find the money."

"Oh, yeah, I bet. There's money lying around everywhere for people to buy land in California. Do they give you all the equipment and farm it for you too?" He didn't understand why they had to keep having this conversation and getting nowhere with it. If there was anywhere they could not afford to live, it was California.

She rolled her eyes at him. "We can make it work. I don't know. I miss home. I miss my mom and dad. It might be nice to settle down. I'm not getting any younger, you know."

He smirked. "Oh, yeah? What does that say about me then?"

"That you're old as shit, I guess." She laughed silently, like she had said something truly hilarious, and squeezed his shoulder hard.

"J, I'm happy—us, together—like this. Just not here in this leaky yurt." She pressed her hands flat on the mattress. "It was fun for a few years, but we're grown people now. Let's do something for ourselves. Is that too much for a woman to ask of her man?"

"I've been *grown* a lot longer than you, and I promise, this is a grown-up job. I like this leaky yurt. A lot better than the funky-smelling dorms in Big Sky. At least we have a door here to keep Giuseppe out."

Alexis sighed again, heavier than the last one. Then she got up, filled the electric kettle and poured a few scoops of grounds into a French press. She put both hands on the counter and took a deep breath. He frowned, confused why she suddenly seemed so unhappy.

He watched her there. She was as tall as he was, near six feet, and he knew her parents had pushed her to play any sport that she would take to—which ended up being none. They had that in common. Just like Jason, Alexis had preferred to spend time outside without the pressure of competition. Just hands in the dirt, watching the plants grow, doing their own thing.

But right when Alexis turned to face him, he understood what was happening. The revelation hit him out of nowhere. His first thought was *how did this happen?* But that was a stupid question. Jason knew exactly how that shit tended to happen. He knew what was going on without her having to say it, but then she did. "Thing is, J, I'm pregnant, and I need to know what we're gonna do about it."

His second thought was intrusive and came in a flash. An image of his mother wobbling, drunk, standing over his father's grave all those years ago.

ELYSIAN, MINNESOTA

It was not quite six but already full dark when Lo watched Blanche head back into her house. Lo set out unsteadily down the street and around the block toward the auto shop. She hoped it was still open, so she wouldn't have to repeat this whole process again tomorrow. It was possible Blanche might not even remember her if she came back the next day; Lo had no idea what to expect from her.

Fresh snow reflected the lights of the city, everything glowing red with taillights, and then the green, yellow and red of the town's one stoplight, which had taken years of city council arguing and a suspiciously large hike in taxes to install. The snow also reflected the humming neon sign that blinked ON SALE/OFF SALE LIQUOR of the town's only bar.

There was something comforting in the reflections, and if not beautiful, then at least a change of scenery. It didn't last long, though, and eventually turned into used-up slush, gray with muffler dioxide, dog shit and dirty boot prints. At least fresh snow covered an ugly street littered with random snow-shaped garbage.

She glanced into Lefty's Bar and recognized everyone inside. Jonas Olafson, who ran a tidy family farm on the edge of town. Lo had been in the same grade as his grandson, Tyr. She liked the old Norwegian names that people gave their kids, even if she doubted their heritage was more Norwegian than anything else—British, Irish, German, Swedish. As far as she knew, everything in town was an equal mix of the same ingredients. Besides, Tyr was a jerk. He had mostly ignored Lo in school and did inane things, like make fart noises with his armpits and shoot spit wads out of plastic straws. She wondered what had become of him. In the very least, he had succeeded in getting out of town. She, on the other hand, had not.

When Lo finally looked up from watching her feet move slowly on the ice, she laughed. The repair shop was called Jefe's, not Jeff's. Apparently, just like Blanche, Lo had never looked closely enough to read the name correctly. She had an excuse for never noticing, though. She'd never actually had a car.

She had to duck low to get under the partially opened garage door and was met with a quiet chorus of car-shop noises: electric whirring, gears being tightened, metal on metal. Somewhere a radio played what she thought was mariachi music, and she heard men speaking Spanish to each other.

No one noticed her until she cleared her throat loudly. An older man in a blue mechanic's outfit hurried over from under a raised car and shook his head. "Sorry, no customers back here. Go through shop door, please." The man was of Latin descent, and Lo scolded herself for only a few minutes ago assuming everyone in town must be the same mix of that Northern European amalgam. It wasn't true.

"Okay, it's just that I have a strange question that might sound crazy and—"

The man shook his head. "No, sorry, no customers here." He moved his hands in the opposite direction toward a door with small black letters that read LOBBY. "John will help you."

He escorted Lo to the door that opened to a small waiting area with gray linoleum floors, fronted by a wall of windows that overlooked the street. A man stood at an old computer, clicking a mouse. He made a confused expression when he noticed them coming from the garage. The older man nodded toward Lo. "She needs help, I think." He raised his eyebrows, shrugged and went back to work .

"Sorry, just give me one minute," the man behind the counter said in a southern accent, a deep voice that caught Lo off guard, not quite matching his age or appearance. His hair was the darkest shade of brown before black. He pushed it away from his forehead as he looked down at the computer. Pale irises reflected the light of the screen as he clicked the mouse on the small laminate counter. He was tall and not exactly thin. It was actually the same physique most of the men around town had, like he had just worked on the farm all day, stopping from time to time to take drinks of raw milk out of the bulk tank. But she had no idea if there were dairy farms in—wherever he was from, and she definitely didn't know anyone else in town with an accent like that.

"You need a mouse pad." She couldn't think of anything else to say. He nodded and gave a polite smile without looking away from the computer. Lo wrapped herself up in a hug and examined the lobby while she waited for him to finish. It was as cold in there as it was in the open garage. Finally, he looked up at her briefly.

"Sorry, we don't use the heat much around here. Not much of an exhaust system in the garage, so, fumes," he stammered before he stopped talking altogether. He seemed flustered, probably surprised to have a customer this late on a Friday night. "The owner figures it's safer to put on a coat than asphyxiate."

The man gave her a shameless once-over, drawing his eyes from her old hand-me-down winter boots, over her tie-dye spandex pants that flared at her feet and were tight around the hips and across her permanently stained puffy coat and her hair, wild like always. She knew what he was thinking—she was a mess, probably a hippie, and at the very least, *definitely* weird.

"Yeah, that's okay. I'm used to the cold." Lo felt herself flush. She looked out the window toward the bar across the street. "Your accent surprised me. You don't hear many accents around here."

He looked into the garage and nodded slowly. "People here have accents. *Especially* you."

Lo was vaguely aware she had a Minnesota accent but couldn't hear it. She only knew what it sounded like when people made fun of them— long, nasally *o* sounds, particular attention to holding vowels and an inflection at the end of words that made everything sound like a question—everything sounded just a little more polite that way.

"Yeah, right, well I guess I meant southern accents. The guys working in the garage have accents because English isn't their first language."

He raised his eyebrows at her and scratched his head, staring at her for a minute. She didn't know what to say. Was it rude to say that English wasn't their first language? She realized she didn't even know if that were true. Plus, she only spoke one language and apparently had a thick accent, at that. Her hands were still frozen, but she started to sweat under her down jacket, her neck felt hot with her hair wrapped into her scarf.

"Did you need something? I mean, did you bring a car here for service?"

"What?" She had completely forgotten why she was there.

"I'm assuming you're here for a reason. Can I help you?"

She nodded her head slowly. "*Mhm.* I mean, yes. I hope you can. See, what I need might sound a little strange."

He laughed then. "Should I be worried?" His accent still held her attention. The cadence was so different from the way most people talked in Elysian.

"Sorry, it's been a weird night." She heard the extended *o* vowel in her *sorry* and felt self-conscious. "The thing is, my car—well, *a* car—won't start. It's only down around the corner on Forest Street. I was wondering if you, or someone who works here, might come look at it and give me an estimate to fix it."

He rubbed the back of his neck. "We don't usually do that sort of thing. There's a tow company in town, just a guy with a truck, really—Luke Olafson, you probably know him. I'd be happy to call him and have it brought in."

"No," she said, too loudly. "No, it's okay. I'm actually broke, and I'm getting a very good deal on this car, so . . ." She faltered, unsure what to do next.

He looked down at the computer. "I'm not sure my boss would

let me leave. I'm finishing up the paperwork for the night. We close at seven."

Tows were probably expensive, even just for a couple of blocks. She didn't want to deal with all that for a free car that might never run. As she stood there in the cold office, still sweating from the awkward exchange earlier, the mechanic from the garage came back into the lobby. He glanced quickly at Lo while saying something in Spanish to the man behind the counter. They talked for a minute, looking at her from time to time, her cheeks burning red.

She was trying to follow the conversation by reading their body language when the older man laughed. "No, hombre. That's not what I said. I said, 'you never do anything at night except go home and eat meals from your microwave. So, go help her.' You need more practice on that Spanish app of yours—I don't think it's working."

"No," Lo blurted out, confused about what was happening between them. "I'm sorry, I shouldn't have asked. I know this is strange. I'll find someone to come look at it tomorrow. Sorry to bother you."

"No, it's okay," the older man said. "John does nothing but work, so he'll go with you. It's okay. He'll bring his tools for an easy fix or give an estimate for repairs. It's all good. We're open until seven, so you have time." The man offered a small professional smile, but his eyes seemed to be laughing.

Lo looked over at John. He was looking down as if he were inspecting the keyboard, his lips pressed together. Finally, he glanced up at Lo, put on a weak smile and told her he would be back with his tool kit.

Alone, she rocked back and forth on her wet snow boots for a minute, then casually walked over to the screen to see what he had been working on. It was a complicated spreadsheet filled with what looked like the cost of repairs or something. She couldn't figure it out, but the boxes full of figures impressed her in some small way.

She was still trying to make sense of the screen when John returned with a brown canvas bag filled with what Lo hoped were tools and not murder weapons, suddenly aware that she had just invited a stranger to walk her down a dark street at night.

"Find any mistakes?"

"Oh, god, sorry. I can't help myself sometimes. Curious by nature."

He lifted a shoulder. "Just back-office stuff. Want to lead the way?" He held his tool kit with his left hand while zipping his jacket up with his right.

Lo nodded, flustered, and pushed the door open. "Thanks for doing this. I'm sorry it's so late. I'm Lois, by the way, but people call me Lo. I'm hoping it's an easy fix. But if not, I was wondering if you offer payment plans, or . . . ?"

"Let's just take a look, and we'll go from there. Make and model of the vehicle?"

Lo was quiet. She was still sweating in her coat even in the frigid air. "*Uh*," she drew the word out a little too long. "I'm not exactly sure. See, I'm getting it for free, and it's been sitting on the curb for a while. Let's just—we're almost there, it's like two blocks away, around the corner on Forest."

She didn't know John and would probably never see him again after the car was fixed, so she told herself not to worry about what he thought of this whole debacle. Still, she felt increasingly embarrassed that she was dragging him out in the cold and that Blanche had convinced her so easily of this plan, all to get a free car that would probably cost more money just to get running than it was worth.

They walked for a minute in silence. Lo hated small talk, but not as much as she hated awkwardness. "So, you're not from here, are you?" she asked, hoping they could talk about anything to distract from how peculiar this situation must seem to him.

"I'm from North Carolina. My uncle and his family live here, though. That's why I came." He breathed into his cupped hands, attempting to warm himself.

"God, you must regret coming to this frigid wasteland. Who is it? I might know them."

"The Blanks. I don't regret it. This is a decent place, good folks."

"The Blanks?" She scoffed. "Funny name. Any kids?"

"Randy, but he'd be older than you."

"How do you know how old I am? Everyone thinks I'm younger than I am."

"All right, well, he's in his midforties. You that old?"

"Maybe," Lo responded.

He stopped walking for a minute and cocked his head. "Something else you don't know? This whole setup is feeling kind of strange. Is this some kind of Craigslist scam or something? Are you planning to eat me for dinner tonight?"

She looked down at the uneven ice covering the ground in front of her. "I'm not sure. I mean, no. I won't eat you. But I'm not really sure whether this is a scam or not. Listen, I know this all seems weird, and it is, because I'm getting this car free. There was an ad in the paper. It's . . ." she hesitated for a minute, "important to me that I don't *buy* a car. Anyway, here we are!"

She tried to sound cheerful as she held out her hands toward the pile of snow parked on the street in front of Blanche's house.

John walked toward the car. She glanced over at him while he took in his next job, encased under a thick layer of ice. He was maybe a foot taller than her—hovering somewhere above six feet. Lo wondered if he was married (no ring), if he still lived with his uncle, if he thought she was a crazy person. Wouldn't have been the first time someone thought that.

He looked from the car back to Lo. She smiled at the car, still holding her hands out toward it like a game-show prize, just as Blanche had done earlier.

John pushed a breath out, and she watched the condensation form in the air as he exhaled. She avoided eye contact. He set his tool kit down gently next to his boots and breathed into his hands a few times. "All right, open up the hood, I guess. I'll take a look at it."

Lo held up a finger in her mittened hand and ran back up to the screen porch. She only hesitated a second before she opened the storm door, ran through the porch and knocked on the heavy wooden door to get the keys. Blanche peered around her shoulder, squinting, trying to get a look at John through the broken sheets of plexiglass that lined the porch.

"Tell that boy to put on a hat on. It's cold as hell. I got an old one of my son's lying around," Blanche said as she stood in the doorway with her oxygen tank, the heat from the house pouring out. Lo told Blanche that he was probably fine and that she would let her know if the car started. "You tell him to come in too. I'll pay him for his work. You both come in and we'll discuss it."

Relieved by Blanche's offer to pay, Lo ran back toward the car, conscious of how cold John must be standing in the street waiting for her. She brought the keys over and tried to hand them to him. He just looked at her.

"What? What's wrong?" she asked.

"Is there a shovel to dig this thing out?"

"Oh, right, you aren't from here. Hold on." She laughed awkwardly, frantically attempting to crack open the driver's side door, which took a gentle and then harder kick to break the sheet of ice that was holding it in place.

"Been here quite a while, still never seen a car this frozen solid before. Can you pop the hood?" he asked.

Lo bit her lip. She decided she wouldn't even pretend she knew how—it would only waste more of his time.

"Well, if you aren't just a damsel in distress."

"Look, I know this is a little unconventional, but Blanche, the lady who lives here, said she'll pay for the repairs. I appreciate you coming here after hours. Sorry I'm not more help." Thoughts kept running through her mind, but she stopped talking. It wasn't like she was marooned on the side of the road. She went to the shop and asked for service, and John's boss accepted the job. Her face felt suddenly hot against the subzero wind.

He unlatched the hood and worked to pull it open, but ice had settled into the cracks. After a minute of watching him pull, Lo walked over, shooed him away and slammed her fist on the seams of the hood as hard as she could. On his next try, the hood swung open when John clicked the hidden latch. He handed her a flashlight, which she held unsteadily while she rocked back on her boots. He seemed to jiggle a few things around. She was still thinking about how she could prove to him she wasn't a damsel in distress when he crossed behind her, sat down in the front seat with the door wide open and turned the key in the ignition. The engine started on the first try.

"The ad said the car was free," Lo murmured quietly, pulling her mitten off with her front teeth as they huddled near the door. She tried to reach for the ad folded in her coat pocket, but her hands were too cold to grip it. The house was dark except for the light of the dimly lit Christmas tree around the corner. John stood slightly stooped with his hands in his pockets, staring at the floor awkwardly. The snow melted in a puddle around their feet and the base of the oxygen tank as Blanche stood in old wool slippers and waved her hands.

"It is free. It is. How 'bout this? You guys head back here for dinner tomorrow night. I bet this fella needs a home-cooked meal. We can figure his payment and yours." Before Lo could say anything, Blanche waved her hands again. "Oh, heavens—I don't mean money. I just need a favor from youse." John lifted his eyebrows but only scratched the back of his head. He seemed to be scrutinizing the house.

They stood near the dining room table that Lo had noticed earlier. It was covered in mail, dirty dishes, ashtrays. There were a dozen circulars full of coupons that had been ripped out, shreds of them lying around the table and floor. The six chairs around the table were all pushed in and framed by the columns of newspapers stacked against the walls. There wasn't a clean spot to sit and eat.

Lo responded, "Sorry, I have to work tomorrow. I'm only here now because the weather shut us down tonight."

"I have to work too," John said quietly as his eyes swept over the rooms of the house they could see from the entryway. Behind the dining table was an open doorway to the kitchen. There sat a small table, cleared for eating, with only one chair.

"Well, all right then—come over on Sunday evening at five. I eat early. Or do you kids work on Sundays too?"

"Only in the morning, ma'am, but you don't owe me anything since it was just a spark plug. It's my pleasure. So—"

She cut him off. "Well, what do we have here? What's this accent? You a rebel?" The room seemed to be getting darker, and Lo wondered if more of the lights on the tree had burned out as they stood talking.

"I come from North Carolina. But you don't need to worry about paying me anything. It was no trouble."

"Well, at least let me feed you supper. I don't like to owe nobody. Sunday at five. Don't be late. I get stomach troubles if I eat too late." Blanche caught her breath in loud gasps as she opened the door to let them out before Lo had a chance to protest.

A NIGHTMARE

For a moment she was experiencing childhood. In the next, she was a grown woman watching at herself as a child. She ran barefoot in a backyard, tumbling through the grass, laughing as dusk turned into evening then faded to dark. Patio lights were strung through the trees above her. Fireflies started to blink and a mason jar appeared in her hands. A miracle, a task. She looked down at the jar and smiled.

She ran through the grass with one hand held in front of her to catch lightning bugs. Did she feel the dewy wetness of the grass? Did she feel the cool night air against her skin as the sunlight disappeared? It wasn't until the jar was full of captive constellations that she realized it—no holes had been punched through the metal of the lid. She knew that if she didn't open it and free them, the fireflies would fall to the bottom of the jar and suffocate.

The truth: things kept captive had no room to breathe. She struggled, but the lid didn't budge. The string lights above her started blinking out, the night darkened. She clutched frantically at the lid, at one moment a child, at others a woman. The lid refused to open. The lights above her blinked dim, then brightened, then exploded in showers of glass.

ELYSIAN, MINNESOTA

Snowmelt rushed down the storm drain in front of Lo's duplex. She had to leap across it to reach the driver's side of her new car. As she unlocked the door, she heard her neighbor's screen door creak open. A voice called out to her from across the street. "Good morning, Lois!"

"Good morning, Mrs. Carlisle!" Lo yelled back. She held up one hand in a wave and managed to drop the keys into the muddy drainage stream below. "Shit."

"What was that, honey?"

"Nothing, Mrs. Carlisle. Hope you're surviving this never-ending winter!"

"Spring's around the corner, dear!"

"Sure it is," Lo murmured as she turned the dripping wet key and finally got the door open.

Even though she rarely drove, she had been sure to send in the form to renew her driver's license just a few weeks ago. May would mark the ten-year anniversary of getting her license. The extent of her driving practice since then was taking Parker, her boss and closest friend, home drunk whenever the situation called for it. So, while she was a legal driver, she felt unsure of herself behind the wheel, as if she weren't exactly qualified for the task.

Lo had walked to the Salvation Army dozens of times, but driving felt different and somehow more limiting. She couldn't cut through the back alley of the thrift store like she did on foot, so she drove around the block a few times to find a parking spot with no other cars remotely nearby.

She wished it was garage sale season, but that was months away. Most of the old women in town knew her, and they usually ended up giving Lo whatever she needed, either for free or for just a dollar or two. Of course, they talked among themselves at the Teakettle, at Lefty's, at the VFW.

One time, Lo had spent ten minutes explaining to Jean Little, a friend of her father's, that she tried not to use money to buy things, preferring things that were discarded by others—that she was what was some people called a "freegan." After Jean confirmed that did not mean "communist," she smiled kindly and then went ahead and told the whole town through a game of telephone. Now everyone knew some version of the story—whether the story was that Lo was very poor now because her father had cut her off, or that she was still going through that teenage rebellious phase (never mind that she was in her midtwenties), or that she was, indeed, an actual communist—it did end up getting easier for Lo to acquire things she needed without having to spend much money.

Elysian was full of gossips; it was one of the few pastimes the town offered. Sometimes she could use this to her advantage—like when it came to getting what she needed for her house. Other times, it stung.

She knew everyone in town had gossiped relentlessly after she was born, when her father brought her back to Elysian. She heard bits and pieces of all the stories through the years, which ranged from the fantastic (he found her in a dumpster), to the tawdry (her mother was an escort), to the tragic (her mother had died in childbirth).

No one but her dad knew the whole truth—not even Lo. All she knew about her mother was that she had been very young when Lo was born and had chosen to let Jerry raise his daughter on his own. Beyond that, he wouldn't divulge much, so Lo had learned at a young age to ignore the gossip around town and get on with her life.

Jean and her friends would save things for Lo under their collapsible card tables during rummage sale season. A casserole dish, an ancient olive-green Crockpot, a wooden-framed picture of a blue-eyed, blond-haired Jesus with a baby lamb.

The retired librarian, Marta Davis, centenarian age, regularly went through her bookshelves and found anything she thought Lo might find interesting. Many of the books were, in fact, fascinating and educational, as Marta had collected texts spanning topics from psychic healing to natural childbirth to Indigenous books and books on the Native history of Minnesota. Marta had bequeathed the lot of them to Lo, and they had shaped her late teens and early twenties in meaningful ways. It was then that she first discovered Wendell Berry.

She still kept a quote of his on a Post-it Note stuck to her fridge: *We must achieve the character and acquire the skills to live much poorer than we do. We must waste less. We must do more for ourselves and each other. It is either that or continue merely to think and talk about changes that we are inviting catastrophe to make.*

Still, most of the stuff they saved for her was junk and promptly returned to the thrift store. She tried to believe they meant well but worried their niceness was a thin veil for pity. They believed her principles were based in necessity—out of being poor—and not in the reality of overstuffed landfills, a polluted earth—that people could make a conscious choice to step outside the rat race of *buying new, buying more*. In the end, she wasn't bothered too much that the women in town judged her as a charity case. At least she wasn't contributing to all the waste.

She thought about these women as she checked out her parking job. The car was crooked and sticking out into the street a few inches, but traffic was slow today—it was slow every day. Once inside the thrift store, she walked with purpose. She needed a tray for her keys and a road atlas to keep in her car. It didn't matter that she had no intention of traveling anywhere, at least for the moment; she still felt it was the responsible approach to car ownership—keeping a map under the passenger seat.

She stopped short in front of the books. There was a title she wasn't

expecting: *Bioluminescent Insects of the Eastern and Central United States.*
She pulled the book from the shelf and tucked it under her arm.

She walked to work that night. She wasn't ready for The Locust's parking
lot yet. The club was on the far west edge of town, across the street from
the grain elevator, the meeting place for farmers in the area. They would
drive up in their combines full of corn and stop in for burnt coffee and
stale donuts. Many of Lo's childhood memories involved sitting on the
muddy floor playing with half-dressed Barbies while her dad chatted
with the other men. Besides the elevator co-op, there was nothing near
The Locust except for an abandoned gas station and a small section of
field wedged behind it. The club itself was simply an abandoned machine
shed someone had sold Parker on the cheap. It was advantageous that
the building was isolated on the edge of town; otherwise, noise com-
plaints from elder townspeople would have shut them down long ago.

When she pulled open the heavy door of the club, she heard Parker's voice in an intense conversation.

"Artie, I practically raised you. I changed your diapers more than
your own mother did, so trust me when I tell you that you have got to
let this go."

Lo's chest tightened. She held her breath and backed against the
door, which was framed by two half walls to keep too much light from
flooding the club when the door was opened. Still, when she was working, she could always tell when the door had opened because even a
fraction of daylight lit up the dark club.

She heard feet shuffle. Parker cleared her throat. "Lo? Is that you?"
She knew that Parker knew it was her. No one else worked tonight.

Lo stomped in and walked toward the bar, a floating oval in the
middle of the open shed, and made a panicked face at Parker while
looking around for Artie, who must have gone to hide somewhere in
the back. "What the hell, Parker? Is he really trying to get me fired?"

Parker sighed and shrugged her shoulders. She wore black cargo shorts and a black hoodie, even though it was freezing outside. Lo made an exasperated groan and shook her head as she walked toward the bar. Parker followed her and sat down at one of the stools while Lo began prepping the area for opening.

"Not really. He's confused more than anything. Don't worry about him. He's convinced you're 'emotionally manipulating' him. This whole mess is *exactly* what I told you would happen. I told you until my damn face was blue. But . . ." She stopped. Lo washed the lacquered bar top, which housed one sunken cooler filled with domestic beer. A taller Coke fridge filled with pop stood behind her. She pulled up a box of potato chips and clipped on a few different flavors to the hanging chip rack— salt and vinegar, plain and dill pickle.

Lo thought about when she and Artie had started dating a few months back. Parker had *actually* supported the relationship. They even joked about how Lo might be able to spend Christmas at their grandparents' family farm out near Janesville. But now that it had turned south, Lo felt like Parker was backtracking as a way to avoid taking sides. She tried not to be offended by this diplomacy since Artie *was* Parker's cousin. But it made Lo feel like more of an outsider than usual. Parker was her closest friend, and now Artie was coming between them.

"But I didn't listen, did I?" Lo said as she mindlessly counted the cash in the till, an assortment of ones, fives, tens and piles of change that always added up to exactly one hundred dollars at opening.

"No, you didn't. And now I'm having to talk myself out of firing my baby cousin who's acting like a little bitch because you don't want to date him anymore."

Lo slammed the cash register shut and looked over to the low stage, a jumble of plywood pieces nailed together and raised a foot above the concrete floor, framed on either side by a set of PAR can lights on black poles. Parker had another pair of lights for their shed at home where Lo had partied, celebrated holidays and jumped off their old wooden dock countless times over the years. Thinking about all the good times out at Parker's house made her more anxious about the drama between her and Artie.

The heat turned on and blasted warm air out of the three broad, open vents in the ceiling. On winter days, Lo lingered under them while she swept. They blew so loudly, the noises of the world seemed to get lost in their hum. The heat ran almost constantly during the winter and still only kept the place barely warm enough. "You know we didn't really date—not officially! And I technically haven't even broken up with him. I've just—" Lo stumbled on her words, "avoided him for a while."

Parker sighed loudly and rolled her eyes. "Oh, for Pete's sake, I don't have time for this. Are you going to run sound for me if he leaves?" She got up from the stool. "I have a club to run. But listen, you owe me for this whole disaster. If I have to get in the middle of you two again—I'll quit. Then where would you be? *Unemployed*. That's where. And from now on, listen to me about this kind of thing." She offered a perfunctory smile and nodded her head with finality like she had solved everything.

"*Mhm*," Lo responded, rolling her eyes. "What would I do without you, my dear?" she murmured as Parker walked toward the back room of the club, no doubt to give Artie a similar pep talk.

Alexis didn't want to talk about the pregnancy while they were at work. There was a lot to do to get ready for planting and a wave of new seasonal workers. Jason, Alexis and a few others had permanent gigs at Markham Farms, but once spring rolled around, they brought in a handful of workers to run the shop, work the weddings and events they hosted and manage the land. This was usually the best time of the year since there were more people to hang with for a few months, and some of their old friends who went elsewhere for the winter were coming back. Things felt different now, though.

Alexis didn't want to talk about it at night either because it seemed like no matter what Jason said, it wasn't the right thing. A few days passed like this, and he grew more and more frustrated. Things had been so good. The pay was fine, the people who owned the farm were laid-back hippies who listened to Jason's opinions and ideas. He and Alexis had been happy. Too happy, he realized. It couldn't have lasted like that. Not with his luck.

Now he didn't know what to do, and he had no one to ask for advice, not that he needed it. It was his life. But even if he had wanted to call someone, his college friends were all living normal lives doing normal shit and wouldn't understand this situation. He could have asked Julia and Malcolm, who ran the farm, but he didn't want them involved in his personal business. His parents were gone—or at least, his dad was gone, and his mom might as well be.

On Saturday, he was eating lunch on a bench in front of a greenhouse when Giuseppe walked by. Jason was wearing a hoodie with a hat pulled over his ears. He was freezing cold, and though it was the warmest day of the year, it was only in the low forties. He should have grabbed his jacket in the morning, but he was too agitated by the tension between him and Alexis.

Giuseppe stopped and looked down at him.

"What's up?" Jason asked.

"What's up with you? Where's Lexi?"

Jason shrugged. "Don't know. Doing something."

"*Hmm*," Giuseppe responded, nodding a few times. "Trouble in paradise?"

Jason groaned and set his sandwich down. The wind picked up a little and blew through his sweatshirt. "Nothing like that. We just gotta figure some stuff out is all."

"Do you want to talk about it?"

Alexis had told Jason how she thought Giuseppe was lonely and that was why he brought over random breakfast food that Jason never ate, like "protein balls" made of peanut butter and raw oats or overnight muesli soaked in oat milk. He was used to people around the farms eating meals like that, but he preferred the simple stuff—eggs and bacon, black coffee.

"Not really." He didn't know what to say to this guy. Giuseppe was a strange cat. He gave off a London-street-punk vibe with his mohawk, black band t-shirts and a beat-up pair of Dr. Martens that he wore every day no matter how cold or hot it was. But he most definitely didn't have a British accent, and if Jason had to guess, he would say that Giuseppe was probably from Omaha and that his real name was probably Carl and that he had worked in a Hot Topic until he decided to reinvent himself and showed up on the farm one day. He was a decent coworker though. Up early, happy to get his hands dirty, not an asshole.

Jason blew out some air. "No, that's nice of you though. We'll be all right."

Giuseppe smiled down at him. "Okay, well, I talked to Alexis and she told me you were going through some heavy stuff, so I'm here if you need me, bruv." Giuseppe turned the corner around the greenhouse and disappeared.

"Bruv?" Jason repeated quietly as he shook his head and took another bite of his sandwich.

"I wish you hadn't talked to Giuseppe before you talked to me."

"It's impossible to talk to you. I just needed someone to listen to me, like, face-to-face. And I am *definitely* not ready to call my mom. He's nice, he's a good listener and he's been through some shit of his own, okay? I don't need your permission to talk to people. I actually went to find Julia, but they were gone somewhere."

"You were gonna talk to our boss about this? Doesn't that seem a little—I don't know—unprofessional?"

"Oh, come on, Jason. It's not like that here. That's why you like this job, right? We can just be ourselves."

"We don't need to put all our shit out in public—to air our dirty laundry or whatever."

"That's what this is?" She pointed to her belly. "Dirty laundry? Are you kidding me right now?"

He put his head down and his hat slipped off. They were standing in the middle of their yurt, both in their boots, on Alexis's new rug that she had picked out at a store in town just a few weeks ago. A whirlpool of bright colors churned below his dirty boots, and he felt guilty knowing she would be upset if they stained it, but he couldn't change the subject now. He stepped off the rug, trying not to draw too much attention to the muddy tracks. It would only upset her more. He'd never seen her this angry before.

"That is *not* what I meant, Lex. I just mean that not everyone needs to be involved."

Alexis bit her lip. "I didn't think this would be so hard, J. You're not even yourself right now. Been together, what, three years, and every day was better than the one before. I mean that. You're usually so chill. You're a good guy. And you love kids! It was literally your job—"

"Yeah, a job I quit."

She scoffed. "You said you quit because the money was bad and all the administrative stuff. You never said it had to do with kids."

"That's not the point. I just didn't see this coming. I don't want to leave here. I don't want to beg people for a loan to buy land that will probably put us in more debt and then have to take care of a kid on top of that." Jason had never really considered whether he wanted to be a dad or not. That was because he never had to. It was always something he understood deep down—that he would never bring a kid into this world who might end up having to deal with the same shit his parents had put him through.

"We could ask my parents, you know. We could apply for grants and other ways to get money. We're good at this, Jason, and you know it. We could make it work, we could—"

"Ask your parents? Are you crazy?"

"I mean, they could give us a small loan. We both have some money saved. We could make it work."

"You act like you know me, and now you want me to beg your parents for money?" Bit by bit, Jason had told Alexis about his childhood. Not everything, but enough. Enough to know that if there were anything he mistrusted more than a PTA mom whispering in his ear that she *was an ally*, it was his experience with family drama. "I will not get involved with that. No way."

She found the chair with her hands first and then sat down, closed her eyes and leaned back. "Okay, then, what do you suggest we do?"

He stood there frozen. He had no suggestions, no ideas, no clue.

He wanted things to go back to how they were before. "I don't know." It was the truth.

"Do you want to have this baby?"

"I never planned on it." He said it before he considered how it would sound.

She let out a long breath. "Then maybe you ought to leave."

"I'm not going to leave you, Lex. I would never, ever—"

"I'll take care of it. I'll do what I need to do, and you can go live your rootless, bachelor, free-from-responsibility life without me."

"I was *not* saying you should—"

"I wasn't asking what I should do. I don't need you to tell me that. All I asked was if you wanted a baby *with me*. I'm not forcing you into anything."

It was the *with me* that killed him.

He would have shared anything with her. She could have asked him for anything that belonged to him, and he would have given it to her. Jason was like that—he didn't waver on things. Didn't need to think long or hard about the decisions he made. Usually, he just *knew*. He felt something inside and knew the answer. That's how he had always felt about Alexis. When it came to her—the answer was always yes.

But he didn't understand what she was asking for now. To turn his entire life upside down, to get an overpriced loan they probably wouldn't qualify for because the government agencies were biased, to beg her parents for some money. To start a family? Suddenly it wasn't just about Alexis anymore, there were too many variables to consider, and now instead of knowing the answer immediately, he felt paralyzed by the questions.

She laughed but it sounded sad. "I actually believed you were gonna be excited about this."

"I just—I need some time to think about it."

"It's been a week. If you don't know by now, then what you need isn't time. We can't wait on this forever, and you might never know."

"What are you saying?"

"I'm saying that I think you should go."

ELYSIAN, MINNESOTA

Lo put on her winter boots, though most of the snow had melted. What was left was a river of dirty runoff headed toward the storm drains and into the lakes. She reached for her keys on the tray she had found at the Salvation Army. It was antique silver, at least it looked like it, etched with ornate filigree. She smiled when she touched its cold metal, just a small token of adulthood. Above the tray hung an oil painting of delicate red tulips with slender green stems on a backdrop of thick and elegant white and gray strokes. As much as she tried to recall where she had found it, she couldn't. It had been at one of the women's garage sales. It was definitely an original but wasn't signed. She wondered where it came from, doubting anyone from around here had painted something so refined.

The sun grew dim as Lo turned the corner onto Forest Street. She saw Blanche open the storm door to let John in and cringed a little, imagining the two of them attempting to carry on a conversation. She felt bad that John was pulled out of his personal life to help her with this car. It seemed unlikely that he looked forward to eating dinner with her, a self-professed weirdo, and Blanche, a particularly strange old lady. Lo couldn't help but wonder if he had a girlfriend, and if she was uncomfortable with him eating dinner with two women—no matter how strange a scene—what with Lo's patchwork clothing and Blanche's oxygen tank. Still, it was his choice whether to show up or not, and he did. Lo tapped her fingers rapidly against the steering wheel as she parked across the street from Blanche's house.

When she opened the front door, she called out, "Don't get up, I'll let myself in," but accidentally pushed the door into John, who was balancing on his left leg while he untied his right boot. He hopped around the room to regain balance.

She awkwardly reached out to help him right himself, then pulled her arms back quickly. "Sorry," she said, "didn't see you there."

She sat down to untie her boots, looked around and decided she would leave them on. The dirty floor was covered in visible spills and scattered garbage.

John must have read her expression because he whispered, "She asked me to take my shoes off." His eyes looked gray in the dim light. He wasn't wearing a coat, just a hooded sweatshirt that read JEFE'S AUTO SHOP across the front with a clip-art graphic of a checkered flag and a race car. Lo wondered how many race cars they serviced at Jefe's. She guessed that number was close to zero since the town was largely populated by senior citizens driving used Buicks.

She looked at him and raised her eyebrows while untying her boots. "This should be interesting." She took her hat off and could feel the static electricity, imagining her curls floating around her head like Medusa's snakes. After she took her boots off, she smoothed her hair down and tucked it into her scarf. When she looked up, John was watching her. "What a mess, huh?"

"No, it looks good."

"What?" she asked.

"Your hair, it looks good."

"I meant the house." She turned away to hide her smile and pushed herself up off the floor.

"Hadn't noticed."

They sat around an ancient TV in the small front room of the house. It had been designed to serve as a kind of sunroom. They were surrounded by windows, but thick maroon curtains embroidered with gold thread left the room devoid of any light except from the TV. They reminded Lo of the nineties, which she guessed was when they were hung. The love seat she and John shared was pushed back into the curtains, and she found it hard to relax, sitting forward so as not to disturb them and find herself covered in a shower of decades-old dust.

They ate frozen pizza from thin white napkins while an old game show played in the background. Blanche sat across from them, in front of the TV, which was pushed into the far corner and shrouded by curtains like a kind of shrine. Behind Blanche's chair was the Christmas tree, which completely transfixed Lo, who found it difficult to look away from its grotesqueness—broken homemade ornaments, a thick layer of dust, half-burnt-out lights from another era—orange, brown, red. It was truly a decrepit fire hazard, and somehow still heartbreaking. Everything in Blanche's house was out of time.

Lo tempered her urge to ask Blanche why they were there—she didn't want to come across as ungrateful. She also wanted to ask John where he lived, what he liked to eat other than frozen pizza and what he thought about bioluminescent insects. Lo looked forward to reading her firefly book later that night. Earthbound constellations, that's what the book had called them. Entomology was much more enthralling than she had expected it to be.

While Blanche was taking the pizza out of the oven, Lo had gone around the house and tried to turn on a few lights. None responded to the flipping of a switch. She noticed a beautiful midcentury light fixture with simple glass and gold trim above the parlor furniture, but there wasn't even a bulb in it. She found an unplugged lamp with a lightbulb and was looking for a stool to climb when Blanche walked out of the kitchen. "That don't work, Bambi."

"What?" Lo asked innocently, holding the bulb behind her as if she had been caught doing something illegal.

"That light fixture up there don't work. Lamp should work, far as I know."

Lo put the bulb back in the lamp and plugged it in. A wall of photos lit up behind her. Family pictures with wildly printed sweaters and pastel backgrounds showed an unrecognizable Blanche with permed auburn hair, her husband—a good-looking Black man somewhere near forty—and a gawky middle schooler whom Lo didn't recognize. Judging by the era of the photos, he was probably quite a bit older than her and surely looked different now—she shuddered when she thought about her own middle school pictures. Still, she wondered if he ever visited town or came by The Locust. Pretty much everyone who came back to town to visit their aging parents made a pit stop at The Locust from time to time.

A little light in a far corner was better than the eerie glow of the half-burned-out Christmas tree, which Lo found increasingly more disturbing as the minutes passed.

She felt even worse about the whole situation when she found out that the "homemade meal" Blanche had promised him was cheap cardboard pizza, but John didn't seem to mind as he took a big piece and sat down next to her on the dusty love seat. His thigh rested against Lo's.

Blanche finished her piece of pizza and wiped her face with a greasy napkin, which she held crumpled in her closed fist, resting on the arm of her recliner. Lo thought she seemed a little nervous as she cleared her throat—more like gagged and hacked—while she reached for a pack of cigarettes with her right hand before pulling back.

"The thing is, I'm dying," Blanche said. John choked a little on his pizza, but Lo only nodded. She'd been thinking about Blanche over the weekend and figured that only a very sick woman would chain-smoke Marlboro 100s while on oxygen. Blanche continued, "So, what I need is a favor."

"What kind of favor?"

"I got emphysema. The doctors tell me I've only got a few months." Her sentences came out in wheezes and short bursts of air. "I earned it smoking since I was just a kid. But that ain't what I need help with. My husband died years ago when my son was a boy. You can see his picture there on the wall—"

"That's your son?" John asked, pointing to a graduation picture framed on the wall in the parlor.

"You got a problem with him already, Rebel?" Blanche asked defensively.

"No," his eyes widened. "It's just—there are no lights in here," he mumbled quietly.

"That's because I like to live cheap. Don't need it lit up like a football stadium. I've lived in this house forever, don't need lights to know where I am." As she said this, she stood up and walked away, dragging her oxygen tank behind her.

"Do you have any idea what this is about?" John whispered to Lo. A clock ticked loudly somewhere in the background. She hadn't noticed it before with the TV blaring, but Blanche had turned the sound low to ask them her favor. They made eye contact while Lo shook her head slowly.

"Here's the last postcard." Blanche made her way back into the room and handed it to Lo. It was a new postcard designed to look old-fashioned with an old-timey downtown scene—mud streets, shops with horses tied out front. Blanche sat back down in her chair and caught her breath. "He works at different farms—organic farms. Drug farms, I suspect." She stopped again and looked at John, apparently expecting some sort of reaction. He said nothing, only sat back on the love seat in what Lo guessed was an attempt to look comfortable in this strange scenario.

Blanche continued, "See, he sent a postcard from Twin Falls, Idaho. I think he likes to remind me of all the places I ain't been before. He used to complain that we didn't go nowhere. He won't call, won't visit, just writes down where he is." She paused to catch her breath and take a drink from a Coke sitting on the TV tray in front of her. "Well, I'll tell you, I called up the mayor's office over at Twin Peaks and asked some questions. Figured out the name of some of them local farms they got." She stopped again and took rapid, shallow breaths for a moment. Lo resisted the urge to tell Blanche that Twin Peaks and Twin Falls weren't the same place.

"Called them all up. Talked to a girl on the phone who said she knew Jason and knew where he was headed. I wrote down the name and the address—all the information she could give." Blanche's breath wheezed as she reached for her pack of cigarettes again and held her hand on them for a second before she pulled it back. She was talking very quietly and staring absentmindedly at the game show on the TV. "Girl gave me his number, but he don't pick up. Never picks up. I contacted the farm in California, and he told 'em he was headed that way, but they don't know when he'll get there. Leaving a message would mean nothing. He never calls back, won't take my calls."

Lo waited a minute for Blanche to continue. She let the pizza grow cold on the napkin resting on her lap. When Blanche didn't go on, Lo cleared her throat. "So, would you like me to call and talk to him once he gets there? Tell him you're sick?" Blanche turned her head quickly as if she had forgotten they were there.

"No, Bambi. It won't work. He'll just hang up on you too."

"What else could I do?"

"You two got to go to California, get him and bring him home so I can say goodbye. I wasn't a good mom, not after Marcus left. I know that, but I never stopped caring for my son—not ever. No mother could do that."

Lo and John both sat silently for a minute, trying to process her request. It hadn't actually been a request but a statement. After a minute, they both started talking at once.

John said, "I'm sorry, ma'am, but I work at the shop nearly every day."

Lo said something about her job and her duplex. She might have mumbled about the new book she was reading. After they had simultaneously explained why they couldn't leave, the room grew quiet except for the clock's ticking, the game show's quiet humming and Blanche's wheezing.

Blanche ignored them and continued. "I know it's a hell of a favor. And I wouldn't ask just anyone who showed up at my door. But I liked Bambi from the get-go. Then I watched you two out on the street getting the car going, and well, I don't care much for god, but I thought maybe that fella was finally showing up for me." She stopped again and tried to catch her breath. "I'll give you money for gas and cheap motels. I can tell you two don't need nothing fancy. I got social security money stashed away. I don't spend much. Should only take a couple days. Then

I don't have to die without seeing my son once more." Her voice lowered until the last line was barely audible. Lo was afraid she had used up all her oxygen.

John glanced at Lo and shook his head gently. She nodded; she knew she couldn't take off work to drive to the West Coast looking for a man she'd never met who didn't want to be found, even if Blanche was on her deathbed—or more likely her death recliner.

"I'm sorry, Blanche. I'm so sorry. This . . ." Lo stammered, "your story . . . it's . . . just, sorry. I work several nights a week, and John is a mechanic at Jefe's. We can't just leave without knowing how long it will take to find him or if he even . . ." she stopped. She was going to say *if he even wants to be found* but stopped herself. Instead, she said, "If he'll be able to leave his new job and come back here with us. I'll call the farm though, I promise. I'll talk to him and try to convince him to visit."

Blanche stared at the TV for a moment then sighed. She hunched further down in her chair. "It won't work. But he's a nice man—he was a nice kid—so if you show up, you can convince him. He's from here, like you."

"I'm not from here," John said. "And I don't think I'd be very convincing."

"No." Blanche shook her head. "No, Bambi is the one who will do the convincing. You're the one to make sure the car runs, and she don't hurt herself. She can't even open the hood or fill the damn thing with gas on her own."

Lo scoffed. That statement was unfair—she was competent. She pictured her beautiful home, her neat stack of firewood, the job she had held for almost a decade. Tempted to outright disagree, she instead turned toward the old tree and let out a breath. It didn't matter, in the end. There was no way they could go. John cleared his throat but didn't say anything else.

"I'm sorry, Blanche. We can't go," she said, watching the tree's lights burn out one by one. "I understand if you want to keep the car."

"Well, take it for now but come back next week. I need to think about it some more. Need to figure out how to get Jason home."

SOUTHERN IDAHO

Wet snow fell on the windshield. The old Jeep barreled down I-84 as the blades of the wipers groaned loudly. Jason held his phone in his lap, clicked the screen, then set it down in the passenger seat.

The car swerved slightly past each exit, like a cat swatting at a mouse. A slight lunge, then a redirection back toward the highway. The whole landscape was ugly and depressing. A few semitrucks passed, full of red-blooded American capitalism made in China, Bangladesh, Mexico. A news report on the radio alerted listeners that trucks were carrying kidnapped women from one state to another.

Without thinking, Jason reached for his phone. The screen lit up. A missed call from his mom's phone number appeared, which aggravated him. He refused to save her number under the name "Mom," but she hadn't changed it in over a decade, and he couldn't help but have it memorized. She had no right to call, but still, she did try from time to time. He could block her number, but that would be petty. Or maybe it would be too much effort, more than she deserved. It was easier to just swipe it away and forget it. No messages from Alexis. Nothing but their two smiling faces, side by side. The heat blowing out of the vents buried the sound of the next news segment. It was colder today than it had been all week.

Alexis asked him to pack up his stuff and then she left the yurt. He didn't see her in the morning even though he walked a circle around the property hoping that it would all somehow blow over. They had argued before, and usually all it took was one puppy-dog-eyed look in her direction and they would laugh it off. Alexis joked that because they were the same height, they were always able to see "eye to eye," so all it took was that one look, and they'd be rolling around in bed apologizing to each other. It was obvious to him that this fight wasn't the same, but still, he didn't understand how everything had fallen apart so fast.

Jason looked in his rearview mirror. An old duffel bag filled with work clothes, shirts slightly stained with soil and grease. Clean, buttoned shirts for going out. A stack of his books wobbled with each turn of the wheel: *History and Class Consciousness* by Lukács, others by Balzac, Zola, James, Mann—the realists. Another stack of books: Baldwin, Baraka, Butler, a well-worn copy of *Invisible Man* by Ellison. Finally, a ripped-up paperback novel, the cover missing completely. He knew that she would notice eventually. It was one of Alexis's favorite romance novels that had been made into one of her favorite movies starring Angela Bassett. They had watched the DVD on lazy weekends when there wasn't a lot to do on the farm and it was too cold to go outside.

He squinted into the distance. The sky was gray, heavy with impending sleet; the ground was gray, covered in dirty snow. A new shade of gray began to fill the horizon as billows of thick smoke, darker than the clouds, filled the air with the smell of burning metal and gasoline. He saw the flames before he saw the truck. There were no people standing in the ditch watching the vehicle burn. There were no people anywhere. No women fleeing the bed of the truck. No sirens wailed in the distance. He reached for his phone and dialed. The operator instructed him: *stay where you are, wait for help.*

Jason drove past the scene slowly but didn't stop; no one stopped because it was clear there wasn't anything anyone could do to help without a fire truck. Instead, everyone slowed down and watched for as long as they could before they sped up and drove away.

He swerved the red Jeep off the next exit and parked in front of a gas station as gray as the sky, as gray as the dirty snow, as all that smoke. The bathroom doors, located in front of his parking spot, required a key tied to a giant piece of wood. He watched a woman with two small kids unlock the gray metal door, clinging to the makeshift key chain. She looked nothing like Alexis, but still he thought of her while he watched the family close the door behind them.

It wasn't like he had options. Alexis asked him to leave. He never wanted to be a dad. He wouldn't do that to a child—make that decision for them. It wasn't fair that children couldn't choose their parents.

She'd even warned him. "*If men aren't on birth control hormones, why should women be?*" He'd agreed with her. Seemed fair. But so much time had passed since then with no scares, no issues. She said something one morning about being extra careful, some app on her phone. They'd run out of condoms weeks before and just hadn't found the time to get into town. He told her he'd be careful. But it was all her fault for looking so damn good, lying there half-asleep and half-dressed in bed every morning, smiling up at him.

He laid his forehead on the steering wheel and tried to breathe normally, resisting the urge to bang his head against the wheel as some sort of release. Some kind of penance. Without looking up, he reached for his phone. He opened it and found what he was looking for. A picture of Alexis, her lips on his cheek. His smile was broad, eyes half-closed. Anyone looking at it would have thought: happy kids, they're going to be all right. He remembered how his cheek had been stained with lipstick for half a day until he noticed it in a bathroom mirror. It really was all his fault.

No new messages.

ELYSIAN, MINNESOTA

Lo was the first one at The Locust on Wednesday night and was relieved
that the gravel lot was still empty as she parked the car. She wasn't even
sure if she should get used to driving it. Blanche might ask for it back.

She unlocked the door to the club, flipped on the first set of lights—
mostly black lights for ambience, the place was always dark—and took a
deep breath. She'd worked at The Locust since the eleventh grade, eight
or nine years now. She could open the place by herself without much
thought. It felt like a second home, even with its noisy vents and sticky
concrete floor. While she restocked the Coca-Cola fridge with pop and
added a few beers to the cooler, she thought about Blanche Peterson
and John Blank.

While she ran the faucet waiting for warm water, she considered the
favor. It was ridiculous, really, to ask a pair of strangers to track down a
grown man living off the grid at a California weed farm. She imagined
her embarrassment, tapping him on the shoulder and saying, "Excuse
me, your mother asks that you return home now," like he was a kid out
past curfew.

She carried a bucket of ice from the ice maker in the back and filled
the small bin they kept at the bar. They didn't serve mixed drinks, so it
was mostly for when someone wanted ice water instead of paying for
a bottle—something Lo encouraged even though they lost a few extra
bucks here and there. Parker didn't seem to mind, at least not after Lo
had preached endlessly about it. Lo even ordered compostable cups,

which usually disintegrated after about an hour, but that was fine because people had a habit of leaving them lying around and replacing them with new ones, regardless of what they were made out of. She had tried to convince Parker to buy the cups that had wildflower seeds embedded in them, but then they laughed for an hour imagining people around town discovering awl aster sprouts clogging up their septic tanks.

After the cooler was filled, she got the broom out to sweep. She had been the one who swept up on Saturday night, so there was nothing on the floor but a pop tab stuck under a bar stool. She thought about her and John Blank packing up the car and driving through the night before finally stopping at a cheap motel. Would they share a room? Surely Blanche didn't have enough money for them to each get their own room. And how far was California? How many hours would it take to drive to Santa Rosa? Would they have to stop two nights? Two nights in a hotel room with a stranger. She shook her head and laughed out loud. It was crazy.

She heard the door creak open and saw sunlight flood in for a moment. "Hi, Parker," she called to the shadow near the front door.

"Hey, you," Parker called back. "You're early."

"Yeah, well, I got a car, so I didn't have to walk."

"Are you kidding? A car? I thought buying a gas guzzler was against your religion."

Lo made a face but then told her about the ad in the paper, which horrified Parker, who sincerely explained to Lo how lucky she was that she hadn't been a victim of cannibalism, to which Lo explained back that nothing that thrilling would ever happen in Elysian. Then Lo told her about Jefe's, about John fixing her car for free and about Blanche's favor. Parker only listened, eyes wide.

"Damn, I remember Jason Peterson. Maybe two classes below me in school. His dad died in a car accident. I still remember the day it happened. Probably everyone does. Or everyone who is old enough does, but you were what—in kindergarten then, maybe not even in school? There was a baby in the other truck." She stopped. "The baby died too. The lady driving that truck still lives in town somewhere. I don't know the details of how it all played out, but Marcus Peterson and that baby died. God, it was awful."

Lo's chest felt tight. "Blanche's husband died in a car accident?"

"Yeah, he ran the paper, I remember. Especially because that news was *in* the paper for months—nothing else mattered in town for a while after that. Mrs. Peterson went off the deep end. I mean, Blanche Peterson was always . . ." Parker seemed to look for the right words to describe her, "an *interesting* woman, rough around the edges, not that I'm one to talk. But I remember my mom being worried about Jason. I guess all the moms were worried, but no one did shit, of course. All gossip. By the time I opened The Locust, he had left town. Sounds like he hasn't been back."

"Seems like it. Said she hasn't seen him in years. I think I'll call the farm he works for and try to talk to him." Lo shrugged.

Parker shrugged back, then asked, "All set here? Need me to do anything else? First show is early tonight, six thirty."

Lo shook her head. "All set."

The first band was not good. Lo was used to high school bands by now—they made up the majority of shows held at The Locust—but this band must have just started playing together. The singer had an okay voice, but she struggled to play the guitar and sing at the same time. They had to start a few songs over, which Lo knew was the best way to kill a crowd. At least there were only about twenty people watching, probably all family.

More people would show up for the last band, Magenta Crush. Lo had seen them play a dozen times already. Their singer was, by small-town Minnesota standards, a star. He was an outgoing kid who would call the club regularly and ask when they could play again. He sang some of the songs in Spanish and sometimes would switch from Spanish to English in the middle of a line. She thought that sounded cool, and she enjoyed working on the nights that they played, partly because they were so much better than most of the other local acts and partly because people actually came to watch them play.

Her thoughts somehow turned to John Blank again, how he had spoken Spanish and English at the garage. She was wondering if she would ever see him again when she looked up and found him standing directly in front of her.

She smiled so wide that she immediately blushed and looked down, opening a cooler and pretending to inspect it.

"Hi," he said casually.

"What are you doing here?" she blurted out. It sounded aggressive, accusatory.

"I'm sorry, am I not welcome here?"

She smirked. "No, sorry. I mean, no, of course you are." She smoothed her curly auburn hair and stood up straight, closing the cooler. "I just didn't expect you to like this kind of music."

"Rock music?" he asked. He was wearing a long-sleeve shirt that said JEFE's with the same logo as his hooded sweatshirt from the other day. She wondered if he wore anything else.

"Well, small-town teenage punk rock, specifically." She tilted her head to the side just a little.

"That's actually my favorite genre. And also, I know Aldo, the singer of the band. He's my boss's kid. He invited me to watch him play."

She clicked her tongue in her cheek and nodded. She hadn't made the connection. Her heart was beating fast, and she looked around the club awkwardly, unsure of what to say next, when Parker walked up. She stood next to Lo for a minute looking back and forth at the two of them. "Is everything okay here? Can I help you?" Parker also had to look up at John, whose height kept surprising Lo.

Lo smiled at Parker politely, attempting to secretly implore her to keep the conversation civil. "This is John. The guy who fixed my car."

"Christina Parker, I'm Lo's boss and best friend in the entire world. You're a real hero." Parker reached out to shake his hand, then stopped and looked at him closely, narrowing her eyes. "Hey, you're Randy's cousin, right? I think we hung out one night, out at that bonfire at his place last month?"

"Yeah, yeah," John nodded, smiling. "I remember you telling me you were the owner over here. That was a fun night." Lo raised her eyebrows but wasn't surprised. Parker knew everyone. Everyone knew everyone, except apparently Lo, who was certain she'd never set eyes on John before.

"It *was* fun. You were with Shay Rose, right? Anyway, I heard you and Lo are going on a little road trip? Fulfilling an old lady's dying wish and all?" Lo's head shot up, and she shook it violently. John only laughed while Lo was trying to catch up with Parker's comment about Shay Rose, a girl from town who was now in law school in Minneapolis (as Lo's dad constantly reminded her), but then the conversation moved on.

"Yeah, believe it or not, that's not the first time an old lady has asked me to search for her estranged son living on a weed farm in California."

Parker scrutinized him for a minute. "Wow, you're pretty funny, huh? Honestly, it's crazy. I was telling Lo all about Blanche earlier. Hard life. I think you two should do it. An adventure! And seems like it would be worth ultimate karma points or something." She was suddenly distracted by someone coming into the club and held up her hand to wave at whoever it was. She winked at John and walked away. "Let's talk later, you two."

"Parker!" Lo called out her name angrily as she walked across the venue toward the door.

Lo offered John a Budweiser on the house, but before she could ask him about Shay Rose or the parties at his cousin's house, she was called away to clean up a spilled drink. By the time she returned to the bar, he had found a seat elsewhere.

For the rest of the night, Lo caught herself looking across the club to where John was sitting with Aldo's dad and some of their friends. Once, John turned his head in her direction, and for a few moments, they held their gaze before Lo remembered herself and got back to work.

He didn't walk up to the bar to tell her good night, just waved while she was counting the cash in the register. From the corner of her eye, she watched him help the members of Magenta Crush roll an expensive-looking amp out of the club and never saw him come back in.

All night, Parker had popped behind the bar to remind Lo how badly she had always yearned for adventure, to assure Lo that she could run the club for a few nights without her, and also tell her every time Artie was glaring at her from the sound booth. Lo only rolled her eyes or responded with a sarcastic smile.

"Why are you trying to get rid of me?" she asked when they were locking up the club for the night. They stood in the small square entryway where tickets were collected. Warm air blew down on them from a vent in the ceiling. A thousand pieces of Scotch tape and pinholes from old show posters covered the wall.

Parker shook her head and played with a nail sticking out of the plywood that framed the entryway, black paint chipping onto the floor. "I'm trying to save you, that's all. What's your plan, Lo? Like your life plan? You say people stare at your hair and your crazy outfits. I know, I know," she said, nodding when Lo dropped her mouth in mock outrage. Parker spoke delicately, as if everything she said was a light-hearted joke. "I see you, Gunderson. And I know you hate it here. Even though it's got the raddest club in south-central Minnesota—you hate this town. But maybe you're too afraid to try somewhere new because you've never left. No, don't get fired up. I know your dad took you to New York City once." Parker laughed to herself while her finger loosened the nail patiently.

Her dad, for her sixteenth birthday, had driven her from Elysian to New York City. They had stayed in a decent hotel right near Times Square. He and Lo had walked Manhattan almost end to end, and she would have kept walking for days to take in the quaint little bookstores, to watch the women with black niqabs that covered their entire bodies slip quickly into busy movie theaters and tiny bodegas, to eat food that she didn't even know existed, to listen to people speak languages she had never heard before. It was one of her favorite memories, certainly her favorite that involved her dad.

"Parker, I can't just pack up and travel across the country with

John. What if he's a murderer? And what's this about Shay Rose? Are they dating?"

"Highly doubt it since she's up in the Cities. Besides, even if they are, you're here right now and she's not!" Parker laughed like she'd made a hilarious joke. "And he's not a murderer. I know his family. Known 'em my whole life. Randy was a high school hotshot, now he's running his dad's farm. And John's pretty cute, Lo." Parker raised her eyes dramatically. "Come on, we both know it. He's a cute dude. I worry about you." She pulled the nail free and put it in between her teeth, so her words came out pinched. "Lo, you need some excitement in your life. And let's be honest, Elysian doesn't have the largest pool of eligible bachelors. Unless you want to get that dating app and let me swipe for you again!" She raised her eyebrows a few more times.

"No, thank you. It all feels weird. Driving across the country—now come on, take that nail out of there. God, I hope you've had your tetanus booster."

"Don't change the subject. And no, it's not! It's a split-second decision! It's a road trip! You'll be back in a week."

"No, it's more than that, Parker. I would have to search for someone who doesn't want to be found. I would have to waste gallons of gasoline and probably buy food wrapped in plastic. That's wrong—"

"All right, I hear you. But it could just be a once-in-a-lifetime thing, right? And everyone should see their mom one last time before she dies."

Lo looked at Parker for a minute then looked down at her feet on the dirty entry mat. Parker made an *Umm* sound as if she wanted to rephrase her statement, but Lo pulled the door handle to leave the warmth of the entryway and stepped outside.

Parker walked behind her and ran into Lo's backside when she stopped short and pointed to her car. "Why is it leaning like that?"

They walked around to the other side of the car, spotlighted by a streetlight above. Lo let out a moan when she saw that both tires on the driver's side were completely flat.

OBJECTIVE SCIENTIFIC FACTS

Fireflies live most of their existences as eggs, larvae and pupae. They hatch and then slowly mature. For years, they consume other insects and decomposing matter in their larval state, simply grubbing around the dirt looking for things to eat. In the northern United States, this may take up to a year longer as weather is unfavorable and development is hindered. When they eventually spread their vulnerable interior wings and fly, they only actually live—luminous and free—for a couple of weeks.

ELYSIAN, MINNESOTA

Parker offered Lo a ride home and promised she'd help figure out the tire situation tomorrow. Afterward, Lo stayed up late wondering if it was time to give up her short-lived dream of car ownership. Blanche probably wasn't going to let her keep the car anyway.

People wanting more than what they needed was what led to so many of the world's problems.

She could walk everywhere if she wanted to, had a good job, a duplex that her father owned outright that she heated nearly for free. What more did she really *need*?

She had been hesitant to get a car, but she hoped it would be a step toward *something*. She wasn't sure what; she just felt it. She could finally get serious about moving to Minneapolis and finding a community that appreciated her. The blanket was wrapped tight around her shoulders as she crouched on the floor in front of the brick wall that stayed cool to the touch, no matter how hot the stove got.

Maybe in the Cities she would feel more connected to the things she believed in, ways to find meaning in life outside of the price of corn and Artie's scowl. In Elysian, she could grow a massive garden from the seeds she saved year after year and rage against two-day online delivery to her fellow employees, buy items secondhand, and read from her revolutionary collection of aging books, but she never really felt *connected* to any movements. Parker told her about co-ops in the Cities, people who biked, rideshared, gardened, protested and lived together in shared spaces.

The woodstove crackled. She opened the door, blew inside as hard as she could, and then reached for the old hair dryer she kept in a basket on the floor and held it into the fire. She waved it around, embers beginning to glow red and orange. This was a trick her dad had shown her as a kid. After spending the first year in her duplex pumping bellows for hours with little effect, she caved and decided that not using the heater was a better trade-off than using an electric hair dryer to get the woodstove hot enough to heat the house.

Lo remembered when she and her dad found the place nearly eight years ago, the week after she graduated from high school. At eighteen she had been a bit too naive to realize that her graduation present—a house—was extravagant. At the time it had actually felt like a compromise, like she was settling. After months of arguing with her dad about how she had no interest in going to college to spend a fortune for nothing, they settled on the idea of a gap year. Lo had insisted the gap year take place in Minneapolis, but he would only agree if she stayed in town where he could keep an eye on her.

Over the years, she learned to live on her own, to keep a steady job, and she had studied what *she* found meaningful rather than checking boxes off some antiquated curriculum. While it was the Wendell Berry quote that lasted longest on the refrigerator, several quotes had come and gone over the years. Ideas from Marx, Bertrand Russel, bell hooks and Keith McHenry had been floating around on scraps of paper as she formed her own personal philosophy, all while she grew more and more complacent in her small duplex.

It helped that she had a nice neighbor too. Mike Bauer, an old friend of her father's, lived next to her in the identical apartment. He was a kind old man whose wife had passed away years earlier. After a fall and a broken hip, he had sold their farmhouse and moved into town. Besides lawn maintenance and landscaping, paint trimming, cleaning the gutters, and general upkeep, her father also tasked her, in lieu of rent, with keeping an eye on Mike, who hadn't lived alone since his early twenties and was becoming more question-mark shaped as the years passed.

Most of all, Lo cherished her woodstove, using mulch from the wood chipper out back that she ran on quiet Sunday mornings, slowly inserting branches and producing chips small enough to keep her house sufficiently warm. Her dad had tried to explain that the central heating worked perfectly fine, but the ritual of spending her weekend mornings using her wheelbarrow to gather branches and limbs from around town became part of her identity.

While Lo fed the woodstove, she regretted getting involved with the car. She set the hair dryer in its basket, which sat next to a larger basket full of chips, and then grabbed the oversized United States road atlas she found at the thrift store earlier that week.

One day, she might need a map. Maybe she'd drive up to Canada to see the fields of wildflowers across the border in Saskatchewan. Or maybe she'd drive to the Black Hills and go camping. She fingered the highways that tangled through the Midwest until her pointer finger landed on Des Moines, Iowa. She left it there for a minute, staring at the little splotch of yellow.

Her phone vibrated from somewhere in the room. She tossed the atlas on the floor and fought an impulse to throw it in the woodstove.

The phone was also from her dad—another thing she felt unsure about. He was adamant she carry a cell phone in case of emergency. Sure, she felt uncomfortable that he paid her monthly bill, but he must have known that she would cancel the service immediately rather than give her own money to a multinational comm tech conglomerate. The only people she texted regularly were Parker, her dad, the neighbor, Mike, who messaged her several times a week to ask if she wanted his dinner leftovers, and sometimes the other employees from work. Artie used to text all the time, but that was over now.

The message was probably from Parker, drunk at Lefty's, asking her to come out. Lo opened the door to the cast-iron stove, added a handful of chips, blew as hard as she could and then got up to look at her phone. The text was from a number she didn't recognize with an 828 area code.

I heard the damsel needs new tires. Meet me at Locust, 6 a.m.

If Parker was drunk at Lefty's, she was apparently with John Blank. Lo rolled her eyes and decided not to respond. She hadn't stopped trying to invent comebacks to John's initial damsel comment from Friday night. The best one so far was (in a sarcastic tone): *So you believe you're the knight in shining armor in this scenario?* She was still brainstorming, though.

And here he was again, trying to paint her as some helpless little woman who couldn't take care of herself. "Whatever," Lo whispered to the phone while scooting back toward the heat of the stove. She opened the door and watched the embers glow like glitter in shades of blue, white, orange, red.

Six a.m. was only five hours away, and on top of that, she didn't need John's help. She barely even knew him. Either she would find free tires or return the car for good.

There was also Shay Rose, who may or may not be his girlfriend. Shay Rose—who never allowed anyone to call her *just* "Shay"—had left town for college somewhere nearby and then gotten herself accepted into U of M Law School. Lo had no idea that Shay Rose ever came back into town to hang out, particularly to hang out with John.

Biting her lower lip, she held her phone hesitantly. Lo had made an Instagram account when the protests over the Keystone XL pipeline were at a fever pitch. She felt helpless sitting in her living room, so she figured the least she could do was support the protesters online. But what if Lo had a car then? She could have driven—it wasn't that far— and joined the protesters. Another reason that a car, while *unfortunately* requiring oil and gas to drive, could also help Lo be a part of the movements that were important to her.

Behind her a wood chip popped. She opened Instagram and searched. A tiny circular picture of Shay popped up, all long blonde hair and straight white teeth. Lo scanned her photos quickly, looking for evidence of John, but there was none. Unable to look away from Shay's life outside of Elysian, Lo scrolled for too long. A dimly lit Italian restaurant tagged in Minneapolis, a sunny picnic by the river in St. Paul, a photo of an empty college classroom commemorating her first day at law school. Lo sighed, clicked the screen black and set the phone down on the coffee table.

On Thursdays, she met her dad at the Teakettle Café to have lunch. Otherwise, she would barely see him. They still did Christmas morning at his house, but over the last few years, she had started joining Parker, her wife, Teresa, and all their friends for Thanksgiving, the Fourth of July and really any other holiday that required social interaction.

So, perhaps out of guilt, or maybe a sense of comfort that she would never admit to aloud, she almost always kept their Thursday dates. She only missed it on the rare occasions when she too hungover from drinking all night at the club with Parker and the gang. But she hadn't done that since her falling out with Artie.

She only ordered a hot tea, the same packets of black Lipton that they had served for the last two decades. Years ago, she had stopped ordering lunch, much to her father's bewilderment. He loved the Teakettle, and they had been eating there together since Lo was a kid. Since then, every week when the waitress put a burger in front of him, he would say something to the effect of, "Now don't start going off about factory farming and the agriculture industry or none of that business, you hear?" She would squint her eyes politely and sip her tea.

But she continued meeting him just to watch him eat and talk about the weather. She looked around at the speckled linoleum floor. The familiar wood paneling tacked with dead fish—bass and walleye trophies from local fishermen. Signs that read: *You Catch 'Em, We Fry 'Em, Life Is Better at the Lake*, and *If My Keys Are Missing, I've Gone Fishing*. Lo scanned the small café and its red vinyl-covered chairs, only a third of which were occupied. They looked like they had once belonged in a Pizza Hut. She appreciated that the owners were thrifty enough to purchase used furniture, and she liked the chairs because they recalled faint but pleasant memories of BookIt.

Lo told him about the ad in the paper that resulted in a free car, and he looked surprised when she mentioned Blanche Peterson. He re-called briefly what he remembered of the car accident, how difficult it had been for the community and the Peterson family in particular. He wasn't much for gossip or reminiscing though, especially about heavier topics. Lo didn't bring up Blanche's dying wish to find her son or the fact that Blanche might want the car back by the end of the week.

She wanted her dad to be excited about it, to acknowledge that she could take care of herself and even find a functional automobile while still fighting against the idea that work meant wealth and that those were the things that made a meaningful "grown-up" life. Instead, he simply nodded and wiped ketchup and mustard off his gray stubble when she mentioned how reliably the old car ran.

Once they were done eating, he used the table to push himself back. The unstable table legs shook, causing his half-drunk diner coffee to spill toward his lap.

Lo was never sure how to handle her father's embarrassing moments. She simply murmured, "Oh, no," then helped him wipe the table with flimsy napkins hoping to escape. She kept glancing toward the door. "Thanks for lunch," she mumbled as she turned to leave.

"Wait! Lois!" he called after her. "I want to see your car!"

She froze.

"Sorry, it's over at Jefe's." Hopefully, that would impress him. He always prided himself in servicing things—his air conditioning unit, his car engine, all the tools in his perfectly organized tool shed. Instead, he leaned a bit, as if tired.

"Now, Lois, why would you bring it there?" he asked, irritated.

"Why wouldn't I, dad? Do you have something against immigrant-owned businesses now?"

His eyes went wide, and he scoffed at her. "Gosh darn it, Lois. I'm too old for your bullcrap. You know I've been going to Doug's out on the highway for near forty years. He owes me for some legal services, decades past, that he'll never pay off at this rate. And here I thought you approved of bartering and all that."

"Okay, I know, sorry." She thought for a minute and then asked,

"Actually, do you think he could get some used tires for me? Two of the tires were flat," she paused, lying, "when I got it. So, I need to replace them, but don't know how much it'll cost."

"Sure, yeah. Come on, it's raining. I'll drive you over to Jefe's. I'll chat with the owner and let them know we've got a tab at Doug's. I want to look under the hood. I could have done that for you, you know. You've watched me fix my own car a hundred times. For free." He put an emphasis on the last two words.

Lo was trapped. She really didn't want her dad's help, but she wasn't going to be able to shake him. And most importantly, she couldn't bring him to Jefe's to see a car that wasn't there. If she backtracked now and told him it was actually sitting with two flats at work, he'd have a few more *pointed* questions for her. Then he'd insist on paying for the tow. And if that happened, for some reason, she'd feel like she lost. Lost what, exactly? She wasn't sure.

"Dad, please don't worry about me. I've got this handled. I appreciate it, though."

"Oh, Lois. I know." He sighed. "Come on, let me help you out. Let's be honest, I've got nothing on the agenda today until *Jeopardy!*, and I got a DVR to record it, just in case." He smiled weakly and leaned on the back of the red vinyl chair for support. Lo stood awkwardly in the middle of the Teakettle while a few quiet farmers chewed their burgers and a mom fed crinkle fries to her toddler.

"All right, Dad, let's go."

She took out her phone and started frantically texting John, wishing she hadn't ignored his two calls earlier that morning.

When they pulled up to the curb in front of Jefe's, Lo walked inside as fast as she could, leaving her dad behind as he slowly made his way out of the car.

John stood behind the computer clicking the mouse and didn't look up right away.

"John!" she whispered urgently, as if her dad might hear her while his slow gait carried him to the front door. John kept clicking the mouse and watching the screen intently. "John! Did you get my texts? I'm sorry about not getting back to you this morning. But I need your help with my dad." This was all she could get out before her dad pulled the front door open and huffed his way inside.

John looked up and smiled. "Hello, you must be Mr. Gunderson!" He walked around the corner of the checkout stand to shake her dad's hand.

"Call me Jerry," he said politely but with an edge. Lo could tell he was preparing for a professional exchange. He came with one goal—to free Lo's car from the belly of the enemy's garage and return it to its rightful place—Doug's Imperial Auto.

Just like Lo, her dad was short, and he had been shrinking the last few years. This put him more than six inches below John's eyeline. She knew that would bother him. She remembered when she first heard the term *Napoleon complex* and had often wondered how she might bring it up to her dad in a way that didn't offend him. She never did try.

"And what can I help you with today, Mr. Jerry Gunderson?" John asked carefully, his deep voice echoing in the small lobby.

Jerry tilted his head a little but didn't comment on John's accent. "Well, I'm just hoping we can get Lois's car towed over to Doug's—I mean over to Imperial Auto—out there on Sixty. He owes me favors, so I prefer to take my cars there. I'll pay you for work you've already done." He reached for his wallet.

John held out his hand as he sat down casually, one knee bent while resting on the crossbar of the stool he was sitting on, the other extended onto the dirty linoleum floor. His tan leather work boots were tied loosely. "No, sir, no cost. I finished Lo's car this morning. She might have told you that I helped her with it last week, and we got it started in front of Mrs. Peterson's house. Just a spark plug. Earlier this morning I fixed her tires. Found 'em at the junkyard out on the highway last night, no problem. So, her car's over at The Locust, ready to go."

She stared at him, her face growing hot. For a reason unknown to her, she had to suppress a grin. Why would he do all that for her? Was he at the junkyard all night?

"Oh," Jerry stammered. "Oh, all right, then. So, you—" He paused, then looked at Lo. "Well, Lois, why didn't you tell me your boyfriend was the mechanic here?"

She laughed too loudly. A single *Ha!* "No, Dad—"

John cut in. "No, sir. Just friends, and it was no trouble. I found the tires over in the junkyard within an hour. Not sure why people don't go there first."

"Well, I agree with you there." Jerry nodded. "But that's awful nice of you to do for a friend." Her dad looked at her again, as if he were trying to convince her that they were dating just by staring at her. Lo didn't understand exactly what type of comfort it would bring her dad to know that she had a boyfriend who spent the wee hours of the morning in the junkyard, but she could tell that it would. Of course, she'd never mentioned Artie to him.

"No, I suppose you are just friends. When Lois finds a boyfriend, he's certainly going to be a communist. I know that. A PETA member. Probably part of antifa, just to make people's heads turn. Or maybe she'll try to rattle me with a girlfriend like her friend over at that music hall."

Lo wished she could laugh at the outrageous things he said but was instead mortified into speechlessness. When he said things like that, she always told herself: *He's old; he's confused; he's scared for my future; he believes he's thinking these things and not saying them out loud.* She tried to practice seeing his frustration as internalized projection, something she'd heard on an audiobook from the library. With her dad, there was always a fine line between ignoring his offensive comments and confronting him. But confronting him inevitably led to her apologizing because somehow he managed to convince her that he only wanted what was best for her, that he simply wanted to help. Still, she didn't want John to hear firsthand what an ignorant old man he was.

An angry comeback was forming on the tip of her tongue when John stood up and walked over to where Lo was standing. He stood next to her awkwardly, and it took her a minute to realize it had been a quiet act of solidarity. She raised her eyes and frowned at John in an attempt to apologize for her father's embarrassing comments.

He glanced down at her for a second, then responded, "Like I said, sir, you don't owe me anything."

That afternoon she found her car in the parking lot with four intact tires. She wasn't sure how to thank John both for the tires and for helping manage her dad.

Unwelcome images of a tall, blonde, blue-eyed Shay Rose picnicking on the Mississippi kept flooding her mind. Had John taken that picture? Lo really didn't want to get in the middle of a love triangle with the town's jurisprudence sweetheart.

Lo cringed when she noticed Artie's car parked out front. Her relationship with Artie had been fraught for weeks and now it was causing trouble at work. Then she remembered how she was *still* living down a mess she made a few years ago with the singer of a band from Mankato, whom she had dated on-and-mostly-off for a year or so. By the end of that relationship, he refused to play the club unless Parker fired her. Why were men always trying to get her fired?

Before she went in, she decided to send John a simple text. Thank you for staying out late and fixing my tires. I appreciate it.

Most nights she stored her phone in a cabinet below the old cash register, but tonight, she left it out. A decent country duo was playing, and the venue was half-full. She served a few cans of beer and then leaned against the cooler and tried not to watch for the light of her phone signaling a message. She avoided Artie's pointed looks from the sound booth. The night was long and unbearable.

After the show she was busy sweeping and could hear Marti, one of her coworkers, finishing up with the till.

"Phone's going off, hun," Marti called. Lo perked up and tried to suppress a smile. "I see Parker's name popping up."

She let out a breath and scolded herself for being tied to her phone, for acting like a teenager. Why did she care about John texting her back all of a sudden? She stopped sweeping and wondered if this sudden interest in John was *all* just a means to gain her dad's approval. People did crazier things for that reason. She'd read that in a book from the library as well. John seemed so normal. And it felt like her dad's dream for her was simply that—for her to be normal. She heard Marti say, "Parker keeps texting you. She wants you to meet her at Lefty's."

"Tell her no."

"I'm not your secretary." Marti laughed, her voice layered with a smoker's rasp, her bleached blonde hair glowing in the black light. She slammed the till shut. "I'm done here, girly. Ready to lock up?"

Parker had texted Lo five times. In the last text, she threatened her job if she didn't meet her at Lefty's. Lo considered for a second and then responded. Fine. Be there soon. It wasn't like she had any better plans for the night.

When Lo pulled her car up to the street opposite Lefty's, the first thing she noticed was John Blank sitting on a bar stool. All she could see of Parker, sitting between John and the old wood-paneled wall, was her hand reaching for a pint of beer. Lo suppressed a rising anxiety and put on her best irritated face as she crossed the street and walked toward the glass-fronted bar, the ON SALE/OFF SALE LIQUOR sign blinking in red neon above her. She listened to its hum for a few seconds before she pulled open the door.

ANTELOPE ISLAND, UTAH

Brine flies swarmed the beach. The horizon line was lost in the pasty gray foam of the lake, which reflected the pasty gray gloom of the sky. Jason knew the mountains were close, but they were mostly hidden from sight. Smoke from a not-too-distant wildfire sat on the beach like a shipwreck, a purple haze that could be tasted.

He stood in the lake, water up to his ankles with his sneakers sinking in the soft mud and salt water. Tourists walked by holding their noses, complaining of the stench. No fish lived in the Salt Lake—not one—but still, the smell of rotting fish engulfed the shoreline. Jason read about it on a glossy pamphlet near the visitor's center. Each year the smell became stronger as the water evaporated, disappeared into the wildfires or the warming atmosphere. The salt content rose, the brine shrimp flourished, the red-necked phalaropes grew fat and fed their young, stabbing shrimp with their sharp, narrow beaks. The flats continued to expand while the lake grew smaller and more buoyant.

He walked farther into the lake until his knees were covered, then pulled his phone out of his pocket, sleek and black. Jason checked his texts again, typed something rapidly, stared at it, erased it and then reread the last message he sent on the morning that he left.

Lex, I don't understand the hell just happened. Are we doing this?

No responses, no missed calls, no new messages. Just silence. There had never been silence between them. Things had always been so easy.

He didn't know how to be a parent. That wasn't his fault though.

Jason never forgot how much of a natural his dad was. Little League baseball games, doctor's appointments, everything taken in stride. But then one day, his dad was gone, and not *all* parents were naturals. It was wrong to gamble with a kid's life like that. The truth was he had no idea whether he would be more like his dad or more like his mom, and he had never intended to find out.

Jason threw the phone as hard as he could, then sat down cross-legged in the cold, clammy water. He filled his chest with air while leaning back, disappearing into a murky gray wake. A lonely baptism. He didn't know if he had ever been baptized. If he had, no one had told him about it. A group of phalaropes chided him with frantic calls, flapping their wings to fly away from the disruption.

As he stirred up soft sediment trudging out of the lake, an older couple stood at the shoreline with heavy binoculars. The man didn't take his eyes off Jason until they were close enough to hear each other without shouting.

"Hey, son, you ought to head back in and get that phone you threw. This is a national park. That thing is full of chemicals that will leach out and harm the delicate ecosystem here." Jason, soaking wet, only looked at him. "And haven't you heard? That lake is full of mercury. Full of it," the tourist continued.

Jason stopped for a second. "I'm not your son."

"What's that?" the old man shouted from shore.

"I said *go fuck yourself.*" He whispered this, mostly to himself.

"What's that? Come on out of there."

"Go fuck yourself."

"What's that? This lake isn't for swimming. You should know that, that's all." The man seemed to have lost his resolve.

A trail of footprints moved through the sandy flats from the shoreline to the parking lot. Jason passed by the foot-washing station, a spot to clean off the sand, the dead fish smell, the toxic mercury, and found his car easily—one of only two left in the lot. But first, he leaned into the window of the tourists' car. He could see the man watching him through his binoculars from the beach. Jason waved and then looked down to examine its insides. A *New Yorker* magazine, a birder's guide, two cups of gas station coffee in the center console. Clean and otherwise completely empty. Out of instinct, he reached for his phone in his dripping wet pocket. He patted it, empty. "Well, shit," he said to no one.

"You guys are crazy!" Lo yelled into the mostly empty bar. The only people in Lefty's were the three of them and Mike Nelson, the old bartender who'd worked there since before Lo was born. He pretended to clean the counters as he listened to their conversation. Lo knew he gossiped with everyone who walked in about everyone who had just walked out. Mike was responsible for spreading news faster than the local paper.

Lo shook her head frantically. The four beers she'd downed in an hour made it feel heavy. She could feel her curls bounce around her face. "I'm sorry, John, but I don't know you, and you might be a serial killer. Parker, why do you want me to travel across the country with a serial killer?"

Parker laughed and hit the bar hard with her open hand. "Oh, stop it, Lo. You're so scared of everything. Didn't you hear the man? Blanche Peterson has been texting him every day. The woman's gonna die. She needs to see her son before she goes. Besides, John is a mechanic, not a serial killer. Nobody's got time to be both. Right?"

"No. Definitely not," John said seriously, leaning against the narrow back of the bar stool. "I know it's sort of crazy, but Ric said it'd be fine to take a week off. We drive to California, convince him to visit his dying mother, and we can see some of the country." He paused and took a drink of his beer. Lo watched his mouth when he talked, the muscles of his jaw clench and release. When he opened his mouth wide to say the *i* in drive, it sounded more like a long *Ahh*. "I thought it was crazy too, but when Parker and I threw back *many* too many beers here last week, she convinced me that it was good karma or whatever. Besides," he sighed, "my real reason for going is because I need to visit my sister in New Mexico. I haven't seen her in a long time, and I owe her a visit. Sort of out of the way, but I guess if we're going that far, why not take a detour . . ." John said this last sentence quietly, then smiled sheepishly. "And your dad would be proud of you. Taking the next step in our relationship."

Lo groaned and pushed him away, but he sat solid in his seat. Parker leaned against the sticky, drink-stained wood paneling, John sat in the middle, and Lo sat next to him. She had to lean forward and look past John in order to glare at Parker, who was giggling hysterically to herself. Did this mean he *wasn't* already in a relationship? Or was he just teasing her? Surely he wasn't being serious.

"Searching for a man who doesn't want to be found in order to return him to his dying mother is *not* a couple's retreat." Lo groaned dramatically. Parker sighed out her last laugh and wiped her wet eyes.

John wasn't *that* funny. Suddenly, it was all too much—the beers that went straight to her head, the coercion, Parker laughing, John joking about her dad. She took twenty dollars out of her purse, laid it on the bar and got up to leave.

"No, Lo!" Parker called after her, but Lo was already pushing the door open into the cool night. Even as she touched the door handle, she knew John would follow her.

She was only two doors down, in front of the hardware store, when she heard John call her name. The shop was dimly lit by a light left on in a small office toward the back. One side of the store was organized with hammers, screwdrivers, tools, and the other half was office supplies, toilet paper, dish soap. Lo knew exactly where every single item was located. She had been into the store a thousand times in her life, finding the correct-sized anchor for a screw so she could hang up a Prince poster in her room, purchasing a tiny jar of superglue to fix her favorite broken coffee mug.

"I really didn't mean anything by it. I'm not trying to embarrass you or anything. I guess—" he stopped and looked into the hardware store.

"You didn't embarrass me. I feel like you were ignoring me—that plan is crazy."

"It's not that crazy." He lifted a shoulder. "When was the last time you left Elysian, Lois? I bet you could map this whole town out with your eyes closed." He was moving closer to her. She stepped away from him. The credit union was behind her now. Its old-timey gold font reflected off the light coming from an old-fashioned lamppost across the street.

"Don't call me Lois, only my dad calls me that. Just because I know this place like the back of my hand doesn't mean it's a good idea to go on a wild goose chase with you—"

"All right, fine. It's crazy. I admit it. It's just that Blanche is hard to say no to. She's going to die soon. And it's not just that—" He stopped talking but kept moving toward her. She kept backing away. He continued, "If we do this trip, I can see my sister in Albuquerque. She and I, we have a complicated history." He paused again and took another step toward her. She didn't move this time. "We could just take a drive, help an old lady out and see some family. I know we don't know each other that well, but I do find you very . . ." He paused like he was looking for the right word. "Interesting." He smiled a little but only looked down at her feet.

Interesting? Her head was buzzing with his offer, and she was definitely buzzed from the beers. Lo knew she ought to say: *you're crazy; leave me alone; "interesting" is not a compliment.* But as she moved her lips to say those things, she instead said, "You're drunk. And I'm not a damsel, you know. I don't need rescuing, not from my own life or from this dumb small town."

He looked confused for a minute but then recognition flashed across his face. "It would just be a one-week thing. We both know the same people, it's not like we're complete strangers. And about the damsel thing, I was only teasing you. I really don't think you're helpless."

She nodded gently and narrowed her eyes. Then she said, "Walk me home, John."

They walked in silence for a couple of blocks. Lo eyed the nearly full moon. The light of it dimmed and brightened in response to wispy clouds that blew across the sky. She could feel John's tension; he seemed nervous. She pointed to her duplex from across the street and told him she could make it there herself. He nodded, but before she could cross the street, he reached out for her hand. The night was cool, but not cold. She wore an old, heavy wool sweater, blue, with white knit stripes on the upper arms that was warmer than most of her coats.

"I'm sorry about what I said back there."

Was he sorry for suggesting they leave everything behind and go on a road trip across the country? Or was he sorry for that lame attempt at a compliment? Or was he reapologizing for his damsel-in-distress comments?

"Listen, it's fine. I had fun hanging out with you guys, and we should do it again—as long as you don't bring up Blanche or driving across the country."

He shook his head, chuckling. "Oh, no deal. I haven't changed my mind. I still think we should go. Pretty set to do it myself if I have to. Blanche texts me every single day, I kid you not. Why isn't she textin' you too, I wonder? And I do need to visit my sister. I meant I'm sorry that I told you you were interesting. What I meant to say, before I chickened out, is that I find you attractive. I think you're strange and interesting and—" He paused for a second. "Do you want me to walk you in?"

"Oh my god, you really are drunk. Aren't you dating someone already?" She stood there laughing while he looked slightly guilty. "Oh, never mind," she stammered, "you get yourself home safely, John." She turned and walked as fast as she could into her house.

Wood chips popped in the stove. She could smell the particular scent of burning birch—so much sweeter than oak. The problem with John Blank was the same problem she'd had with Artie Parker.

After things had gone from bad to worse between them, Lo made a pact with herself to find a man who could understand her. She was tired of having to explain every facet of freeganism, every fact she had gathered about pollution, production, climate change, and then teach it like a lesson in school to the men she dated. There hadn't been many men, but that was partially because she hated feeling like it was her job to spell it all out—as if she were the one who needed to explain herself—not the people who lived without a care on their minds. She knew that getting involved with John would demand the same repetitive arguments about sustainability and capitalism. She owed it to herself to find someone who accepted this part of her without judgment.

She tried to read her firefly book. *Ellychnia corrusca*. Winter fireflies that didn't glow. How strange. She was suddenly distraught at the thought of a fireless firefly and held her breath to keep herself from crying. This was a trick she had learned in middle school, and it had served her well all these years. She set the firefly book down and pulled out the massive road atlas from the thrift store. She flipped through the pages once—the Midwest, the Southwest, California. Then once again, she turned the pages slowly, looking at the tangled mass of highways. She traced her finger down I-35 from Albert Lea to Des Moines. She wondered how long that drive was. Two hours, maybe a little more?

She knew what she had to do.

The next morning, Blanche appeared surprised to find Lo at her front door but welcomed her in out of the cold. The house smelled like cooking pizza, and Lo wondered if that was all she ate.

"You decided to take the trip, Bambi?"

"Well—" Lo hesitated. "Actually, I'm here about something else. See, this might seem strange, but you mentioned that my dad, Jerry Gunderson, and your husband were friends, right? You said you remembered the day I showed up in town. The thing is, I don't know much about where I came from or who my mother was." At first, Lo only knew a name and that she was from Iowa—the only two things her dad had ever divulged. Eventually, she gathered enough courage to search the name on the internet. She found an address listed in Des Moines and a business profile for sales work at a local manufacturing company. That was it. "I was wondering if you had any information or remember anything else about her." Lo's heart was pounding. She had rarely mentioned her mother to anyone, much less an eccentric stranger.

"Oh," Blanche hummed, wheezing a bit as she did. Then she sighed heavily. "There were things that happened. Some secrets. Thing is, my memory from those times—my mind—is hazy after all these years."

Lo nodded. "Okay, I just thought I'd ask is all."

"I forget most things, but I do know who will remember."

Lo climbed three concrete steps and then knocked gently on the plastic window panel of Mike Nelson's storm door. The sun was high in the sky and reflected off the house's white plastic siding so that she was slightly blinded no matter where she looked.

The inside door opened. Mike was wearing a tight t-shirt that accentuated his belly. His long silver hair—normally tied back in a ponytail—was messy, smashed against his forehead and haphazardly tucked behind his ears. He was holding a microwave dinner tray with a fork sticking out of it. From behind the screen door, she heard him mumble, "Lois Gunderson?" She smiled awkwardly.

"You forget something at Lefty's last night?" he asked, not unkindly.

"Uh, no. It's nothing like that. I just have a few questions I was hoping to ask you."

So, it was that day in Mike Nelson's dark living room, the murmur of *The Price Is Right* in the background, that she learned everything he knew about her mother and father. She ran her hands back and forth on Mike's old orange sofa. The polyester fabric was soft to the touch and made a gentle *whoosh* sound as he told her about her father's first wife, a teacher who left him for the principal of the school in the next town over. That was old news. A detail of her father's life that she was aware of but hadn't much considered. But she did discover many details she'd never known about her young mother—a Minneapolis waitress—and other details she might regret knowing for the rest of her life.

"Fifty thousand dollars?" she repeated, in shock.

Mike nodded. "That's what I heard. Gave her fifty grand and, far as I know, never saw her again."

When she left Mike Nelson's house, she held back tears long enough to say goodbye and thank him for his time. On her way down the front stoop, Lo, flushed with embarrassment, flicked tears away from her face with her fingers.

She took the long way, wandering around town until she found herself standing in front of her childhood home. She felt like she was seeing it for the first time. The paint was chipping along the wooden siding, which was starting to warp and grow soft through many long, wet winters. Patches of brown grass were visible under drifts of melting snow. The curtains in her old bedroom were drawn closed. The same purple linen that she'd hung in high school were now sun-faded and a shade of pale gray.

All she could think to do in that moment was text John: I'll go.

A NIGHTMARE

Lo dreamed of a small box turtle. It was upside down, wiggling its arms and legs, not urgent—but desperate. Almost futile. She bent over to pick it up but suddenly felt frightened to touch it. She tried to right it, but her hands shook; she could only bring herself to touch it with one finger. It kept rolling too far, rolling over again onto its back. She was making no progress. Was she hurting it? There were no sticks, no branches to use in place of her own shaking hands. The animal was powerless in the tumult. She used her foot, but kicked too hard, so the turtle circled around and landed on its back once more. She knew she had to reach out and grab it in order to save it. Your home is on your back, you are your own home. The harmony in your life is fleeting quickly, where will you take it—this one life? But she couldn't overcome her fear before the turtle disappeared into something else, some other dream that was forgotten by morning.

ELYSIAN, MINNESOTA

John reached out hesitantly and took the envelope from Blanche, fat with cash. Her other hand rested on her oxygen tank. She was not frail, despite her condition. Her arms were solid as she slowly pulled her hand away from the money.

"That's too much," Lo said. "All we need is cash for gas. We'll sleep at rest stops, and I'm going to pack food."

Blanche waved her hand dismissively. Her breath wheezed, and Lo wondered if she could hear the oxygen tank leaking a slow hiss. "Take it. If you don't use it, then fine, bring it back, but I don't need it. I don't need nothing." Blanche's dark orange hair had faded. Her roots were a shock of gray, and the other inch or so had faded into a pale yellow. Her muumuu was a white terry cloth, stained with a spectrum of colors.

John tapped the envelope of cash rapidly against his thigh. In her first meeting with him, he had seemed so relaxed and confident in the small lobby of the auto shop. She realized now that it might have simply been his low voice and slow southern accent that hid a deeper restlessness.

Blanche sat in her recliner facing the TV while John and Lo sat on the love seat. She could feel the vibrations of his heel tapping quickly against the floor and imagined all the dust he was stirring up with his nervous energy. She tried to take shallow breaths and covered her mouth with her sleeve. John looked at her strangely. She gestured toward the door, ready to go.

They had discussed everything ad nauseam. They asked a few questions about Jason, but Blanche couldn't answer them. All they had was the contact information of the farm in Santa Rosa where Jason was supposedly headed. Lo wished she could reassure Blanche that they'd bring Jason back to town, but she knew she couldn't make any promises.

During the visit, questions for Blanche sat on the tip of Lo's tongue. John left the porch and was walking toward the boulevard when Lo asked quietly, "Did you know about my mother?"

Blanche stopped short. They were the same height, eye to eye. She didn't look surprised by the question, only tired. "What do you mean?" Blanche wheezed loudly and her hand gripped the tank, squeezing tightly. "No one talked about anything else for damn near five years."

"No, I mean the details of—" She didn't know how much to share. If Blanche had forgotten what she knew, what did it matter?

Blanche hacked out a laugh. "I can't remember anything anymore. Mostly just big things. Big moments, old faces, whole days, but not single details. Those have all"—she waved her hand up the ceiling—"flown away." As Lo pushed the porch door open, Blanche said, "The only person who could tell you the truth of it is your mother. All you kids need to call your mothers. Tell Jason that when you see him. You too, Rebel, you hear me?"

Lo brushed past John, who had been waiting for her on the curb, but he called after her. "Lo, I want to talk about what you said the other night. About me having a girlfriend or whatever."

She shook her head. "No worries. I'll text you later," was all she could get out. She couldn't deal with John right now. Blanche was right. The person she needed to talk to—the only person who could answer all her questions—was her mother.

They met at the shop early Saturday morning. John planned on giving the car a thorough service with an oil change and whatever else he could tinker with to get them ready for a cross-country road trip. At first Lo stood awkwardly while John bent under the hood. She enjoyed watching him work.

After a minute, he stood up and wiped his hands with an oily rag and cleared his throat. "I'm not anybody's boyfriend, Lo."

"That's not what I heard." She pretended to be uninterested as she looked around the shop for nothing in particular.

"What did you hear? Something 'bout Shay Rose, I suppose?" Lo only nodded and kept looking at anything but John. "She's like—" he faltered. "She comes into town, and we hang out. Really, maybe once a month, and now that she's in law school, you know." He shrugged. "Might not see her much anymore. Thing is—it's not serious or anything."

Lo wasn't sure how to process this. It's not like she had any claim on John and technically had not even broken up with Artie yet. Besides, did John think Lo would be cool with being Shay Rose's in-town backup? All she could think to say was, "It's cool."

Eventually, Lo moved to the lobby where she sat flipping through her firefly book. It mostly focused on the glowing lightning bugs out east. She read that species in the western United States rarely glowed as adults. Only a few pockets of different species here and there could light up. But *all* glowworms—fireflies in their infant state—were bioluminescent. This meant that even fireflies that didn't light up the coastal California twilight still had glowing larvae, buried just below the surface of the soil. She was reading a paragraph about bioluminescent algae when she heard the door from the garage open.

She expected to hear John tell her that the car was not safe for a cross-country trip, but she looked up and saw Ric, the garage owner, smiling at her from behind the computer. She smiled back and nodded. "Hi," she said politely.

He started moving the mouse around on the service counter then sighed dramatically. "Everything okay?" she asked.

"It's okay. Just not sure how to work this thing." He laughed, but Lo worried he might blame her for taking John on this road trip. Maybe he should.

"Sorry if John leaving for the week makes work harder here. I'm still not sure we should even be going, actually."

Ric looked surprised for a minute, then shook his head back and forth. "I told him to go. Not really because of the woman and her son. But John told me the whole story of his sister. I told him, 'You should go out and see the world. See your family. Meet a girl.'" He shrugged then waved his hand nonchalantly. "So, he's finally listening to me. We don't need him here. Ha! He mostly stares at the computer all day. Aldo, my son, you know him. He's good with the computer too. Me—not so much." He shrugged and then sat down next to her.

She had a sneaking suspicion he was going to warn her not to break John's heart or something like that. "Well, I promise we'll hurry. It'll be a quick trip."

Ric seemed to be lost in his own thoughts for a minute, then stood up as a customer walked into the lobby. "You two have a good time. Play loud music. Play Magenta Crush."

"I'm Lo, by the way," she said.

"Yeah, I know your name. We hear it all day long."

SOUTHWESTERN UTAH

The Jeep was as old as him, rusted red with a flat back and boxy edges. Jason stopped for gas in Cedar City. A kid with round eyes sat in a minivan and stared at him as he held the gas pump. When Jason noticed her staring, he tipped an imaginary hat her way and took a bow. She smiled only slightly, then looked back toward the television in the car that played something bright and slightly hallucinogenic.

Were there somehow more children in the world than before? It seemed so. They were everywhere he looked. Moms, dads and kids had taken over the rural highways and crowded byways of these United States.

Jason didn't know a lot about his dad because after his death his mom had refused to speak about him. Though she had kept every single back-catalog edition of the town paper that she could get her hands on. She didn't only save the paper, though. She also kept a shoebox full of small tapes on which his dad recorded notes, interviews and exhaustingly thorough Vikings' stats. Jason had moved that box safely up to his bedroom one afternoon while his mom was nowhere to be found, and as far as he knew, it still sat there twenty years later.

In the crumbling gas station, Jason found a compact voice recorder similar to the one his dad once used. Along with it he bought a pack of batteries, a pack of Marlboro 100s and a lighter.

In the car, he put the batteries in the voice recorder, packed the cigarettes with a few hard slaps to his open palm and put one in his mouth.

It smelled like his dad. Jason picked up the voice recorder, pressed the record button and immediately felt stupid. He hit the stop button, threw the recorder and the cigarette down on the passenger seat and started the car.

A work arrangement was waiting for him at the end of this trip, farther out west, but he wasn't in a rush. He needed to clear his head and whatever it was that had compelled him to buy a seven-dollar pack of cigarettes he didn't even want to smoke. He needed to shake whatever it was that brought up all these memories of his dad, two decades later.

It was time for Jason to see all those places he wanted to but hadn't yet, to visit some old friends, to get his head right after everything that had happened with Alexis. Time to start over.

His pointer finger moved away from I-15 and followed one highway, then another, moving east toward Bryce Canyon. He folded up the map of Utah, fresh off the shelf of the gas station that probably sold a lot more phone cases than maps.

As he drove, he reached for his phone. He kept forgetting it was sunk somewhere at the bottom of the Salt Lake. Eventually, mindlessly, he picked up the voice recorder and hit the button.

"I haven't watched a Vikings game in ten years. Lex grew up a Niners fan but now she hates football. We find better shit to do on a Sunday afternoon. Sometimes she sits and reads romance novels—she's into that kind of stuff. We go to town and check out the movie theater, eat some Chinese food, get stoned, lay next to the river. Did we ever eat Chinese food together? I don't remember." Jason pressed the stop button. He didn't know what else to say.

The screeching noises coming from under the hood made him nervous as he handled the curves, his eyes scanning the red rocks covered in patchy, scant snowfall. A few times he hit the dashboard. It didn't make the noises stop, but it didn't seem to make them any louder either.

He slowed down when he passed the welcome sign: BRYCE CANYON NATIONAL PARK in shades of stone and brown framed by a pine forest in the distance. Alexis would have demanded he stop for a photoshoot, but without his phone, he had no camera. Maybe he could find a disposable camera at another ancient gas station. But maybe not. Who would look at the photos anyway?

Jason parked the Jeep and walked to an overlook, brownish-red spires of rock in every direction. A wooden sign explained that the natural formations were called hoodoos. Hoodoos demonstrate the power of water in reshaping stone and altering the landscape. Penis-shaped red rocks that were chiseled into being, infiltrated by something as tiny as water molecules. Changing slowly over time. Something that seemed impenetrable and permanent was altered so completely by something so minuscule, tiny as a fucking molecule.

Jason looked around and inhaled the dry desert air. He squatted and scraped his fingers through the red dirt, packed hard by the sun. Pine trees flecked the view. As he made his way back to his truck, he watched the tourists huff with difficulty in the thin oxygen. They looked blankly toward the blue sky. They squinted blindly toward the red-rock formations in the distance. No one seemed to notice him. They seemed to notice nothing, really, not even their own shadows on the trail.

ELYSIAN, MINNESOTA

In six hours, John would knock on the front door, and they would load up Lo's car and drive across the country. She'd already packed her backpack with rolled socks, clean underwear, a few pairs of leggings. She'd purchased most of them on a single trip to Mankato with Parker and Teresa, who sometimes went to check out the local venues and find new acts willing to play The Locust. Colorful bell-bottom leggings and oversized t-shirts with pictures of wolves howling at the moon or cat heads floating in space were Lo's typical picks. Parker teased her about their loudness. Lo could never explain how it was the *normal* that was continually pushing in on her, trying to trim her down to size, squeeze her tight and fit her into what it offered, which never felt like enough. Even if her only way to fight back was an ugly t-shirt that cost a dollar.

She crawled into bed and set her alarm. Her backpack sat by the front door. A canvas tote filled with apples, sandwiches, jars of peaches and a bag of kringlas. And a full jar of pickles sat next to it.

Earlier that evening, a group of three women from town had knocked gently on her front door. Lo smiled courteously when she found Melinda, her neighbor; Jean Little, a friend of her father's for possibly their entire lives; and another woman she eventually recognized as her middle school English teacher. They heard she was leaving town—from whom, she had no idea—and wanted to bring her a bag of kringlas leftover from their book-club luncheon earlier that day. They were apparently feeling chatty, even while the cold wind whipped through as they huddled on Lo's front stoop and began to analyze the section of *Bleak House* they had discussed that week. Mostly they talked about how they still remembered folks with smallpox scars. Lo listened politely, nodding, never having read the book and not knowing anything about Dickens, except that he was responsible for the boring black-and-white movie version of *A Christmas Carol* that her dad loved so much.

She had wondered vaguely if they expected her to invite them in and lay out the route of her trip for their approval. They likely wouldn't have approved, though. Since they were first weaving their way south to New Mexico to visit John's sister and then heading northwest to Santa Rosa to look for Jason—an awkward triangle. Eventually, she explained that she had to finish packing and watched them file down the sidewalk shoulder to shoulder. Lo figured they would head to the VFW for fervid gossip about her wild cross-country trip to fulfill Blanche Peterson's dying wish.

"God, they're obsessed with me," she said to herself as she shut her front door.

She was ready to get out of town.

MINNESOTA/IOWA BORDER

"So, I've been thinking about Minneapolis since Parker has a friend who lives in a co-op up there and offered to hook me up with him." Lo said this with more assurance than she felt. John nodded as he ran a finger across the seal where the window met the door. His long legs bent so one knee rested on the passenger door and the other was near the shifter. Lo had been resting her hand on top of it while she drove until his leg grazed one of her fingers and she moved it away.

The ground was mostly flat. Cornfields flanked the side of the highway to their right. On the left, a gas station would pass by, an exit for some small farm town she'd heard of but never visited, an outlet mall, an ugly billboard, a McDonald's, a patch of oaks still winter brown without buds or leaves. Then they'd be surrounded by empty cornfields on both sides again, with only a few feet of ditch separating the road from fallow dirt. She knew that's where the fireflies congregated every year once the weather warmed. She'd seen them floating, blinking in all the ditches that bordered the highways.

Everything still felt familiar. The fields were just brown mud now. No one had planted yet. Some had been cleared to prepare for it, and some still held half-chopped, weathered yellow stalks of dead corn. They'd be cleared soon enough. It was the same every year.

"You plan to leave Elysian?" he asked.

"*Mhm*, definitely. I can't stay there. Everyone knows more about my past than I do. And they all think I'm a communist weirdo." She smirked and expected a laugh or at least a chuckle, but John only looked out the window.

"I like Elysian. The people are mostly 'conventional.'" He used finger quotes. "That's true. And it's also true that you're not." He chuckled then, but Lo didn't. "Not like they're really conservative or anything, voting-wise. Maybe even a few communists around town if you wanted to start a club or something. Think you're misrepresenting them in that department. They mean well. Helpful, nice, predictable. The lakes are full of fish. Lefty's got cold beer."

"That's all you need? Fishin' and beer?" She asked in her best southern accent. "Sounds like a country song. I guess you are a true southerner."

"I don't think that's true."

He shook his head and looked past Lo, out her window, where a semitruck drove by. She tried to act natural as she cruised at five miles below the speed limit. The car started to shake when she got up to seventy, but John told her not to worry—it was just old. Still, she set the cruise at sixty-five and did her best not to swerve away from trucks as they flew past.

"No, that's not all I need. Though, I do like fishin'," he said, laying the accent on thick like she had tried to. "And I do like beer, but I am not a *true southerner*, whatever that means. I like Elysian. I got some family around me, my uncle and all them. I know where everything is. I never get lost. I know who I'm working with and got a good job. I meet nice people." She could feel his gaze on her, but she kept looking forward, both hands on the wheel.

"Just give it time. Burn a few bridges. I can barely even go into work anymore without my—" she stammered, "I guess he's my ex-boyfriend— trying to get me fired."

This made John smile. "Oh, you don't got to tell me about any of that. Parker already did."

"What?" Lo demanded, a little too loudly.

John laughed in response. "Pretty sure I got the full rundown on your dating history, your high school report cards, your favorite foods. Parker talked at me all about you for a few hours one night."

Lo's face burned red, and she could feel her hands start to sweat against the vinyl steering wheel. The day was mostly overcast, but she suddenly wished she had a pair of sunglasses to hide behind. She saw a sign flash by: DES MOINES 90 MI.

"Jesus. Sounds like Parker. Once I started dating her cousin—not even really dating—she told us we were both fired if we split up and caused any drama. Which of course we did."

"Yeah, she told me that. And she told me y'all haven't actually broken up. Don't be mad at her though. She told me 'cause I asked. But she couldn't tell me what it is you really want, though—like I'm sure eventually you'll want to get a job, right, when you head out of town? I imagine you wanting to be a veterinarian or marine biologist or political lobbyist for local farmers or something important like that."

Apparently, he hadn't listened to Parker very closely. "No, not at all," she responded. "Actually, I think people finding their identity in work is a product of a sick capitalist culture. I would never base my worth or my dreams on a career. I'm more than a job. I'm a human being. So, I don't base my life goals on a future income or anything like that. I aim for contentedness in my surroundings, peace in my heart and a sustainable balance with nature. That's all." She sat up straighter in her seat.

"*Hmm.*" John nodded slowly. "That is interesting. I wasn't—" he stopped for a minute, still nodding, "expecting such a passionate response. I guess I shouldn't be surprised about anything, not with you." He said this too casually, too suggestively, as if she were a puzzle he could solve with a little work.

It was frustrating, and she wasn't interested in playing his games. He wanted her to do the work, to flirt back, to ask him why he cared so much about getting to know her, but she wasn't interested in playing some cat-and-mouse thing with him.

The facts were that they were both currently entangled in other relationships, that Lo was going to leave town anyway, and on the off chance she didn't leave town, she couldn't be stuck with both an angry Artie *and* an angry John once their relationship inevitably ended.

Minnesota Public Radio played quietly in the background. Subdued chatter and intermittent laughter. Silence settled in, and neither of them spoke for a few minutes until she could feel John watching her. Lo side-eyed him with her best scowl, but the car started to swerve toward the ditch in the direction her eyes were looking. She overcorrected and nearly swerved into the next lane, where a mom in a minivan panicked and honked. John tensed, but she thought maybe he was holding back a laugh. "Stop looking at me, Bambi. Just keep your eyes on the road."

"Fine. I'm fine." She nodded, gripping the wheel. "Thank you for never calling me that again."

John smirked. "No deal. That name was given to you by our generous benefactor—Miss Blanche. And hot damn, it suits you, doesn't it?"

She glared at him for a brief second, only as long as she was willing to look away from the interstate. She looked back at the road and turned the volume up on the radio.

"No, it doesn't. Well, what's your nickname then, John Blank?" She asked, her voice raised over the radio, now blaring a quiz show. "Rebel? Jack? Johnny?"

In the corner of her eye, Lo caught a quick look of surprise cross over his face. But he only shook his head. "Never had one."

A LIST OF NAMES

Fitful Light
Lamplighter
Night Traveler
Belly of Fire
Light Beetle
Lantern Tail
Firetail
Ember Insect
Firelight
Surging Light
Spark Bug
Sun Fly
Flash Fly
Firefly
Lightning Bug
St. John's Beetle

KEARNEY, MISSOURI

Lo pulled into a gas station outside of Kearney. She had driven for five hours, and her hands were sore from clinging to the wheel. Even though they had filled up the gas tank an hour ago, they agreed to top it off while they were stopped. It was John's turn to drive since Kansas City was coming up and Lo didn't have much—or any—experience driving through big cities. John went to prepay since they were using cash. Lo took the chance to text Parker. This is so awkward. He's a passive-aggressive flirter and I don't like it. Just want to get to CA and find Jason.

Lo sat in the passenger seat and held her phone in her right hand and used it like a drum to keep a beat on her left palm when John came out of the gas station carrying a full plastic bag.

When he opened the driver's side door, she immediately said, "I'm sorry, did you just buy all that? Look at all that plastic! I told you already, I packed all this stuff." She pointed to the back seat where she had a cooler filled with snacks she had brought from her house—food from her winter garden like spinach salad and cooked sweet potatoes, apples, water in reusable glass jars. He set a plastic bottle of tea down in the driver's seat, mumbled, "Sorry," and then shut the door. He started filling the gas tank when Lo opened the passenger door and found herself face-to-face with him. Actually, face to chest. She looked up.

"John, I told you I brought stuff for us to eat." He only nodded. "Okay, you're just going to keep nodding while you destroy the environment and fill the oceans with your plastic pop bottles?" A middle-aged

man in a fedora stood near his SUV, cleaning out the trash from his car—
an empty bottle of water, a crumpled bag from a fast-food restaurant. Lo
could tell he was trying hard to look inconspicuous as he eavesdropped
on their argument.

"It's tea."

"What?" she asked tersely.

"It's sweet tea." He sighed and seemed to choose his words carefully.
"I realize how important this stuff is to you—"

She scoffed, cutting him off. "It's not *stuff*. It's facts. Facts that people
choose to ignore while the planet becomes toxic, landfills overflow and all
the bugs disappear." He looked at her confused, but then took a breath
and squeezed the pump as if he could make the gas come out faster.

"Okay, I understand this—these facts—are important to you. I just
wanted a tea and some chips. I apologize?" The inflection that turned
his apology into a question infuriated her.

"This is exactly why I didn't want to do this. Look at all this waste."
She pointed hopelessly toward the garbage bin next to the gas tank,
trash spilling over the top. The man that stood next to them was discon-
necting his own gas tank, frowning. "Half-empty plastic water bottles.
Water! It comes out of faucets for free! I just—I can't keep watching
people ruin the planet. And I could never be with someone who doesn't
understand that."

John scratched his neck with one hand and closed the door to the
gas tank with the other. She was standing in front of the open passenger's side door. He walked toward her. She backed into the door and
raised her head to look him in the eye. Very quietly, he whispered, "I'm
sorry. I just really like sweet tea."

She pursed her lips tight and tilted her head. Her phone vibrated
in her hand. She looked down and scanned quickly. Poor Lo. He's practically in love with you. Like love at first sight shit. It's stupid! You bought the
tix. Now take him for a ride. Just relax!

John seemed to be inching closer and closer to her. Lo made a dis-
gusted sound and held up a finger to stop him. He was close enough
for her to touch his chest, so she tapped it once. He reached up and

held her finger in his hand. Her eyes widened but all she said was, "No more plastic crap, please."

He shrugged and let go of her hand. "Yes, ma'am."

John was crossing the front of the car when she said, "And while we're at it—quit flirting with me. I don't like it." He stopped short and looked a little surprised. The man next to them started his car and drove away. A sound came out of John's throat like he was going to say something, but then she noticed his face change. He never said anything, just pushed out a breath and nodded once, then walked to the driver's side door.

The weather warmed a little as they headed south. Minnesota hadn't hinted at spring. Here, buds on the few trees near the interstate exit teased Lo with virgin blossoms. Bees and wasps collected around the trash bins, children wore t-shirts and didn't have to worry about rivers of snowmelt. She thought about texting Parker back but felt the situation with John had been defused somehow, so she simply slid into the passenger seat.

Once she shut the door, John said softly, "All right then, here we go." She only offered him a half smile along with a gentle roll of the eyes—an acknowledgment that she knew he was attempting to ignore their awkward tension. Lo sighed, confused, and suddenly missed her woodstove, her boots neatly arranged by the front door, the comfort of her own home.

He followed the directions on the phone's GPS, and they kept heading south.

NEVADA/CALIFORNIA BORDER

"Her eyes shine like gold in the sun. It's cheesy to say, I know, but it's the truth. I never minded rain or whatever, but once I met Lex, I only wanted clear skies because I'd never seen anything like her eyes when the sun is shining. She's always laughing, cracking jokes, taking things easy. Smart, too. Got her degree in agriculture and can work magic in a garden. I've got so much to learn that she already knows . . ." Jason hit the stop button and threw the voice recorder down into the passenger seat.

At first, he'd been tempted to throw it away at every stop, embarrassed by how often he picked it up. But once he got talking, he could say as much about Alexis as he wanted to. He liked remembering all the good times they'd had before everything went to shit.

He started to remember things about his dad that he'd forgotten, too, like how they would fry eggs and bacon on the pancake griddle on Saturday mornings before his mom woke up. Whenever memories of his mom intruded, Jason pushed the stop button and turned back to the scenery.

The old Jeep had moved west out of Utah, through Nevada and into California. Signs for Death Valley appeared on the side of a narrow highway. He turned his wrists to the right, then both arms flexed hard. The power steering kept failing. He had serious doubts whether the Jeep would make it through this trip alive.

After Bryce Canyon, Jason had decided on Death Valley, and the literature teacher in him couldn't ignore the metaphor no matter how hard he tried. Not even fifth graders would have missed it. He was feeling sentimental, but angry at himself for it. He missed Alexis. He felt awful. He wasn't ready for Santa Rosa, where he was hoping he could stay on for a few years. Or maybe he wasn't ready to give up the voice recorder, which he now planned on throwing away once he stopped for good.

There would be no baptism today. The water that was currently evaporating in the wildfires in Utah had evaporated in Death Valley forever ago. The saline valley glimmered white in the pale yellow sunshine. The sky reflected the colorlessness of the flats. The wind blew hard and collected in miniature salt dunes.

Jason's red Jeep pulled into a parking lot flanked by mountains. Trash littered the concrete. Styrofoam cups, burger wrappers, cigarette butts. He sat in his car for an hour, watching families come and go. He watched a mother pour bottled water over her toddler's head. The kid laughed and clapped wildly.

He watched the mountains in the distance. Distance wasn't a finite thing. It was dependent upon a certain vantage point. That was something he had taught to elementary school students. The displacement of parallax made understanding anything from a distance a relative construct. Distance was relative to all the people streaming out of trailheads, relative to the garbage in overflowing trash cans. Relative to everything. Maybe even relative to death itself. The distance he was from his dad might appear fixed, but somehow, he felt closer to him than he had since he died. The distance he felt from Alexis was supposedly relative too, but it felt permanent and infinite.

He looked at the map, and his eyes moved from Death Valley to Twin Falls and back. He reached compulsively for a phone that no longer existed. His eyes scanned the distance on the map up and down the continental United States, not more than a few inches on the page.

He opened the car door, then stopped, one foot close to landing on the concrete. His eyes went dry and immediately started to burn in the salty wind. Heat surrounded him as if he had just opened an oven door and put his whole body inside. Everything was wrong. He tried to take a deep breath and flexed his extended leg, but it never touched the ground. After a minute, he pulled it back into the car and shut the door. The Jeep left the parking lot and headed west.

WEST TEXAS

"Did you ever see them—the synchronous fireflies?" she asked, flipping through her book in the growing dark. "You grew up in the Great Smoky Mountains, right?"

John shook his head. "The Smokies? They're up on the border of North Carolina, spilling into Tennessee. We never went to the Smokies, especially not to watch bugs. Had plenty of opportunities for that without taking a long drive." He gripped the steering wheel and squinted at the road signs as they passed.

Past Kearney, whenever she offered to drive after they stopped to fill up the gas tank, he told her that he didn't mind doing it. While she did appreciate that—she had realized almost immediately that she didn't like driving on an interstate full of semitrucks and people streaming movies on the phones in their laps—she worried he thought that she wasn't a good driver. While she conceded that this might be the truth, she didn't like the idea of John thinking it.

While he drove, Lo watched out the window, taking in the scenery. As the hours passed, the budding spring green of the lower Midwest had slowly faded into shades of brown. By the time the sun set and their first day driving turned into night, a monochrome of rusty-orange rocks and chunks of ocher-colored clay replaced the empty cornfields she was used to. The excitement of the newness tightened her chest—the kind of constriction that happens when some beauty and some novelty collide.

"A lot of bugs where you grew up?" she asked, immediately regretting it. A dumb question. There were probably a lot of bugs where everybody grew up.

He nodded, then asked, "You ever been to North Carolina?"

"Huh?" She was squinting, attempting to catch any scenery she could in the silver moonlight. "Uh-uh. Never really been anywhere. Well, once to New York with my dad, over to Mount Rushmore, all around Minnesota, obviously, and up into Canada once. That's it."

His fingers tapped the steering wheel as he took turns stretching each leg. Lo watched him surreptitiously. "Need a break? You've been driving all day."

"*Mhm*, I've been looking for a gas station or somewhere to stop. Not a lot around here, but Amarillo's coming up, so there'll be something." He said this as his finger pointed toward an exit sign that listed a single gas station. When they pulled onto the off-ramp, the sign listed the gas station as two miles away.

"I hate when they do that," Lo complained. "If the gas station is more than half a mile away, it shouldn't be listed on the exit sign."

"I don't know if there's much choice around here." He turned left while Lo watched his hands on the wheel. He had complied with her request to stop flirting with her. He'd been polite and a little too quiet, and for some reason, this made Lo feel like she needed to make up for the lost energy. She'd done this by finding different radio stations as the signals became static, by reading to him from her firefly book and by asking superficial questions like what his favorite subject in school had been (Spanish and shop class—no surprise) and what his favorite food was (he couldn't decide, so he listed about ten different things including pizza, lasagna, Mexican food or anything that came off a grill) and his favorite band (some country singers she'd never heard of, along with a few classic rock bands). He'd tried to turn the questions around, but she simply replied, "Hey, I ask the questions around here."

They pulled into an unlit and empty gas station and got out to stretch. Lo was afraid they'd run out of gas in the middle of nowhere, but John didn't seem worried. She understood the implication though.

If they couldn't find a gas station open this late, they would have to spend the night in Amarillo.

Their plan had been to drive straight through to John's sister's in Albuquerque so that they wouldn't have to pay for a hotel—or share a room. As she watched John reach his hands over his head to stretch his back, she thought maybe it wouldn't be that bad to get a room with two beds. They could keep talking and she could ask him more questions about his past and his family. So far, she'd only covered the easy stuff, likes and dislikes. Books, TV shows, favorite constellation (Orion, though she had been rapid-firing questions and hadn't expected an answer to that one).

Like some kind of magnet, maybe due to the vast scope of the lonely West Texas night or the relentless noise of chirping crickets, Lo found herself drawing closer and closer to John on the concrete slab of the small gas station while he looked out over the expanse. Except she happened to be standing directly under his elbow at the same moment he lifted it to point at something in the distance. He hit her face, not violently, but still, it hurt.

"Oh, Jesus Christ, I did *not* see you there, Lo. I'm sorry," he said, slightly panicked.

She tried to laugh while her eyes watered. "I'm okay, it's okay."

"You scared the shit out of me," he said, while at the same time, maybe out of impulse, he put his arm around her while looking down at her face in the pale light. "Is your nose bleeding? I can't see anything. I think your nose is bleeding." She smiled up at him politely and extricated herself with some difficulty.

"I'm fine. You were going to point to something before I ran into your elbow?" she asked, feeling the bridge of her nose for damage. The air smelled overwhelmingly like dust and the reflective prisms of spilled gas that glowed faintly purple on the concrete.

"Look," he pointed north. Lo glanced up and saw them—blinking lights.

"A city?" she asked.

"Doubt any small town out here would light up like that. An oil refinery, maybe? You see the blinking red lights there?"

"Can I see your phone?" she asked.

He looked at her curiously, took his phone out of his back pocket and handed it to her without saying anything. This felt intimate, something a couple might do, but Lo didn't hesitate as she asked for his password, which he shared. When she opened it, a text message to his sister, Deb, lit the screen. She read: I will always feel bad about what happened. She tried to act casual as she found the internet browser, open to a boring shopping site full of random car parts or some other parts Lo didn't recognize. She glanced up at John, who was still watching the glowing lights in the distance.

She found what she was looking for. "Yep, it's a refinery," she said. "Gross."

"Gross? You do know where I work, right? I change people's oil every day, yours included. This thing isn't getting great gas mileage, you know. Literally worse than my truck." A single floodlight was wired above the gas station door, which spotlit her car and backlit John as he faced the refinery. He had been using a lighthearted tone as he jogged in place and rolled his neck from side to side, so she pretended to ignore his comment and kept reading about the refinery, then scrolled through pictures of its glowing lights, which were somehow beautiful.

"Don't you think getting a free car that was rusting on the side of a road is better for the environment than buying a new one?" She looked over at him in the dark, but he didn't respond. She hated the pollution and risks that came with oil and gas drilling and understood that John was partially right. Now she was part of the problem, one of the people who chose convenience over sacrifice. Still, the gold-and-red lights blinking on the horizon felt like a siren's call. It was hard to look away now that she had seen them.

She resisted a strong urge to check his texts, to go through his photos, skim through his apps. Whose calls did John Blank miss? What was he googling in his free time? Were there any pictures on his phone besides walleyes and expensive cars? Was there more than one see-you-when-I'm-in-town kind of girl who John texted with?

"It is pretty, though, glowing out there in the distance," she admitted, "but I wish it wasn't cloudy. I bet the stars out here are unbelievable."

"Bet they are. A lot of stars out where I live by the lake too."

"Oh, yeah?"

"You could come see 'em sometime."

"Better not."

He laughed. "Well, that's your call."

She scoffed as she turned back to the car. "Can't risk it. You might actually break my nose if we're alone in the dark again."

OBJECTIVE SCIENTIFIC FACTS

Lightning bugs consume oxygen, which then mixes with a natural enzyme in their small beetle bodies called luciferin. This enzyme glows yellow and generates a cold light, almost perfectly efficient. For decades the flying beetles have been studied and dissected because, of course, humans are rapacious in understanding how they might harness the insect's natural technologies. Luciferin is named after Lucifer, a name many might recognize from certain religious texts. However, Lucifer simply means light-bringer in Latin and was a name used to signify the planet Venus, which rises at dawn with the sun.

TEXAS/NEW MEXICO BORDER

"Should get there around four," he said as he shut the car door. They had found an open gas station off the interstate, a massive truck stop that sold blankets, DVDs, stuffed animals and iced tea, which Lo was beginning to realize John was addicted to. He had asked her permission this time, which embarrassed her.

"Don't ask me," she argued, "ask the floating plastic island in the ocean."

They discussed options for tea containers, and Lo agreed that aluminum cans were better than plastic, but glass would be best. It was midnight, and he had already been driving all day, so he probably needed the caffeine. "Should we just stop, do you think? Can you make it four more hours?" she asked, unsure of what answer she hoped for.

"I'll be all right. The tea'll help. You can read more from your book if you want," he said, as they pulled back onto the interstate and headed west. Lo couldn't see much scenery unless it was illuminated by the light of a passing billboard. Mounds of jagged red rock, small scrub bushes— it was beautiful to her, even in the dark. She sighed, thinking about all the views she was missing. "Or not, you don't have to read if you don't want to," he said.

"What?" she asked. "No, I like reading. I didn't think you liked listening. I just hate missing all these views. I might not get to see this highway ever again, since we're going a different way back up."

"Yeah," he agreed. "Do you want to stop at a hotel so we can see it all in the morning? That's fine by me. Blanche is paying."

Lo felt a flush of warmth but shook her head. "No, it's all right. Your sister is expecting us, plus we'll save time and money—you know we shouldn't spend Blanche's money unless we really have to. As long as you're okay to drive," she added.

He didn't respond, just kept heading down the freeway as the radio signal turned into crackles and high-frequency beeps. Lo listened to them for a minute, trying to make sense of the chaos. She reached for the tuner at the same time he did. Their fingers met, and somehow he twisted his wrist so they were holding hands. They made an arch, sort of a game, for a few seconds. Lo laughed a little, as if it were funny rather than alarmingly erotic. She pulled her hand away from his and started playing with the radio while John put his hand back on the wheel and looked straight ahead.

She found a station that played old country music on a frequency in the high eighties. In Elysian, this was the polka station. She had always believed anything below ninety-two was for the elderly. Lo didn't know any of the songs, but they were pleasant and seemed to fit with the landscape that she couldn't see but could imagine—sage brush, covered wagons, westward expansion. That last one unsettled her. The car was quiet for a long time before John interrupted her thoughts about the colonial ills of Manifest Destiny.

"This is the sort of thing I listened to growing up," he said when the song changed to a woman crooning about her heartache.

"Oh, yeah?" she asked. "I've never heard any of this before. I don't think my dad ever changed the radio station from MPR, like ever."

"There was no public radio in my house. Only the classics—Jimmie Rodgers, Hank Williams, Jenny Lou Carson." He pointed to the radio. "That's who this is."

"What do you have to apologize to your sister for?" Lo blurted out, then raised her eyebrows at her own forwardness. "Sorry," she said quickly. "When I looked at your phone, a text message was up on the screen. I just . . ." she trailed off.

He waved his hand away in the darkness. She wondered if he wanted her to grab it again. Instead, she folded her hands under her thighs and listened to her own breath while John seemed to consider his words.

"Yeah," was all he said for a minute. Lo watched him expectantly. His profile glowed whenever they passed brightly lit billboards, and she could make out his black eyelashes in silhouette. She forgot what they had been talking about as she watched him blink in the passing shadows.

He took a deep breath and continued, "I'm actually glad you brought it up because I've been thinkin' I need to talk to you about it all day. Just to let you know what to expect. Deb and I, where we grew up, it's—" he paused. "It's pretty hard to explain and sounds wild."

"Okay," Lo responded, holding out the syllables carefully in a sing-song voice.

"A snake church," was all he said.

"*Hmm?*"

"You know—we grew up in a snake church, where people hold poisonous snakes to prove that God will protect them and that they're true believers."

"I'm sorry," Lo said, "I'm confused. *Um*—what?"

"'They shall take up serpents; and if they drink any deadly thing, it shall not hurt them.' Ever heard that verse? Maybe not. Okay, well, there was a documentary about it you might have seen. I never watched it, but I heard about it. It wasn't made in my church or anything, but what I'm saying is my parents would take my sister and myself to church twice a week and people there danced with snakes. Diamondbacks, cottonmouths, rattlers."

"I—" Lo reached up with both hands and straightened the part in her hair, scratched her scalp a bit and then held the ponytail with her right hand as if this ritual could help make sense of what he was saying. She tried to make out John's expression, but it was too dark.

Lo imagined the Lutherans in town holding venomous snakes. She'd only attended occasionally growing up—old ladies in slacks and knit sweaters drinking coffee from tiny Styrofoam cups, quietly singing along from the same old songbooks that were used before any of them had been born. "So, you grew up holding snakes to prove that you were a good Christian?"

He shook his head. "No, they don't let the kids do that part. But there was other stuff too, you know. Preaching what I understand now was very frightening for a child to hear. I think it messed me up a little." He exhaled and gripped the steering wheel. Behind him, an ad on a billboard flashed by with only the words JESUS SAVES. Lo might have been caught off guard by the coincidence, but religious billboards had been constant for the last hundred miles or more.

"Okay, that is—" she was going to say *crazy* but stopped herself. "Interesting information. And I have at least ninety questions. But what does that have to do with your sister? It can't be your fault how your parents raised you. Isn't she older than you? What could you have done about it?"

He shook his head. "It ain't that. It's—something happened."

"*Ain't?* I like when you go full southern." She hadn't meant to change the subject, maybe only lighten the mood.

John grinned, and the mood did change a little. "Are you flirting with me now, Bambi? That's against the rules."

"No, it's not." She shook her head. "I make the rules."

"Don't I know it?"

Lo couldn't see him raise his eyebrows, but she thought she heard it in his voice. He rubbed the back of his neck with his left hand, and she felt the urge to rub it for him, to relieve the tension of driving all day.

"Ha. Ha," she said sarcastically. "All right then, what happened that you have to apologize for? I mean, it sounds like a traumatic way to grow up, and you can't be responsible for your parents' choices. Trust me—I read a lot of books about that."

"Well, it's kind of a long story."

"We've got four hours," she said as she settled into her seat, bending her knees and bringing her feet to the dash. She turned toward John. She pulled her thick auburn curls around to one side and then looked at him expectantly. "Is your neck sore?" she asked innocently.

"When I was little, I never knew any different. We grew up in a small town in the mountains, and every Wednesday night and all day on Sundays, we were at church. People usually held snakes during service, but only rarely got bit, for whatever reason. It was normal to me. When Deb came to my high school graduation and asked me to leave town with her—I said some things I shouldn't have. I was ignorant and young. I haven't seen her since then, even though I meant to. I finally saw what she saw. I understood what she meant about our parents. We've talked on the phone since then but never in person. And I need to apologize for that."

"Wait, wait, wait. That was *not* kind of a long story, John! Context, please! First off: what the hell is a snake church? Secondly, can you start from the beginning? Where had Deb been all that time? Why did she want you to leave? What did you say to her?"

KIND OF A LONG STORY

It's not like what people think. We weren't fancy southerners in our Sunday best strolling up to a steeple on a genteel plantation, and then we all passed snakes around. Not like that at all. My mom wore regular clothes—jean shorts and tank tops—and when she felt the Holy Spirit, whatever you want to call it, she danced and spoke in tongues. The church was more of a broke-down shed up against a mountain face on the highway. The pastor would preach straight from the Bible. It was all very literal. Like you took the words from the Bible and that was it—even the verses about handling snakes and drinking poison. Yeah, the pastor drank poison from time to time. A few times people got bit, but not often. I never knew anyone who died from the snakes or the poison, not while I was growing up.

The church didn't have a denomination or anything. I know there are Pentecostal snake churches, and my dad would know about the history of the church and how all that fit together. But I wasn't ever that religious. Even when I was proud of my church and the snakes looking cool and dangerous in the cages near the pulpit, I was never "moved by the Spirit," as they called it, or anything like that.

I didn't worry too much about it though. I was just a kid. Figured when I got older, I'd understand God better. But what I came to understand as I got older was that our church was just one tiny congregation on the edge of town and that the rest of the area was full of plant stores and hippie communes and just regular blue-collar folks. What had been my whole life as a kid started to feel less and less "normal."

So, anyway, Deb was always into TV, just obsessed with high school drama shows, *Dawson's Creek* and *The O.C.* and whatever else. I don't remember much, I was younger than her, but I knew she liked watching TV and that was supposedly a bad thing. Some of the other kids in our congregation were allowed to watch but not us. She would watch at friends' houses and whatnot.

The kids in school had no idea what my family was into—you know—religiously. We knew enough to keep that private, so did most of the other kids from our church who went to public school. I remember she told me that some Christians believed the Bible was just stories, not history. That families on TV would go to church and sit quietly and smile and then eat a picnic lunch. That they didn't yell in church, dance with snakes or condemn people to hell—all kinds of stuff like that. But I didn't really care. I just shrugged her away.

She was always making my parents angry. At first, she tried to get my mom to watch one of her shows about what she imagined was a "normal" Christian family. I think that's what she wanted us to be, just normal, like the rest of the folks in town. Obviously, that didn't go over well. My mom made Deb write out some verse about false idols or something, repeatedly, until she was crying. My dad would near punch holes in the walls he'd get so fed up, and once he locked her in her room with a padlock on the outside after she stayed out all night.

I didn't want to deal with any of that. I didn't mind going to church and sitting in the back and listening if that's what it took to keep my parents from yelling. Deb was always acting like she was the only smart one, trying to explain to my dad what the Bible meant, even though he'd been reading it every day his whole life. This set him off. He wouldn't even let Deb cut her hair because of a specific verse about women, even though other women in our church didn't abide by that. So, he wasn't about to let her interpret the Bible for him. I just stayed out of it.

Deb graduated and left town that same day. She'd been working at the public library for years, just helping the librarian restack books and whatever. She had saved her money and apparently, without anybody in our family knowing it, applied to college in Arizona and got in. To this day I don't have one clue why she chose to go all the way out there. I was fourteen and cared more about finding worms to use as bait than anything else. She never said bye to me or nothing. Just left.

I didn't see her again until four years later. Still went to church with my parents and all that, but did start to wonder about the snakes, the drinking of poison.

My first serious girlfriend, Graciella, was from a Mexican family. They were Catholic. I was pretty naive about the world, but I knew enough to keep it a secret, to keep it between us. I was in eleventh grade and those were probably my two main goals in life—to not make my dad angry and to hang out with my girlfriend. I was worried that if he found out, he'd be mad since she wasn't from the church, and I could take a guess that he wouldn't want me datin' a Mexican girl, to be honest.

I don't know how it used to be down there before my time, but things changed fast when I was growing up. My dad wasn't into all that change, so I didn't want to rock the boat.

Anyway, as I'm walking down the aisle to get my diploma, I see Deb sitting there in the bleachers. I must have stopped in my tracks because I heard the kid behind me telling me to keep walking. So, Deb finds me before my parents do and pulls me into some empty hallway. She whispers, real fast and urgent-like, all these things about abuse and violence, ignorance and racism, she's going on and on. Tells me she finished school at Arizona State and that she's applying for jobs, so she can support me while I get on my feet. I hadn't seen her for years and barely knew her, quite honestly, when she was living at home. I was scared that if my dad found us, he'd do something to her. Then he'd take it out on me, blaming me somehow for her showing up. I just wanted to get away from her.

I was scared. And annoyed. I was trying to be proud of myself with the diploma in my hand. I was not about to leave my entire life behind to pack a bag and flee from my hometown with this woman that I barely knew. So, I just spewed all the things I'd heard my dad mutter and the prayers my mother prayed out loud—I called her a philistine, a heretic, Jezebel, whore, devil worshiper, democrat, stuck-up, the list went on. I just said anything that I could recall my parents saying. I didn't ask her one question. I didn't ask her what she'd been doing, or what she went to school for, or why she cared about me at all. I just ranted and raved and called her names. It's hard for me to admit it, even now. It was ugly. I think she figured I was feeling how she felt on her own graduation day—desperate to leave town—but I wasn't there yet.

When I stopped, she was crying but quiet, just tears coming down her face. And I saw my dad standing there at the end of the hallway, nodding his head and grinning. I felt like my heart went cold or something. Deb walked off, and I haven't seen her since, though we've talked, of course. My dad came and tried to shake my hand, but I was so confused and—so I just pushed it away and left.

After that, nothing was the same. I couldn't unhear any of what Deb said. I never saw my dad the same way. And one day a couple of years later, he and I were out washing his car, which is a thing we did together on the weekend. I was twenty or so, just working at a small car shop during the day and still living with my parents. Well, out of the blue, I talked to him about my girlfriend from high school, her background, being Catholic. I don't know why I brought it up because we'd already broken up by then. She moved off—had bigger plans. Anyway, I was struggling at home and maybe I was looking for a fight—a reason to leave.

It might have been the heat, or it might have been that I was finally listening to what he actually said, or maybe he thought I was old enough to "hear the truth," but he said a bunch of stuff about how people of different religions and races shouldn't be in relationships together. I don't remember him ever being so straightforward about it. At that moment I thought of Deb, and all the things she warned me about over the years, all the people around town who went about their lives without the weight of all these rules my father had put on us. These people I passed by on the highway every day just living by their own rules. I was jealous of them. I thought about all those awful things I said to her, and I felt sick.

I started coming up with excuses not to go to church. I think both my parents were waiting for me to be "filled with the Spirit" and grab a snake. I knew they wanted me to find a girl in our congregation, which was very small and not particularly promising at that time. They surely would have let me put a trailer on their land and stay forever. That would have been my life. That scared me. I had to get away. I thought I better just do what she did—just get in my car and drive away. I do miss it from time to time. If it wasn't for my dad, maybe I'd go back. But his personality, his beliefs, are too big. He'd drown you out, if you let him.

My dad's brother Luke had left town, met a Midwesterner and was farming with his father-in-law. He wasn't exactly disowned or nothing, but my dad didn't like to talk about him much. I asked a few questions, figured out where he lived. My mom, she's all right. She had the address tucked away somewhere and didn't ask too many questions about why I wanted it. I thought if Uncle Luke could get away from all of it, he could help me do it. I figured if I stayed in North Carolina, my parents would still expect me to visit, go to church, stop in for holidays. But I was wanting to do what Deb did and cut myself off.

I called Luke up, and he knew what I was asking: can you get me out of here? Offered to let me sleep in his basement, told me we could fix it up a little together, all that. And then I left. Never went back. My mom calls sometimes, but that's it.

And one day the phone rang, and it was Deb. I hadn't called her because I was still embarrassed, but she had the decency not to hold that day against me.

Now we talk on the phone, and I have apologized. You know, real quick and embarrassed, and she swept it under the rug. Blamed my parents. But I can feel it—in my chest—the things I said to her, the grin on my father's face, her own face with all the tears. I'm going to apologize and tell her she was right about everything, that she was always smarter than me, and that she probably saved my damn life.

MISSION BEACH, CALIFORNIA

The Jeep, flecks of salt still clinging from Death Valley, made its way through the busy streets of San Diego and found a spot in front of a massive modern house a few blocks from the ocean.

"Dad, you would have liked Kevin. Despite the fact that he's a Cowboys fan. Can you believe that? That would have pissed you off, but he's a good kid. Funny too. He was always pushing for MSU to get a Black frat. They eventually did after we graduated. I got an email about it back when I used to check email. Not like I would have joined it when I was in school. I was never the joining type." Jason stopped for a minute and looked out the window. "Though who knows what I would have been like with a little guidance or a little anything. I thought maybe I could offer guidance to the kids I taught, you know, that's why I wanted to teach. Anyway, you might not be aware, but Mom really fucked things up after your accident."

He surprised himself. That was the first time he'd said anything about his mom in years, and it was enough. She wasn't worth the trouble. He hit the stop button and slid the recorder into the glove box on the off chance that Kevin would glance into his car and ask him about it.

Jason opened the door and stretched his body. He rinsed his mouth with mouthwash and spit it out near the front tire, resting his hand on the hood of the Jeep.

When he pushed the sleek black doorbell, he waved into the camera right as the door opened wide.

"Damn, Jason! I didn't know whether you were gonna show up or not. Kept telling Trish you probably passed right by. Why didn't you call me back?"

Jason shrugged. "Hey, man. Sorry, I threw my phone in a lake."

His friend nodded sagely. "Okay, all right. I hear you. I get it. I'm just going to say it, J. Shit happens—happened to me in college with some girl I barely knew. It's tough. Anyway—" Kevin held his hands toward the open door. Inside was a massive foyer with a circular table in the center that held a bouquet of flowers. Beyond that, Jason noticed a wall of windows on the back side of the house.

"This house is wild, Kevin." Jason hesitated at the door, then stopped entirely. "I'm hungry. Let's get some tacos."

Kevin looked at him for a minute, then nodded. He was shorter than Jason, a little rounder around the midsection than he had been in college. "Sure, you're the one who's been driving for days. I'll text Trish, maybe she can meet us on the boardwalk."

The two of them walked in bright sunlight toward the beach. They talked about the good old days back in college, but Jason's nods became less enthusiastic as the blocks passed.

Kevin talked about the apps he had developed and then asked Jason whether he was still subbing or tutoring or if he had finally given up teaching for good.

"Nah, a whole lot of good that degree did me," Jason said as they sat down in flimsy plastic chairs at a taco joint with a view of the beach. A group of pale women in massive sun hats and beach wraps hid under patio umbrellas, their bags sprawling onto the sidewalk, forcing people to sidestep them into the street. Their smell was permeating the air— suntanning oils, perfumes and laundry detergent mixed with the scent of the ocean from across the street.

A mother came out of the taco shop holding a newborn baby. She sang softly into the child's ear while pacing up and down the sidewalk past the two of them. Jason watched for a long time and wondered what the baby smelled like before he snapped out of it.

"What is it?" Kevin turned around to see what Jason was looking at.

"*Hmm*? Nothing. I saw a cat."

Kevin snorted. "Watch out! Beach cats are everywhere!"

A few tall palm trees lined the view. One was shading a person napping in a dirty sleeping bag, a shock of greasy orange hair sticking out of the open end. All their belongings were in a bag tied to a dog's collar—a large brown German shepherd that panted on the small patch of grass between the boardwalk and the sand.

The silence stretched out between them and was turning into an awkward pause. Kevin jumped in, "Man, I was actually stoked when I heard you walked out of that classroom and never went back."

"Wasn't that dramatic. I finished the year, and I doubt they were surprised when I told them I wasn't coming back. Make five K more where I am now with a hell of a lot less bullshit."

"Nice man, very nice. But you know you could do even better than that, right? I'm serious. I could get you a job, and you could work your way up to the top like me. They don't even care what kind of bachelor's degree you got, as long as you got it. You saw my house, dude. I'm talking *that* kinda cash."

"Nah. It's cool. I like being outside. Don't think I could handle sitting in front of a screen all day." Jason tried to imagine what he would do with a four-thousand-square-foot house but gave up once all the imaginary rooms were filled with grow lights.

"You make your own schedule, bro. Honestly, I could set you up. Could be like the old days back at MSU. Can you believe we got out of there? And look where we are now!" Kevin held his hands up to the Southern California sun.

"Huh, yeah, got out of Minnesota and haven't been back since. But I got a job lined up, so I'm good, man. I chose this line of work on purpose, so like I said, I'm good."

Ten years had passed since they'd seen each other—those days of drinking cheap beer and feeling like big shots on campus were distant history. The extent that the two of them had kept in touch through the years was a random text chain of albums they were currently listening to. Jason thought they'd be able to pick up where they had left off, but he realized Kevin was like a stranger to him now.

"Right. Okay. So now you're headed back to Santa Rosa? Thought you loved Idaho."

"Couldn't stay there. Not—not after. She actually—" he faltered, "asked me to leave."

Kevin nodded sympathetically. "Ah, I see. Sorry. Oh shit, they got shark on the menu here! Is that legal? Let's do this!"

After lunch they walked the boardwalk along the beach, the long way back to the massive modern house flanked by identical massive modern houses. As they approached Kevin's house, both men reached for their keys.

"Want help grabbing your bags?"

"Ah, no thanks. I actually got to hit the road. I took a couple detours on the trip already. So, they're expecting me up in SR. I got friends there I need to catch up with before I get back into the routine." Jason hoped this was true. He knew a lot of people who skipped around, working the same few farms year after year. He thought he'd needed a friend, but he knew now that person wasn't Kevin.

"You can't be serious? You're staying, right?" Kevin wasn't trying all that hard to be convincing. "Man, Trish will be so mad that she missed you. She's always getting held up at work."

"Yeah, wish I could have said hi. She was my friend before you were, you know." Jason smirked. He and Trish had actually gone on a few dates before Kevin swooped in, but none of that seemed to matter anymore.

Kevin made a few attempts to dissuade him all while holding the front door of his house open, looking anxious to get back inside.

Jason came up with excuses and offered weak smiles until Kevin relented.

"Well, tell Trish that I'm sorry. I'll catch you guys again soon. Maybe we can surf next time."

"Yeah, definitely. Stop by anytime, man. *Just call first.*" Kevin laughed and then pushed the massive door open. "See ya, J."

Jason was alone on the street with a few palm trees and parked cars. There was nowhere to go but Santa Rosa.

ALBUQUERQUE, NEW MEXICO

An awareness filtered to the surface—the car had finally stopped moving. Lo heard the shifter click into park. A streetlight created a reddish glow behind her closed eyes, but she couldn't bring herself to open them. All she wanted to do was curl up in the seat and sleep a little longer, but she felt a hand on her leg. The gesture didn't feel like *Lo, wake up, we're here*; it didn't feel like a platonic squeeze. There was something more, even if it was only on her end, in the way her body responded. She jumped a little, startled, and opened her eyes. Her first impulse was to move his hand away, but somehow, instead, her hand landed on top of his and she let it rest there. After a second she gently lifted his hand onto the shifter and sat up.

"Scared me," she whispered. "Are we here?" Her throat burned, maybe from not brushing her teeth, maybe from spending hour after hour conversing with John, but most likely from running out of water after dinner but refusing to let him buy her a bottle, even though the last gas station's bathroom faucets were crusted with black mold, so she couldn't drink out of them.

It was almost five in the morning. John parked the car in the small lot to the side of what Lo assumed was Deb's apartment complex. She admired the brick building, which was house-like, but too large and uniform to be a single-family home. The side of the building was lined with rectangular windows, most dark, but a few glowing with string lights or the flashing colors of a TV screen.

John hadn't moved since he woke her up. He sat gripping the wheel, looking like he was either praying or had fallen asleep. "Are you okay?" she asked, her voice still hoarse.

"It's just been so long since I've seen her," he said into the dash.

"Would you rather find a hotel? Call her in the morning to meet for breakfast or something? That would be less intense than staying the night."

He sat up and rolled his shoulders back, stretching. "It'll be all right. I think I'm delirious. Let's go find some beds to sleep in. You were kicking around like crazy over there. Thought you might get me in the face as payback for your nose."

She tried to laugh but her voice didn't work, so she just shook her head tiredly. At one point, she had woken up with one leg across his lap and had little memory of kicking it up in an attempt to get comfortable. She wasn't surprised, though. She regularly woke up on the floor after falling out of bed during the night without even noticing. The few nights she had spent with Artie were followed by days of him teasing her about how she attacked him in bed all the night. She eventually concluded that she just needed her space.

John pushed the door open and stepped outside. It was much colder than Lo had expected. When she thought of the Southwest, she thought of desert, sunshine and saguaros. But it wasn't much warmer in Albuquerque than it had been in Elysian. She shivered and wrapped herself in John's sweatshirt that she had been using as a blanket.

John was getting their backpacks from the trunk when Lo heard the building's front door swing open and saw a woman standing under the porch light. "Cain? Cain?" the woman whisper-yelled from the stoop, looking in their direction. Lo's eyes went wide with this very-early-morning case of mistaken identity until she heard John say, "Hey, Deb."

"Cain?" Lo asked quietly, but John either didn't hear her or pretended not to. Deb practically ran to where their car was parked. The siblings looked at each other for a minute under the streetlight, just nodding and grinning at each other until Deb broke into a broad smile. Lo felt slightly awkward, like she was intruding on a private moment, as she watched the two of them hug each other for the first time in over ten years.

John had to look down at his sister, who apparently hadn't inherited the same genes for height. Lo was tired and cold and moved toward John without thinking, until she noticed Deb watching her with a dreamy expression on her face. She moved away and stretched a little.

"Come on in. It's freezing out here. I'm so glad y'all made it safely. I'm just—so glad. Come on in. Grab your stuff. All right." Her accent was somehow thicker than John's, even though she must have been away from home for close to fifteen years.

Lo attempted to smooth her hair and rapidly blink her eyes, which burned. She imagined they were red and bloodshot. She pictured her hair standing on end like a troll doll's and figured her breath smelled awful on top of all that. Not much she could do about it now.

They walked into a hallway, which was aggressively lit for five in the morning. Deb turned to Lo and held out her hand to shake it. "Oh, hey, I'm sorry, I should have introduced myself right away. I'm Deb, Cain's sister, and he's told me so much about you." Deb smiled brightly, her faded purple hair in a short bob brushing against the collar of a fuzzy black robe.

Lo's laugh came out in a hoarse gasp. She cleared her throat. "Oh, wow, well, I've heard a lot about you too. Thank you for letting us stay. And sorry to wake you up like this—I feel bad." Deb grabbed Lo's arm dramatically, and she had to fight the impulse to shake it off.

"You have to know, I'm so glad you're here. So glad." Deb tried to smile while tears welled in her eyes. "I'm sorry. I can tell I'm freakin' you out. I'm a touchy person. I touch people." Deb laughed and led them to a door near the end of the hallway, which was interspersed with gold-painted radiators and built-in bookshelves that were empty except for one fake plant sitting lonely on a single shelf. "It's just that I've been hoping Cain would visit for so long, and he's finally here, and with you, his—friend," she tripped over the word. "It's just amazing. And y'all can meet my boyfriend—common-law husband, he likes to remind me—Raul. He's got to get up early because he teaches sixth grade, so he's sleeping. But he's super excited, and we're gonna go all out for dinner tomorrow night."

"Oh," Lo said, not wanting to disappoint Deb, who seemed like she had been awake for hours drinking espresso. "Well, I think we have to get on the road, actually, at some point tomorrow." Deb led them into her apartment, which was more appropriately lit for the time of day with a pink salt lamp and wall sconces dimmed low.

The apartment was nice but not fancy. Wood floors, light gray walls. A set of beams created a faux entryway. A simple jute carpet, fraying a little, covered the floor in the living room. A vintage-looking couch that Lo pinned as a thrift-store find was facing away from them, toward the small TV perched on a coffee table, centered between two windows. The decor made Lo feel immediately more at ease.

"Nope," Deb shook her head. "Sorry, not gonna happen! You have *got* to stay the night, just one night. Like, no question. Come on, Cain, it'll be a blast. You have to meet Raul, and I can show y'all our neighborhood while he's at work. It'll be great! Good! It's settled!" She looked back and forth pleadingly from Lo to John.

Lo looked down at her stockinged feet and pressed her big toe into a burl in the hardwood. They still had to find Jason Peterson, convince him to visit his dying mother and then drive back home so they could both get on with their lives. She also felt uncomfortable staying at a stranger's house, expecting them to pay for dinner, or even worse, expecting Lo to spend her own money on overpriced bar food or fifteen-dollar drinks—which she would have to refuse no matter how rude it seemed.

On the other hand, there was Deb's pleading face. Plus, they had just spent nearly twenty-four hours in the car—John driving most of it. Lo felt bad—John hadn't seen his sister for over ten years. Deb was pretty much the only reason John wanted to take this trip.

Watching Deb's sincere expression, it suddenly mattered a little less to Lo how quickly they returned to Elysian—the wet spring snowmelt, the same ten streets she'd traveled her whole life.

John set his backpack on the ground with a thud and rubbed his eyes. He spoke up, "I wish we could, but—"

"We can," Lo heard herself interject. "You guys haven't seen each other in a decade, right? I think we could stay for one night. I mean, we got here in a day, and we both have a week off work. As long as we leave really early the next morning . . ." she trailed off. Deb reached over and pulled Lo in for an unexpected hug. She stood stiff and awkward in the embrace. Deb made an *Mmm* sound and then whispered, "It's all right, just ease into it." Lo eased, just a little.

"Okay, but who's Cain?" she asked into Deb's shoulder.

Deb showed Lo the guest room while apologizing to John for calling him his given name, which he despised for biblical reasons. Lo only vaguely recalled that there was a story about brothers called Cain and Abel, but not enough to understand the significance or why John hated it. It was apparently their dad's name, which didn't help.

"Cain was a murderer, which somehow intrigued our grandmother, Lord knows why. Pretty messed up. Anyway, Johnathan is my middle name. So—John." He shrugged and blinked his eyes comically slow. Lo would never judge him for a family history he had no control over. She had no idea where her own name came from and was too afraid to ask her dad, in case it had something to do with her mother—or maybe in case it didn't.

"Here, John, you take the bedroom. You must be cross-eyed after driving the whole day," Lo insisted, but Deb and John shook their heads simultaneously.

"It's fine, Lo. John can sleep on the couch. I wasn't sure what your . . ." she looked at them with twinkling eyes, "situation was. So, I made up the bed but kept some stuff out on the couch too. I wouldn't want to make you uncomfortable with Raul moving around in the morning making coffee and stuff."

Lo brushed her teeth in the brown-tiled bathroom, clearly dated from a time before any of them were born. Still, she liked it. It had character with its tiny ceramic sink and stand-alone shower tub with tiny claw-foot pedestals. She had been anxious all day, missing her duplex. Lo was proud of how she had taken the time and initiative to make herself a home that she loved, full of quality, long-lasting goods. Her dad's massive Victorian house was filled with disposable kitchen gadgets and plasticky comforters likely made by children in far-off sweatshops. Homes like that felt distressing and uncomfortable to her. Lo couldn't really explain it, only that life felt even more synthetic and counterfeit when it was full of what wouldn't outlast a single season before it found a landfill, let alone a single human's lifetime. It created an inexplicable but deep, existential dread that sat in her core. Deb's home felt thoughtful though. Careful in a way that wasn't wasteful or excessive.

Lo realized she'd been thinking all of these thoughts while staring at herself in the mirror in a daze. She blinked hard, smoothed her hair and crept out of the bathroom. John probably needed to get ready for bed too.

It was almost one in the afternoon when Lo woke up. Sunlight filtered through brown burlap curtains. Half-awake, she wondered if they were homemade and whether Deb knew how to sew. She heard voices coming from the kitchen and hoped to slip into the bathroom to get cleaned up before anyone noticed her. She found her bra in her bag, changed into a simple summer dress, blueish tie-dye printed with white flowers, and then remembered how cold it had been the night before. She pulled on a sweatshirt, and it wasn't until she was wearing it that she noticed it was John's. It was too big for her, but she liked the familiar Jefe's logo and ridiculous clip-art race car. She didn't love the way John's clean clothes smelled, strong like perfumed laundry detergent. But he had worn this one yesterday up until he let her use it for a blanket, so it smelled like him too.

As she stepped out of the bedroom door, she glanced up and saw John looking at her, a slow smile crossing his face. He was holding a cup of steaming coffee, and Lo could hear Deb murmuring quietly from somewhere in the living room. Lo crept into the bathroom, brushed her teeth and considered the clear shower curtain that circled the old claw-foot tub. Something about a clear shower curtain in an apartment with only one bathroom seemed suggestive and hinted at an intimacy Lo had not yet experienced or ever witnessed growing up. When she was a kid, it was just her and her dad, and they had kept a wide berth. Since then, she'd always lived alone, with all her romantic relationships defined as on-again, off-again. Every relationship in her entire life had felt more awkward than intimate, if she was being honest.

She wrinkled her nose a bit and felt the thick plastic between her fingers. Of course, Lo wouldn't buy a plastic curtain—hers was made from fabric she found at the thrift store. She had hand sewn it. She never could figure out how to work the ancient sewing machine that one of the old ladies in town had sold her for a dollar fifty.

Deb served Lo French-press coffee in an old Christmas mug, along with a plate of croissants and fruit. She flitted around in circles, offering Lo anything she imagined she could possibly need. An extra toothbrush? A razor? Some cream for her coffee? Lo was touched and smiled politely but stayed quiet so Deb and John could continue with whatever conversation they were having before she interrupted. She didn't feel like it was her place to begin a round of questioning about their childhoods, the snake church, their parents, the fateful graduation day, and how Deb had spent the last ten years of her life in New Mexico in this adorable apartment with her common-law husband, but she was very curious. She hoped they would answer those questions without her prompting.

But at first, Deb kept asking Lo questions about Elysian, The Locust, Parker, and about being a freegan, a word that Lo wished John hadn't communicated to Deb.

The main reason she didn't like to use the word was because she wasn't part of any official group, and so on some level, felt fraudulent.

She'd read some books on more sustainable living from the library, but she'd never signed a membership form or even met another person who identified as such. She also didn't know if she was good at it—being freegan—since she had no one to compare herself to. So, these conversations always led to Lo feeling alienated or defensive.

But Deb didn't dwell on Lo's beliefs and philosophies long, especially because Lo was anxious to hear more about the siblings, so kept her answers short and played coy. That was when John informed Deb about their long drive, when Lo had asked him hundreds of personal questions but refused to answer any herself.

"I see," was Deb's only response to this as she eyed Lo, nodding conspiratorially. Deb eventually sat down long enough to drink yet another cup of coffee. She still wore her robe and had light purple bags under her eyes that matched the color of her hair. Lo began to suspect that Deb and John hadn't slept at all. Then Deb chirped, "Lo, what do you want to do with your life?"

"What?" Lo asked, caught off guard. John froze, his hand on the French press, and made a low groaning noise. Lo's head swiveled toward him, her eyes narrowed. She didn't appreciate the notion that she was a kind of loose cannon that could be set off by a simple question.

"You know, like what's your dream job? Your dream home? Dream husband?" Deb wrinkled her face in a cute but suspicious way.

Lo smiled politely. "Well, my first step is to get out of town. I mean, the town I grew up in. But beyond that, I really don't want to be defined by work or a career. It's something I believe is harmful about American culture—but that's just me. I think people should be proud to do all kinds of jobs—or no job. I don't know. There's a co-op in Minneapolis I've been thinking of joining, maybe look around for some local organizations through that. I—" She stopped and took a sip of her coffee.

Deb had been nodding enthusiastically and didn't miss a beat when Lo trailed off. She eventually turned the conversation around to the plan for the day. A walk around Deb's neighborhood, a detour through the park to the grower's market, then dinner and drinks at home—*spicy mezcal margaritas*—three words that Deb wailed enthusiastically. Lo agreed that the day sounded promising but felt like a spicy beverage was counterintuitive. She told Deb that she'd never been to New Mexico before or ever drank mezcal, all of which had Deb buzzing with excitement.

As the conversation died down, Lo sipped her coffee, which had grown cold, and ventured, "I didn't mean to interrupt your conversation earlier."

Deb squealed and brought her shoulders up around her neck as if Lo were a toddler taking her first step. "I'm sorry, but your accent is really just so cute. I can't get over it! I'm sorry. I don't mean to tease you. I think it's adorable." Lo laughed, halfhearted, and took another sip of her coffee.

"I have an idea," Deb announced. "Let me take a shower and get ready. You look so cute, like you just walked out of an ad for some hip mall store with your Birkenstock clogs and your boyfriend's—I mean, friend's—hoodie over your indigo-dyed dress. So cute. I gotta go get cute. Then we'll head out. Once we've all had a margarita or three, we can swap stories. That way Raul won't miss anything either. We can share stories all night. But that means *share*, darlin'." Deb pointed at Lo and narrowed her eyes, then laughed and stood up, pushing the chair back loudly.

While Deb was in the shower, John told Lo that he'd woken up around seven thirty, after he heard Raul leave out the front door. Deb had gotten up to send him off for the day, so the two siblings had talked the entire morning—apologizing for what went wrong, commiserating about childhood, filling in memory gaps and gossiping about any news they'd heard out of their small hometown. By the time Lo woke up, they had exhausted the topic.

All Lo could do was ask him if it felt good to catch up. John had a distant look on his face as he stared out the window, open wide to the cool spring air. "Yeah, it did. It felt good," he answered, then turned his gaze to Lo and offered a self-conscious smile. "Might have been nice to get more than two hours of sleep. But thanks for agreeing to stay tonight," John said, squeezing her shoulder playfully. He sat close to her, resting his bare foot on the crossbar of her chair. He was wearing gym shorts and an old t-shirt, thin and gray with a faded Minnesota Twins logo. His hair was matted and covering his forehead, and he seemed so much lighter than he had the day before.

By the time they walked out the front door of Deb's building, groups of schoolkids wearing backpacks trailed along the sidewalk that lined a large grassy park across the street. It was a charming view, if not for the messy string of telephone poles. But then Lo noticed a flock of small birds with bright blue heads and creamy white bodies perched on the wires and made a slight *Aww* sound. Of course, Deb couldn't take credit for the birds, but even though Lo had only just met her, she got the sense that Deb was the kind of person who, if she were a character in a children's movie, would have the ability to call up a throng of charming wildlife creatures with a single note.

"Raul should be done organizing his classroom and doing whatever he needs to do in an hour or two," Deb said as she pulled the front door closed behind her. "Y'all be careful coming out here without keys. I honestly never know if it'll be locked or not."

Lo smoothed John's hoodie as they left the apartment building while Deb explained the history of the complex. John never mentioned her wearing it, so she didn't bring it up either.

"You all right?" John asked.

"What? Oh, yeah. Just tired."

"Shit, me too." Out of the corner of her eye, Lo saw John reach for the sleeve of his sweatshirt that she was wearing. He held the cuff for a second. She stopped and turned toward him. He had been walking so close behind her that he almost tripped over the toes of her shoes. They both laughed a little.

"Thanks for letting me wear your sweatshirt," she said, looking up at him.

He smirked, "Never said you could, actually."

"Oh," she made a circular shape with her mouth and extended the word. "I see how it is. Well, sorry not sorry, then."

Deb showed them where she worked. It was a job that both impressed and confused Lo. According to Deb, she worked at a foundation that helped families of low socioeconomic status build wealth. She had been a communications major in college and told Lo that she always wanted a job that *mattered*, so she had applied to several nonprofits and other programs after graduation. She landed the job in Albuquerque, where she helped families find home and business loans, get a handle on their bank accounts, organize budgets, save money and find investments. All things that Deb called "financial literacy." Lo listened with wide eyes. These were things her dad had always insisted that she know; things she always rejected knowing. But Deb clearly believed she was helping people create the life they wanted, a more financially stable life, even if it was centered around capitalist transactions.

Lo thought about wealth inequality and pay gaps and all the false promises capitalism offered but kept it to herself, smiling politely as Deb described her job. She thought about asking Deb how many times she had actually witnessed families escape poverty in a machine that was seamlessly constructed to keep them from doing just that, but the group turned a corner and so did the conversation.

They walked past a few restaurants and shops. Deb smiled at John from time to time, like she wasn't quite sure what to say to him. She pointed out fat squirrels and petted people's dogs as they walked by. Lo wondered if Deb would have insisted on stopping for a late lunch, or a drink or a latte at her favorite coffee shop if a different girl had been visiting with John. He might have already informed Deb of the sweet tea incident. All these thoughts were swirling through her head when she realized Deb had stopped talking and was looking at her, waiting for a response to a question Lo hadn't heard. She just smiled and nodded, which seemed to appease Deb.

They saw hundreds of people biking—people biking in suits, in dresses, in workout clothes with their dogs running beside them on leashes. Lo watched a tattooed mother carrying her toddler while a fat orange cat sat in their stroller. She heard many different languages and accents. She noticed a Latin grocery store selling tamales, a brewery selling organic shrub sodas, and a Lebanese grocery store with a massive cooler filled with hand-rolled dolmades. Deb bought a carton and asked Lo to try one. Lo asked for a second one.

They walked to a massive community garden, and Deb showed Lo the square that she and Raul had planted over the last few years—a neatly tended plot of orange dirt. "If y'all stay a few more days, you could help us seed!" She squeezed Lo's shoulders in a side hug and tilted her head to the side, a frown on her face, to show that she understood that wasn't going to happen. Lo had the notion that Deb's touchy-feely nature ran in the family. Maybe John hadn't been that flirty after all, maybe it was just a weird family thing.

Deb led them back through a park where schoolkids still sat on the grass or kicked soccer balls back and forth. She pointed out their apartment complex, visible at the far end of the park and across a busy street. It was close to five, and the city was starting to feel more crowded than it had when they first left Deb's house.

The grower's market consisted of a dozen pop-up tents spread out in one section of the park, mostly along the paved sidewalk where kids blew past on bikes. Lo's legs tingled with goosebumps in the breeze. "Deb, you're so lucky all of this is right across the street from your house." Lo handled a portion of de-pricked cactus paddles next to a sign that read: STRAIGHT FROM GARDEN $4 A BUNDLE.

"I know! It's one of the reasons we got the place. We love this neighborhood like it's our child. You really should see it on the weekend—three times as many vendors. Mondays are the slowest."

There was produce Lo had never seen before—fresh and dried peppers of all sizes and colors, dried herbs to burn with signs promising they could clear negative energy, herbs for cooking, spices she'd never eaten. There were informational booths for a politician, a women's nonprofit and some kind of jog-for-a-cause charity. The last booth displayed stones and crystals, some smooth and round and some jagged and raw. Lo touched every rock on the table while Deb picked out produce with John. It wasn't that she believed the stones *did* anything, necessarily. They were just so enthralling, and they all came from this very planet, the same planet where humans extracted oil and gas so greedily that the ground quaked. She asked the vendor where the crystals came from with a sudden fear that they were also extracted greedily from the earth.

"I find them myself!" The woman said, eager to have an interested customer. She was white with dreadlocks tied up into a strip of cloth that matched her long skirt—green with small white flowers. "My uncle has a hundred fifty acres with the Rio running through some caves. Perfect for crystal hunting. A lot of jasper, as you can see." She pointed to a brownish-orange rock striated with gold stripes.

"They're pretty," Lo said. She was trying to work out how she felt about this table of rocks. Rocks from the land—now here in the city for sale—when John walked up beside her.

"I used to hunt for gems when I was a kid," he said with a smirk. "Mostly just found mica that I pretended was gold."

"Really?" Lo asked. She hadn't pictured John as an imaginative child.

"Yeah, I was pretty rich too, because it's everywhere. The trails and river bottoms sparkle in the sun." John seemed lost in thought for a minute while he fingered a large piece of rectangular jasper. "Can we have two of these?" He asked the girl without consulting Lo. She narrowed her eyes at him, but he ignored her and paid eight dollars for a pair.

"Just so you know, jasper is a nurturing stone and can ease worry and stress. Here you go!" The woman handed John his change.

As they walked away, he slipped one of the stones in the front of his sweatshirt that Lo was wearing.

"You can't complain about spending a couple dollars in support of a local hippie selling all-natural rocks that heal emotional wounds, can you?" he asked. She still wasn't sure how she felt about rocks

for sale but reflexively stuck her hand in the front pocket and fingered the cool stone, smooth on two sides and rough on the jagged,
narrow edges.

"I don't actually speak Spanish," Raul responded to John's introduction.
A look of embarrassed surprise crossed John's face before Deb cut in.

"His mom is from Ohio. I mean, she's white. So, he never learned
Spanish."

Lo distracted herself with a pothos plant sitting on the corner of the
bar that separated the living room from the kitchen. A few hung in her
duplex that were gifted as cuttings from her neighbor, Melinda. Lo had
stuck them in cups of water until they grew roots. They were so thrilled
to be alive that they exploded once they were planted in soil, so she
was able to keep cutting and rooting until she had several plants growing around her house. She thought about her little duplex and thriving
houseplants as she ignored the awkwardness John created when he introduced himself to Raul in a foreign language.

Deb laughed it off and responded to John in Spanish. They were
laughing about whatever she said when Deb turned to Lo. "I took Spanish in high school, then minored in it. Speak it much better than him,
though." She nodded toward John with a sarcastic smile on her face.
"But I need it for work. Speak it more than English."

"Huh, maybe it's a gene or something," Lo said without thinking.
It was interesting to her that two siblings from rural North Carolina
would both speak Spanish at work.

"A gene for speaking Spanish?" Raul asked skeptically.

Lo's cheeks flushed pink, "Oh, no. I mean, like in their brain—for
language learning."

Raul frowned. "Don't know who they would have gotten that gene
from."

John's brow furrowed, but he didn't respond. He stood slightly
stooped with his hands clinging to the back of a dining chair. Lo made

eye contact with him briefly and tried to both send support and ask for it in a single look.

Deb, standing over a cutting board chopping cauliflower, laughed. Just a single *Ha!* "Ain't that the truth, babe? Surely not from our parents. Or really, who knows?" Lo watched in awe of Deb's skill of turning an awkward conversation around into something harmless, even thoughtful. "They probably didn't offer Spanish when they were in high school, forever ago. Times have changed—thank the Goddess—at least a little bit."

"That's true," Raul agreed. "Who knows?" He shrugged and the awkwardness was mostly defused.

Lo asked Deb if she could help with dinner.

"I cut! Raul cooks!" she exclaimed as she washed small bits of cauliflower off her hands. "But you can help make the drinks! Spicy mezcal margaritas!"

The four of them each drank a few cocktails while an Indian-inspired cauliflower and potato dish simmered in a pan on the stove. A warm, earthy smell filled the apartment. Lo had to alternate a sip of her drink with a sip of water. She had never been good with spicy foods. Raul pulled out a ball of dough from the fridge and began rolling it out to make fresh naan, while Lo sat on a stool belly up to the bar that separated the living room from the kitchen and watched him.

"I'm jealous of your skills," Lo said when he turned to set a dirty dish in the sink.

"Hey, you guys visit again soon, and I'll show you how to make it." Lo was surprised he would offer that invitation considering her and John's earlier comments couldn't have made a great impression on Raul.

Lo laughed quietly. "Okay, so you're inviting us back?"

"Of course," Raul replied, smiling. "You know Deb is dying to get John to move here. It's all she talks about."

She was only getting to know John, but the thought of him moving across the country triggered a pulse of anxiety. She didn't say anything, unsure of how to respond, and so continued to observe Raul, who was too distracted to notice that his comment seemed to rattle her. His hair reminded her of how the boys had worn it in high school. It fell around his ears but was dramatically parted, swooped to one side and held in place with gel. She imagined that Raul hadn't changed his hairstyle since then. But he had thick black stubble on his cheeks and jaw and had shaved what Lo *suspected* to be a hip mustache, even though mustaches only reminded her of pictures of her dad from the nineties. Raul was still in his work clothes, and Lo tried to imagine him teaching preteens from a dusty chalkboard when Deb set another drink in front of her.

"Three margaritas before dinner? I'm already drunk," Lo protested in a louder voice than normal.

"Yeah." Deb nodded. "Exactly."

Lo and Raul got into another disagreement during dinner, but the drinks helped to lubricate Lo into the discussion with less abrasiveness than usual. It all started when he told Lo that he was glad to have another vegetarian to cook for.

"I'm not a vegetarian," she responded, too assertively. "Vegetarianism is like a religion. It's a myth that makes people feel better about themselves so they can pretend they have some control over the state of the world."

Raul had his drink to his lips and almost choked on it. John looked at her for a second and then laughed to himself, shaking his head at his plate of food, which he had barely touched.

Deb, of course, responded graciously. "What? Lo! Tell us exactly what you mean." She looked luminous in the light of half a dozen candles burning in the center of the table. Her lavender hair was pulled back into barrettes decorated with white daisies.

"I mean, this food is *really* good. And, yes, the factory farming industry is destroying the planet, but so is industrial agriculture. And people can *pretend* that doesn't happen since they've already given up meat. But entire wolf packs have died because of wheat farming. And bunnies in lettuce fields! And the dead fish or pigeons that go into the soil of all their precious vegetables. If not dead animals, then petroleum-based fertilizers, which harm the environment *and* the soil *and* the food *and* the humans. Vegan organic farming is cool but so hard to do on a large scale. Plus, it's all so expensive. And plants are alive, by the way! They're just not anthropomorphized like animals. It's all a myth, like religion." Lo could tell she wasn't being as coherent as she normally might be. She'd also never articulated this particular argument before; it was a far leap beyond the perfunctory explanations of anticonsumerism that she repeated robotically whenever asked about her lifestyle around Elysian.

Raul crossed himself, scoffing. "Okay. Well, what about all the corn fields and pesticides and herbicides that are only used to feed cows that should be eating grass? What about cow methane? If everyone would stop eating beef, that would do some real good, right?" Lo shrugged, refusing to give an inch.

"I mean, maybe. But they'd eat something else shitty. Replace it with what? More wheat fields that destroy more wildlife habitats, killing off species after species? Oh god, or should we plant soybeans everywhere? And then spend the entire budget of a small country just to tinker with it in a lab, using a ton of carbon, all so it can taste just like meat? That money would be better spent doing good somewhere else. And don't get me started on palm oil! I'm just saying—" she slurred, taking another sip of her margarita. "The answer is sustainability, regeneration. It's a circle. Death. Life. We only pretend we can escape it." She took her finger and made a wobbly circle.

"Like *The Lion King*?" John asked.

"Don't get smart with me, mister." Lo pointed her finger at John. He shrugged innocently.

Raul, to Lo's surprise, was nodding his head. "All right, I mean, I hear what you're saying."

Lo made eye contact with him, stunned by his response. "What do you mean?"

"I mean, yeah, it's something to think about. Not that I'm going to start eating little baby piglets or anything. I've always known industrial agriculture was a mess. Deb and I, we make sure we're doing what we can. But you know, we also try to *live*."

"I live," Lo said defensively, as if he had been insinuating that she did not, in fact, *live*.

"If we're being honest, which, I can see that we are,"—he held up one finger while taking a drink—"based on how quickly you made a correlation between vegetarianism and religion and the woes of industrial agriculture and dead wolves, then hear me this: Maybe you should lighten up a little? Seriously. Since I met Deb all those years ago, she's reminded me not to attach myself to my ideas."

"Detachment," Deb chirped.

"Right." Now it was Raul's turn to slur his speech. "It's how she—we—make sure we don't get wrapped up in fanaticism. After how they grew up, well, you know that story." Lo nodded. "Deb could explain it better—"

Deb took this as her cue. "It's not like you need to listen to everyone's opinion, like people who are hateful or ignorant. It's just a way to step back from your own beliefs so you don't trample people over with them. Humans create rules and belief systems to make sense of the world, right? Or to feel less scared about the fact that we're just floating out here on a rock for no apparent reason, or maybe to feel superior to others, some form of self-righteousness. Perhaps like vegetarianism, as Lo suggests. They think that they're doing something that makes *sense*, you know? Something that will either keep them from doing harm or keep them from being harmed. Our parents believed they were saving us from eternal damnation, for example, and this allowed them almost complete sovereignty over us. To them, fear of the devil justified all their poor behavior. But in the end, it's possible that humans end up doing harm no matter what, or you know, they harm their children or those around them just by existing with all these rules and ideas. Like with cults. Or climate change. So, we might all just take a step back and detach from everything we think we know. All that shit's getting us all in a whole heap of trouble, isn't it? Anyway, it's just something we like to think about." Deb smiled, lifted a scented candle to her face and sniffed it, making a moaning sound as she set it down. They all watched her in silence for a minute.

"Well, it's something *you* think about! And then share with me." Raul wrinkled his nose at Deb in a small precious way. "I'll think about what you said, Lo. And you can lighten up. And we'll be even." He said this with a smirk and then took another drink. Everyone laughed except for Lo. She shot a look at John, who looked away, still smiling.

She didn't say anything, emptying her drink in one gulp.

Once the plates were cleared, the four of them sat around the table sharing stories, just as Deb had promised Lo earlier. They had nearly finished a full bottle of mezcal by the time she was finally getting to hear more about John and Deb's parents, their sometimes charming and often dysfunctional childhoods growing up in a small town in the lush green mountains of North Carolina. Raul talked about his childhood in Ohio with his single mom, who apparently called every week to ask when he was moving back, and he talked about his dad, who he hadn't seen much as a kid because of the distance but who currently lived right down the street.

Lo, who usually tried to say as little as possible about her background, found herself oversharing. She talked about how, whenever she had asked about her mother or felt upset when she was little, her dad would drive her to the closest Walmart and let her pick out a toy or a book or a new DVD, but how this ritual eventually made her feel lonelier, less seen and less heard.

The four of them finished the bottle of booze by taking swigs in turn. Lo was still unsure of the smoky mezcal flavor. Raul put the empty bottle in the recycling bin, making a show of it for Lo. Then they carried outdoor chairs to the courtyard, nestled between twin brick buildings. Lo didn't say anything about the Myth of Recycling and how only a small fraction of the things Americans believed were recycled actually were. She figured she could save that for next time.

Once outside, John talked about recurring nightmares he had as a kid. How the devil would tempt him with sinful things like a television set and, as he got older, premarital sex. Sometimes, the devil would lead him to hell and read a long proclamation of his sins, which included dreadful things like lust, playing video games and masturbation—all things his pastor had preached against. He would wake up just as he was thrown into the fiery lakes of hell.

Lo couldn't take her eyes off him as he recounted nightmare scenario after nightmare scenario that included the devil, hell and John's body burning in a fiery pit. Instinctively, she reached out for his wrist to comfort him, and as she did, he rolled his hand flat on his leg so she could take it. Lo took it, only slightly self-conscious of Deb watching them, smiling.

Lo had never had a conversation like this before. She had some girlfriends in high school, and they used to tease each other about who their crushes were, but it was never anything this honest. Parker was a good friend, but mostly they joked around, never too serious. She knew that Parker considered her beliefs about the environment and capitalism a form of naivete. Even when Parker took her suggestions at The Locust, like stacking compostable cups next to a water cooler, Lo felt like she was being placated, not really *heard*.

So, it was during a lull in the conversation that she blurted it out. "My father paid my mother fifty thousand dollars to have me—I mean he paid her not to abort me. And then also to leave, so he could raise me alone. Or maybe he didn't have to pay her to leave because she wanted to. I don't know for sure. He was fifty. She was in college."

John nearly fell out of his chair. Deb stood up and squatted next to Lo's. "Oh, wow." She put her head in Lo's lap and sighed. "I'm sorry that happened. Actually, I'm glad it happened and that you're here now, but I can only imagine how difficult that was to process."

Saying it out loud should have embarrassed her or made her upset. But tonight, it felt good knowing that others had heard her secrets. They didn't try to sweep it under the rug, like everyone else had her whole life, whenever the topic of mothers came up in conversation. Instead, they commiserated with her in the cold desert moonlight. John squeezed her hand.

"I had no idea about your mom, Lo." John sat at the edge of the bed while she stood in the center of the room, wobbling and wide awake at four in the morning.

"It is what it is. But actually, there's something I've been meaning to bring up. What would you think about stopping in Des Moines on the way back? I found my mom's address a few years ago and since the theme of this trip seems to be family reunions—you know . . ." She trailed off.

"Shit, yeah. Of course, if you want to do that, I'm along for the ride."

She found herself moving closer to him.

John said in almost a whisper, "I was thinking about something earlier. You ever heard the saying 'ripe fruit falls quickly'?"

"Huh? Uh-uh, must be a southern thing."

"Oh, I don't know about that." He laughed quietly as she pushed her way in between his knees. They were eye to eye now and she could feel his fingers rubbing the length of her hips on either side.

"Well, what's it supposed to mean? What's it got to do with me?" Their faces were inches away. She studied the blue of his irises and noticed a gold rim around the edges. He hands were coming up under her dress now and she leaned in closer.

"Well, we're the fruit." He was smiling so broad that she blushed. He pulled her in closer before she had a chance to respond. "Falling fast."

"Don't be dumb," was the last thing she said before they fell onto the bed together.

OBJECTIVE SCIENTIFIC FACTS

The flashing lights of the firefly are a mating call, an insect striptease. He blinks and prays and blinks some more, hoping a libidinous female will adore the patterns, the effort, the energy he puts off. The female is coy initially—waiting, watching from a distance, clandestine, tucked behind leaves and brush. She needs to know that he's got what it takes before she will join him in the dance.

SANTA ROSA, CALIFORNIA

Jason drove slowly down Fourth Street, examining the brick storefronts, bookstores, art galleries and trendy restaurants. The Thai place was still open, three years later. The local bookstore, dog salon and a bunch of other restaurants were all the same. He bobbed his head slowly as he drove, music low, windows down.

There were hills off in the distance, looming. The trip had been mountains, salt, desert, ocean and now hills with only hints of peaks. The miles had worn him out, but he couldn't really say why. He no longer knew what to tell the voice recorder but couldn't bring himself to throw it away.

He picked it up again and tried, "So, anyway, here I am in Santa Rosa. Gonna get my old job back and put my head down for a bit. It's been nice talking to you—or whatever." He shook his head, set the recorder down in his lap and rubbed his forehead.

The farm got closer and closer until he could see the white roofs of the grow houses at the top of a hill, then lost sight of them again when he got too close. The gate was locked, so he stopped.

This was where Jason and Alexis had met four years ago. She was a year out of college. They flirted and hung out around various campfires and in random bars around town before she left for Big Sky. A couple of months later, he heard they were looking for help at the farm she was at, so he up and left without so much as a day's notice. He knew at the time it was the right thing to do. They didn't last long at Big Sky because the shared dorms didn't fit their new-couple frame of mind. Together they found the spot in Twin Falls, which had been two and a half years of what Jason considered *the good life*.

All of this flashed through his mind as he pulled up to the gate. When they were both working there, they would push the button to reach the office, the gate would open, and they'd casually flirt before they went their separate ways for the night.

Things were different now, and a gatekeeper sat in a small shed. Was he wearing a uniform? Was that a gun on his hip? Jason scrutinized the man as he stood up and approached.

Jason's long fingers danced on the steering wheel, which was rubbed gray with wear and starting to tear on the bottom seam, a thread hanging loose. He put the car in park and rested his head on the steering wheel. He heard a knock on the window and looked up.

"You lost?" the gatekeeper asked.

"Me?" Jason asked, as if the gatekeeper could have possibly been talking to someone else.

"Are. You. Lost?" the gatekeeper asked through clenched teeth.

"No, I work here. Chill."

"Don't recognize you. You need to call the office or leave. Can't have people loitering at the gate. You hear me?"

Jason had rested his forehead back on the steering wheel while the gatekeeper spoke. Somehow, no choice felt like the right choice. He heard himself say, "*What the fuck am I doing here?*" Without lifting his head, Jason rolled up the window. When he finally looked up, the gatekeeper only glared at him, his pink face and neatly trimmed blond hair with specks of gray only a foot from the Jeep's window. Jason shifted into reverse, cranked the wheel and hit the gas. After he clicked the shifter into drive and pulled away from the farm, he watched the gatekeeper in his rearview mirror for a few seconds. Then he drove away.

"Okay," he repeated the word a few times. "All right, okay, okay. Now what?"

Lo panicked as she felt a hand caressing her stomach and then moving up toward her breasts. She didn't open her eyes at first, just rolled to her side and stretched a little to indicate she was awake.

John moved closer, and she could feel him behind her. Her heart beat rapidly. He moaned and buried his face between her naked shoulder blades.

"Lo," he said, hoarsely. "You didn't tell me you had Orion's Belt on your belly."

"Huh?"

"You have the belt, three moles at the same angle. Then one mole above it. That's the arrow."

"*Mhm*. Listen, John—"

"Lo," he said, his voice not quite working yet. He moved her hair off her shoulder and rested his chin there, forcing her head down into the pillow. She continued to panic while attempting to appear civil.

Last night, halfway through her second drink, she had accepted the inevitability of this outcome. She had every intention of sleeping with John by drink three, and after a few more, could barely wait to get him into bed. She reminded herself of this as she took deep breaths and tried to ignore the feeling of John's hard penis on her lower thigh. He was so much taller than her.

"Lo," he said again. "Are you freaking out right now?"

"I am."

"Would you like me to go get dressed?" he asked.

She only murmured, "*Mhm*."

Her face burned red as John got up, naked behind her turned back. She had insisted that John share the guest room with her because they had a long drive ahead of them. He needed to sleep in a comfortable bed. There were several other reasons that she believed sounded extremely convincing at the time.

In the end, they had probably stayed up until five or six in the morning, and now it was nine. She was hungover and embarrassed. As she had been quite drunk the night before, Lo began to worry that Deb and Raul had heard moaning from their room. She groaned inwardly—all she could do was bury her face in the pillow and breathe. In the moment, she'd wanted John to know how exactly how she felt. So, she'd told him, many times. Over and over, in fact, and very enthusiastically. Now she made her body tight, curling up as if she could become tiny and her embarrassment wouldn't fit inside anymore.

"Lo," John said again as if he couldn't stop repeating himself. "We don't have to make it a thing, all right? I mean, I'm glad it happened, but we can just go on like it didn't. I—I understand if you need time to—"

"Okay, John. It's okay. It was great. We better get on the road. I'm going to get the jars from the car and fill them up with water."

What did she really want to say to him? Was *god, that was fun* on the tip of her tongue? Should she admit that last night—the dinner, the conversation, her and John together—was the most fun she'd had her entire life? Or did she want to tell him it would never work, that it was a mistake to even try? That she was moving out of town anyway? Maybe she should say that it would never work out because he was a car mechanic from North Carolina who loved sweet tea and was emotionally scarred from being indoctrinated as a child, and she was a stubborn freegan from a broken home in rural Minnesota, who was only alive because her father paid some lady not to abort her. She tried to clear her head. She took a deep breath and got out of bed, naked and unthinking. John raised his eyebrows and pressed his lips together. She answered with a scowl, pulling the sheet up as quickly as she could.

Deb was in a better mood than Lo had ever been in her entire life as they packed up the car and hugged goodbye. Deb sent them leftover rice and vegetables in empty pickle jars with wooden takeout chopsticks. She filled another two empty jars with coffee and carried them out to the car for the travelers, her black bathrobe over sweatpants and a sweatshirt, tied loosely around her waist. It was a cold morning, and light snow fell.

Tears filled her eyes, and she made both Lo and John promise to come visit again someday soon. As Lo opened the door to drive the first leg, Deb held the car door open.

"I'm serious, Lo. Come visit. Or hey, y'all could move into the guest room for a while. Think about it! An adventure! I'm dying to have family in town. We eat with Raul's dad every Sunday, and I always wish I had my family here too. But really, John is my only family. And, well, now you too. We could work the garden. I know a bunch of music venues or if you wanted, we could find a nonprofit you're interested in. I know a ton!" Deb smiled weakly and let go of the door. Lo wondered if it was possible she hadn't heard anything last night. Though she'd only known Deb for a day, that definitely seemed like the sort of thing that she would bring up shamelessly over morning coffee.

Lo started to shut the door, leaving it halfway open as she said her final goodbye. "Okay, Deb. Thank you, really, for everything."

Then Deb and John said their goodbyes. At one point Deb sobbed, and John hunched over and wiped both sides of her face with his hands. She pushed him away playfully, and that was that. John got in the car, and Lo started the engine without knowing exactly where she was going.

She found it hard to believe they could do another full day of driving. She was hungover, and coffee didn't seem to help. It only made her stomach twist and gurgle. They listened to the NPR station until it disappeared, then John fiddled and found a country station, which Lo tolerated.

She had been worried about driving through Albuquerque, but it was only a few minutes to the interstate, as John's phone led her north and then west. It was past morning rush hour, so the streets weren't too crowded as they left town.

Deb had *insisted* that they drive through Laguna, so Lo pulled off the interstate for ten minutes and drove around what felt like the scene of an old Clint Eastwood movie that her dad would like. A white stone chapel stood at the top of the hill. It was beautiful, and Lo imagined that no town could feel more different from Elysian, which was surrounded on all sides by lakes. There was a consistency to Laguna that Lo appreciated, white adobe homes that fell in step with the brown landscape. This was something that had always upset her about Minnesota—such a lack of design for such a beautiful place. A massive billboard advertising an urgent care would block a lake view, a flashing casino marquee might hide a blooming crab apple, a slew of plastic-paneled houses breaking the horizon.

They didn't stop to walk around since they still had a sixteen-hour drive ahead of them. If they could manage it in one day—tired, hungover and both slightly embarrassed—then they would have four days to convince Jason Peterson to visit his sick mother and head back to Elysian before either of them missed an extra day of work. It was a twenty-eight-hour drive from Santa Rosa, California back to Minnesota, and she figured it would take two of the four remaining days to complete. So, really, their time was limited. She ran these scenarios through her head while John said nothing, only looked out the window as Lo pulled back onto I-40.

"We're not going to talk about it, then?" John asked after two hours of quietly tuning radio stations. None of the frequencies seemed to have much reach, so he was continually adjusting stations to find the one with the least static. It had taken them both several minutes to realize they were listening to Christian rock before they reached for the tuner simultaneously.

Lo almost said *Talk about what?* but held her tongue. She sighed dramatically and straightened her posture, leaning forward over the steering wheel. The truth was, she had mentally rehearsed something and was preparing to deliver it.

"Okay. Please just hear me out. I've felt a lot of pressure from you— knowing that you are clearly interested in me. It's been confusing for me.

You're just so forward. That's weird. But besides that, what's the point of this? Of us? I'm planning on moving to Minneapolis. From what you said about Shay Rose, you haven't been content being with someone who's up in the Cities while you're in Elysian. Why start something just to end it? And what's worse is if I decide not to move. Then what? That would be awful."

She could feel him staring at her. "What?" he finally asked. "Awful?"

Lo opened her mouth, shut it, then fumbled. "I mean, Artie hates me, and I have to see him all the time. Imagine if you ended up hating me, and then I would have to see you around town, it'd be awful."

"To see me around town?"

"I mean—when we broke up and then ran into each other." This was not going as she had planned.

"After we broke up?"

"I'm sure I saw you a few times around town—at Lefty's, at the diner, the store. And it wasn't all weird and awkward before, and I do not need any more of that in my life right now."

"I never saw you."

"Whatever. You couldn't know that."

"I promise I would not forget seeing you. I remember very clearly seein' you for the first time at the shop. Very clearly."

Lo's face flushed. "And this," she waved toward all of him, "this constant flirting. What am I supposed to do with that?"

"What can I say, Lo? I like you, all right. I liked you from the minute I saw you, that's how I know I never saw you before. Should I be mean to you instead? Should I pretend I don't find you attractive? All right. If that's what you want. I guess you think I'm comin' on strong. I guess you need space to figure out your feelings, but you sure as hell didn't need space last night. 'Oh my god, John, you're the best. You're so good. You're so big.'"

"Oh my god! Shut up! I did not say that. I was drunk, and you know it. You were drunk too."

"Right." He looked out the window. She wasn't sure where to take this, and she really didn't know what she wanted. Did she want to pull the car over so she could climb onto his lap in the passenger seat and make out? Or should she stop at the nearest airport and get a ticket home? Obviously, she had sent John mixed signals, but that's because her own feelings were mixed up as well.

"John, I'm just—I'm confused." She took a cue from Deb, suddenly, without thinking it through. She tried simply being honest. "Part of me wants to pull over and make out with you right now. My body is like *hell yes*. But my mind—my mind knows better. That part of me wants to never see you again and avoid a whole mess of unnecessary drama. The thing is, I haven't dated much, but when I do, it always ends *very* badly, partially because the men I've dated don't understand me or my values. And I can't deal with that right now. The bottom line is I want to leave Elysian, and I can't let anything or anyone stop me. I'm scared that'll happen if we do this—this *thing*. That's the truth. I don't know what I want. I need time to figure it out."

She glanced over at him without taking her eyes off the road for too long. He was smiling slightly. "I appreciate the honesty. And if you do want to, you know, pull over—then that's a yes from me. I consent." She smacked him with her right hand, but he didn't turn away. Instead, he caught her wrist and bit gingerly into her forearm. "Woman, you need both hands on the wheel. This ain't safe." She pulled her hand away, jerking the wheel only slightly with her other hand. "Lo, I'll just follow your lead. So, lead the way as you see fit." John laughed and went back to tuning the radio.

The world was green again about an hour into Arizona as lone pine trees began to grow thicker into pine forests. Lo wondered at the beauty of the mountains while John kept insisting that she pull over to let him drive, probably because as she craned her neck to take in the views, the car swerved along with it.

In Flagstaff, they switched, and Lo was able to watch the forests and mountains of northern Arizona pass by. She had expected

Arizona to be desert, red rocks, lifeless—but that wasn't what she found in the thick pine forests and rugged mountains. It was only in the midfifties, and Lo rolled down the window and stuck her hand out into the fresh air.

They both cheered a little when they crossed the border into California, back down out of the mountains and into a harsh desert, but Lo had already been dozing in and out of sleep for hours. She caught a glimpse of John's eyes as he drove, red and drooping, and knew they had no chance at making it another six or seven hours. Lo took John's phone again, since he had much better service and unlimited data, and searched the map.

"I have an idea," she told John, who only nodded and said *Okay* very slowly as if what she was suggesting was a dangerous explosive that needed a delicate approach. She rolled her eyes at him, pressed a button on his phone and lifted it to her ear.

They made it to Joshua Tree fifteen minutes before it closed for the night.

The man on the phone seemed surprised that they still had an open site available and told her that they should hurry because it was first come, first serve.

They didn't have much in the way of camping gear, but together they finished Deb's leftovers and shared a bottle of cheap wine that Deb had snuck in the bag she packed for them. They passed it back and forth, but neither felt like drinking much. Instead, they sat on the hood and watched the stars. Lo had never in her entire life seen more of them— purple, pink and brilliant—bright enough to reflect off John's clear irises. He pointed out Orion first, and Lo thought about him touching her belly just that morning.

"Don't you think it's wild that the two of us met in that little town in Minnesota and now we're out here camping in the desert?" John asked as they figured out how best to arrange the car for sleeping.

Lo shrugged. "No. That little town is the only place I've ever met anyone."

"*Hmm*," he said quietly, nodding. "Not me."

John fell asleep quickly in the backseat, legs scrunched, facing the dusty cloth interior. Lo leaned the passenger seat as far back as it could go, using John's sweatshirt as a blanket. She watched his back rise and fall in the starlight and listened to his quiet breath. The windows were cracked open, and she could hear the desert wind, like something from an app designed to help people sleep. They were surrounded by brown rocky cliffs, small misshapen Joshua trees and the open desert. She reached out instinctively to touch John's hair but couldn't reach the other end of the car from where she was laying. Just as her plans to leave town were unfolding, here was this guy with his sweet tea addiction and stupid blue eyes. Life was starting to feel like a test that she was worried she would fail no matter what answers she picked. She was too tired to keep worrying about it, though, so she curled her hands under her head and drifted off.

Lo screamed as she held her toothbrush and baking soda in one hand and a jar of water in the other. She pulled her bare feet back into the car and tried to catch her breath. John jolted awake, hitting his knees hard against the passenger seat that was still fully reclined.

"The hell?" he asked. "What—are you okay? What happened?"

"It's okay! I'm fine. It was a scorpion! It's just, they're the same color as the ground, and I just put my foot down and—" She took a deep breath. "I'm okay. It didn't get me. But holy shit, that scared me. I totally forgot that scorpions existed until right now."

He laughed a little and rubbed his eyes. "I need some coffee."

"Scorpion aside, I don't want to leave." She surveyed the landscape. The sky was electric, bluer than she'd ever seen it. There was something about the light of the California sun, the way the shadows fell; it was different, somehow more exacting.

"I can feel it getting hotter by the minute, bet it's scorching during the day," he said, lying on his back and attempting to stretch his legs. He looked at his phone. "It's six thirty, Lo."

"I couldn't sleep any longer." She tapped him on the forehead with her toothbrush and then slipped her shoes on.

She didn't say a word when John came back to the car with two coffees. She needed it after such little sleep but couldn't bring herself to thank him for the colorfully printed Styrofoam cup. Instead, she took a sip and smiled politely.

"I almost bought you a cowboy hat. Instead, I got you this." He opened his hand, and in it was a brown scorpion encapsulated in a glass half-circle on a small plastic base that read JOSHUA TREE NATIONAL PARK.

She smiled despite herself. "I'll keep it on my bedroom floor to remind me of our trip together." She turned it around in her hands, feeling the weight of it. "John," she scolded him, "this cost $14.99." Lo pictured the stockrooms full of thousands of kitschy tourist gifts that eventually collected enough dust on the shelves of peoples' homes to justify the trash bin.

"*Shh*, Bambi, don't ruin the moment." John started the car, twisting the AC toward cool. He was right about the day getting hotter.

She ignored the nickname and examined the map on John's GPS app. "It's eight hours, minimum, to Santa Rosa. We have got to find this guy tonight and convince him quick, otherwise, we'll both miss a day of work."

They took I-5 even though John insisted they should take Highway 1 up the coast or the 101, which they both knew from the popular song that played on the radio constantly when they were teenagers. John sent Deb a picture of the road sign since *The O.C.* had been, at one point in her life, her most meaningful connection to the West Coast. Lo wouldn't have called the last two days "wasted," but she felt a sudden urgency to complete their mission and find Blanche's son so they could return to their own lives. It was easy to feel untethered on a cross-country road trip with a near-stranger, even if he was starting to feel more and more familiar to her.

John drove all day as Lo fiddled with the radio or studied the map, checking if there were alternate routes around spots with heavy traffic.

When they drove on the outskirts of San Francisco she saw the bay; its glinting blue water moved her nearly to tears. She didn't want to tell John she'd never seen the ocean before, so she just looked out the window, straining on both sides to take in as much of it as she could.

As they passed exits for Sausalito, Lo was reading about Alcatraz on John's phone when he got a message from Shay Rose. The phone vibrated in her hand, but she wasn't sure whether John had noticed it or not. Words flashed across the top of the screen: Coming home this weekend. Anything going on?

Lo's first impulse was to delete the message, but it disappeared from the top of the screen as quickly as it had come.

"You got a text from Shay Rose," she said casually.

John cleared his throat and nodded. "Wasn't a nude, was it?"

Lo scoffed loudly. "Oh my god, John. No! She just asked what you were doing this weekend. Does she send you a lot of nudes?"

He only laughed, but Lo felt the urge to throw his phone out the window. "If you know Shay Rose at all, you know she's not sending nudes." He stopped talking for a minute, and she could see his Adam's apple bob in a swallow. "At least not this early in the day." He laughed again, but Lo didn't think it was very funny. "What do you want me to do with the message?" he asked quietly.

Lo considered the question, her tongue moving slowly across her teeth, crooked on the bottom. "Well, that's up to you, I guess. I'm not your girlfriend."

"*Hmm*, you're something though."

Lo made a dismissive sound and shook her head gently. "I don't know. I guess just do whatever you want. It doesn't even matter since we're not in town anyway." She smiled sweetly and held her hands out flat as they passed by a small bay lined with houseboats, indicating how "not in town" they were. He nodded in agreement, but Lo wondered if he had hoped she would tell him to delete Shay's number and never speak to her again.

"What do you like about Shay Rose?"

"Huh?"

"I'm just curious. I've known her since we were little. You two seem so different, is all. I'm just wondering." She tried to keep her voice light.

"I'm not going to tell you what I like about Shay Rose."

"It's not that big of a deal. Just tell me, I'm curious."

He shook his head. "I'm not thinking about Shay Rose right now. She's nice, you know. But it was just a few nights here and there, whenever she was back in town. It's not like I miss her when she's gone or anything, you know what I mean? It's not like—it never felt like how it feels when I'm hanging out with you. She doesn't yell at me nearly as much, for one thing."

Lo tried not to smile. "I wouldn't say I *yell* at you."

"Fine. She doesn't *scold me* nearly as much. But I still prefer hanging out with you. Hell, I actually think I like it when you scold me. Kind of turns me on if we're being honest here."

She laughed out loud. "All right, that's enough honesty for today." But Lo couldn't help herself. Without much thought, she deleted John's text thread with Shay, then turned her gaze back to the view.

When they arrived in Santa Rosa, John drove through town slowly as if they might spot Jason Peterson walking down the sidewalk. The main thoroughfare through town was pleasant. It reminded Lo of the most affluent neighborhoods in Minneapolis. Tree-lined streets with brick storefronts, patios serving overpriced cocktails, people walking curated dog breeds on leashes that cost more than her entire outfit.

It was nearly seven at night when they pulled up to a gate at the address Blanche had given them. A security guard greeted them from a guardhouse near the road.

"We're looking for someone—a friend," Lo said, trying hard not to sound suspicious. She had no idea that the farm would have a locked gate, let alone a security guard carrying a gun in a holster.

"Visitors have to call the office," he said, as if the phrase were re-corded from a prompt.

A black walkie-talkie sat on a small plywood table, which was apparently how they called the office. Lo looked at John sidelong and kept her distance from the gatekeeper when she realized he could have simply brought the walkie-talkie to their car instead of forcing them to huddle into his tiny shed.

The gatekeeper pushed a button on the side of the walkie-talkie. "Gate to office. Over."

"Office here. Over."

"Got some folks looking for a friend. Over."

"Who they looking for? Over."

The gatekeeper looked at Lo now, as if this was her cue.

"Jason Peterson. Over."

The gatekeeper gave her a hard look, then said the name into the walkie-talkie. John hung his head, a slight smile on his face.

"Yeah, actually bring 'em in, would ya? Over."

The gatekeeper told John to move the car off the road, closer to the small guardhouse, then brought them into the farm on a four-wheeler. It was a short drive down a gravel driveway to the front office, which was just a small ranch-style farmhouse. Lo saw massive greenhouses, all white with no windows, snug in the rolling hills. It was a golden dusk, and even the bright filmy walls of the greenhouses looked beautiful reflecting the sunset.

When she thought of large-scale organic farming, this was not what she had pictured. She wasn't that into marijuana, mostly because it was expensive and still illegal in Minnesota. But in her mind, she had imagined this place much more hippieish and relaxed with wandering cows and women in long flowing skirts, not a man with a pistol and an ATV prowling the perimeter. Of course, she hadn't necessarily expected a massive weed farm to be open to the public either.

The gatekeeper escorted them into the office but didn't come in. An old man with a white beard and a dirty red baseball hat sat at a large empty desk. Lo could see a camera feed connected to the front gate on one monitor, but all she could hear was *Wheel of Fortune* blaring from a small flat-screen TV mounted to the wood paneling. The room looked like it had once been carpeted. Lo could see the glue still stuck to the concrete.

"I'm not going to waste your time. Jason isn't here, but I wanted to ask if you knew where he is and if he's all right. I saw him yesterday. He pulled on up to the gate but then left. He called me a week ago, maybe two, telling me he needed his old job back. Sounded a little down. Can't get him on his phone now. We got a lot of turnover here, and I was happy to have him back. But then he just drove off. I thought maybe he needed to head on over to Walmart or something—forgot clean underwear." The man laughed at his own joke. "But he hasn't been back." He looked to John and Lo as if they could explain Jason's disappearance.

Lo only shook her head, disoriented. John curled his neck back and looked up to the speckled ceiling, a broad florescent light blinked and dimmed spastically as the night darkened. Lo could imagine the humming sound it was making, a sound she couldn't hear over a commercial reading the side effects of a prescription drug: *increased blood pressure, anxious or suicidal thoughts, death.*

"So, that's a no? Haven't heard from him? Why are you looking for him?"

Lo made a sour face; she wanted to leave. She didn't want to be standing in this sad office with the loud television and this man who didn't know where Jason Peterson was.

John cleared his throat. "Actually, we don't know him that well. We—well, she grew up with him in Minnesota. We're from his hometown." John's accent certainly wouldn't help their wild story make any more sense.

Lo cut in. "His mom asked if we would find him. She's very sick, and his phone is off. We don't know where he is. Do you think we should be worried about him?"

Here she was, standing in a dingy office on a weed farm in California with an armed guard waiting outside, looking for a man who had no idea who she was and probably wouldn't want to speak to her if he did. She had traveled all the way to Northern California, and now Jason Peterson was nowhere to be found, and they had no way to get in touch with him. This was pretty much what she had expected to happen, but now that it was happening, she couldn't contain her frustration. Lo was tired. And she was confused about John, whom she could feel watching her—namely, why she was so attracted to him. And why now, when she was ready to leave Elysian for good? And why, of all the women in the world, did it have to be Shay Rose? She felt tears sting the corners of her eyes, and she bit her lip.

The man cocked his head to the side. "He'll be all right. Don't worry now. Funny guy. Nice kid. If you find Peterson, tell him I'll hold his spot for a few more days, but we need to bring someone in soon."

Lo nodded weakly, then they headed back out to the porch where the gatekeeper was waiting for them.

SANTA ROSA, CALIFORNIA

"Hold on a minute. I'm nervous, sorry. I haven't done this in a while. I asked Fred for the expired stuff from the store, so now he just drops it off on my porch."

John nodded. "No surprise there."

"What does that mean?" Lo snapped back.

"It just means that you've got a great setup there in Elysian, what with the owner of the grocery store personally delivering free groceries to your front porch."

"Well, they're the expired ones, okay? And this was your idea."

"It was only my idea because I don't want to buy you a dinner that you'll hate eating."

"Just stop, John. I'll find us something, and we can bring it to the hotel." She shook her head as she surveyed the back alley of the grocery store. She was still in disbelief that they couldn't find a hostel to stay at, though the hotel she found on John's phone was much cheaper than the other places in town. "We need to figure out how the hell we can find Jason Peterson now. You said Blanche still hasn't texted you back?"

"Yeah, she just did a minute ago. She said she would call the girl in Idaho again. We'll see if she gets back to us tonight."

Lo sighed. "Okay, I think if you just boost me up, I can check out the dumpster and see if it's worth going in."

John shook his head but opened the passenger door. Lo was touched that he was even entertaining the idea. Even if he did so begrudgingly.

The giant blue dumpster was greasy to the touch and smelled like old cardboard. The same moment that John bent down, his fingers interlaced so Lo could step on them, the back door opened and a man wearing an apron and holding a cigarette stepped out. He looked at them, irritated. They straightened up and did what they could to look inconspicuous.

"You know that's illegal here?" The man glared at them, head tilted down, eyes up, like a teacher scolding students for shooting spit wads.

"What? It's illegal to collect wasted food?" She tightened her messy bun that had started to droop and attempted to win him over with a gentle smile.

"Don't blame me, honey," he said, lighting his cigarette. "Dumpster diving is illegal in Santa Rosa city limits, and you're on camera." He blew out smoke and then pointed to a camera positioned above the back door. "Y'all better scat before the security guard heads out here. Try the free store over near the train." He turned his back to them, leaning a shoulder against the dirty stucco wall of the grocery store, as if to let them know that he was finished with the interaction.

They didn't talk on the drive to the free store. Lo followed the directions to a less tree-lined, less brick-fronted side of town. They found a spot on the street to park, and Lo noticed some people leaning against the few bedraggled pine trees in the area. They were nothing like the tall narrow pines at home. These were many-limbed and had broken branches poking off like spikes in every direction. Some of the branches grew at a vertical angle—straight up or down. They were unkempt and dangerous looking but also wonderful. She took John's arm, but he pulled away.

"I'm just a little uncomfortable here," she whispered as they stepped onto the street to avoid walking directly over a man who was stretched out on the sidewalk eating an apple under a streetlight that had just blinked on.

"Okay. Me too, but that's because we shouldn't be here."

She scoffed. "It's not that—I mean, I'm sure these are nice people, John. We shouldn't judge them—"

"That's not what I meant. We shouldn't be here. *You* should not be here. You might actually be the richest person I know. I mean that. Your dad and his law firm, big-time county judge, all that."

She stopped short and looked at him, shocked. "What does that have to do with anything? *Big-time* county judge, really? Of *big-time* Le Sueur County? And his money's not my money, John."

"Right." He lifted a shoulder aggressively. "But it is. He pays for your phone, right? Your apartment—"

"No, he doesn't!" she lied, her voice rising. A man leaning against the wall of a low building watched them mildly. She stood on the curb, staring at the store across a quiet street that she wasn't ready to cross, but she also didn't feel comfortable having this conversation three feet from a stranger.

John rubbed his eyes. "All right. I'm sorry. All I'm saying is it doesn't feel right that we would take this free stuff from people who need it just because your dad's money makes you uncomfortable or whatever."

"Oh my god, *whatever* yourself. Money is a bullshit construct that brings destruction, corruption and environmental degradation. It's a hundred million bandages covering everyone's pain and suffering that they refuse to look at!"

"Right on, sister." The man on the sidewalk nodded along with Lo then lowered his head as if he hadn't been listening to their conversation.

"Fine. Maybe you're right. But I'm not going into that store. You can go if you want, but I'm going to buy some food in town for myself. I'm sorry."

Lo stood staring at him with her eyes narrowed. She turned to look at the store at the same moment the lights went dark. A minute later an employee was locking the front door.

"Fuck," she whispered, tilting her head up toward the streetlight. "Fine. Whatever. I'm starving. Blanche can buy us dinner tonight. We've barely spent any of that money anyway."

"Thank you," he responded, then held out his hand toward Lo, offering his arm. She looked at him for a minute, head down and eyes up, the same way the man at the grocery store had looked at them. She strode past him and walked to the driver's seat of her car.

"Just get in," she said, her back turned to him. "I'm driving."

"I'm serious," John said, laughing. "Deborah was a badass in the Bible. The day I learned that Deborah was some kind of feminist judge and military strategist or some shit, I was mad at my parents for six straight months. I—honestly—I'm still mad about it." He shook his head and took a drink of his beer. Out of principle, Lo hadn't ordered anything but tap water, but after she tried a sip of his Thai beer, she ordered one for herself. The line between vile materialism and sheer curiosity was much more easily blurred outside the borders of Elysian, where everything was familiar and there was nothing new that might stimulate said curiosity.

She'd forgiven John for his comments about the free store, partly because it had closed anyway. But also, she let it go because deep down, she worried that what he said was true. She knew without ever saying it aloud that her dad was one of the richest men in town. Of course, big fish in tiny ponds weren't really *that* big. His money wouldn't mean much in California, but in the more modest town where they lived, Jerry Gunderson had a comfortable life, and as a result, Lo's life had been comfortable as well. That didn't mean she needed to be complicit in a predatory capitalist system—she just wasn't clear whether that privilege required a responsibility she didn't quite understand but John seemed to hint at.

They sat on the patio under a set of string lights. Both were mediocre at eating with chopsticks and had to ask for forks to eat their noodles. John wore a long-sleeved Twins shirt that had the exact same logo as his t-shirt he had worn at Deb's house, while Lo still wore his sweatshirt. It was a cold night; there were so many more cold nights on this trip than she had prepared for. She was realizing that Minnesota didn't have a monopoly on cold weather, though she didn't imagine Santa Rosa had many subzero blizzards.

"So, when did you start going by John then? When you moved to Minnesota?"

He nodded, taking another drink of his beer. "Yup. My parents got mad anytime I complained about my name. Something about how Cain served God's purposes in his own way, how it was a family name, all that. When I moved in with my uncle's family, they never questioned it when I asked them to call me John. Who would want to be named after one of the most famous murderers in history?" He scratched his head. It was meant to be lighthearted, but John got a serious look on his face and set his fork down. "Do you think Deb is happy? Did Raul seem like a nice guy, to you? A bit of an asshole, right?"

Lo scrunched her face and thought about it for a minute. "Well, if he's a jerk, then so am I. We were both arguing, and actually—" she said, struggling for a minute, trying to come up with the right words. People passed by—men holding hands, women in big trendy hats and tasseled wool shawls. Massive dogs, tiny dogs, dogs in strollers, kids pushing dogs in strollers. The strong scent of marijuana floated by in wafts from seemingly out of nowhere. Lo knew she didn't fit in at this fancy downtown Thai restaurant on the West Coast attempting to eat prawn noodles with wooden chopsticks, but she was enjoying herself regardless. "I actually liked Raul. Even when we had differing opinions, he was willing to listen and even learn. I think that's rare. I think they are both—" She paused and admired John in the glow of the hanging lights. "Rare. Deb's a gem."

The waiter came over and John ordered a second beer. He made an inquisitive face at Lo, raising his eyes just a little. She nodded slightly, warming inside at that small, intimate gesture, and feeling only a little bad about the price of another beer.

They had made it all the way out to Santa Rosa only to have missed

Jason Peterson by a day. And Blanche had given them a fat envelope full of cash to fund their wild goose chase, so she tried not to feel guilty about getting one nice dinner.

As the waiter brought out their second beers, John set his hand out on the table, flat and open like an invitation. Lo hesitated for a minute, watching his open hand, but eventually brought her own hand up and ran a finger the length of his open palm. He cleared his throat. "I guess I think you're rare, Lo." He said this slowly, perhaps testing her current attitude, and then took a drink of his beer with this free hand. She looked down at the table and wrinkled her nose. "I mean it. You are. You kinda—" He paused for a minute and tilted his head side to side. "You're smart and you care about stuff. And you're a great travel companion. Five stars and all that. And," he stammered, "you look so fuckin' good right now, sitting there in the sweatshirt you stole from me. I'm glad we're here. It's been fun." Even in the dim night, she could see him blushing. He cleared his throat.

Her heart beat so out of tempo that she worried she needed medical care. She coughed awkwardly. "Why do you keep saying these things? It's dumb. It's so cute when you're all sentimental and embarrassed like that. I really hate it." She couldn't suppress an awkward laugh, more like a giggle than she was willing to admit.

She couldn't keep that promise to herself. The force that pushed them together once they stepped inside the rented room was unavoidable, magnetic. That night at a cheap hotel on the side of a rolling hill, they made love. And *yes*, Lo would be too embarrassed to say those two words out loud together in sequence, but that's what happened. She was shocked at how easily he could hold her up, her back pressing against the dingy brown motel room wall. Much more sober and much more alone, hundreds of miles from anyone they knew, she moaned into his ear as he moved against her, "*Thank you. Thank you. Thank you.*" If he had asked her what she was thanking him for, exactly, she wouldn't have been able to explain it.

SANTA ROSA, CALIFORNIA

The interior and exterior of the hotel were shades of brown, but the rate for the room was a third the price of the neighboring chain, and there was a hint of self-loathing in the cheap polyester bedspread that was fitting for his circumstances. Jason set two things down on one of the two double beds: his duffel bag full of clothing and one book. A well-worn paperback, the cover missing.

For a few minutes, he stood in the center of the room, unmoving. He looked at the old phone resting on the table between the beds, a relic from another time. The phone was brown like the rest of the room—a light tan. Each button was worn with use and stained with grease. Jason moved toward the phone, picked up the receiver, then set it down.

He dug the voice recorder out of his bag and lay down on the bed. He hit the record button.

"Once you were gone, she stopped coming home most nights. *Pokémon* was the only kids' show on TV after school. I mean, I was getting too old for that shit, but it was that or *Charles in Charge*. When it was nice out, I dug around in the backyard, hoping every night she would come home and make dinner. When it was too cold, I watched *Pokémon* and got used to feeding myself whatever was in the kitchen— less and less as time went by. No more eggs and bacon, just cans of beef stew and saltine crackers. I don't even remember what else, mostly microwave dinners. The bartender at Lefty's would drop off two-gallon buckets of potato salad and coleslaw once in a while. I forced myself to eat it, but really, what kid likes coleslaw? I did all right though." He shrugged. He didn't need his dad feeling sorry for him after all this time.

He sat for another minute, picked up the receiver and held it to his ear. Jason pushed the number one and then ten more numbers and then immediately pushed the button to cancel the call. There was no sound in the room except for the dial tone beeping past his ear and into the silence.

At the pool in the center of the motel, he could see the doors of all the other rooms. He watched one couple silently unlock their door with an old metal key. The guy was wearing a Twins shirt. Jason didn't like that, for some reason. One old man sat next to the door of his room and smoked a cigar from the balcony—definitely illegal in California. The heady smell filled the cliffside. It was getting later now, and a few stars were visible above him. The motel was far enough outside of the city and halfway up a hillside, so they could see a couple stars but not many. There had been an infinite number of stars above their place in Twin Falls. Too many, maybe. An overwhelming number.

He got in the pool and swam several laps, back and forth. The chlorine burned his eyes a shade of pink. The smell wafted from the water, and he remembered floating in the lakes in Minnesota. There was no pool where he grew up, but his mom and dad had taken him swimming at the public-access beach on summer weekends. After his dad died, he went with friends, girlfriends, on a few school trips maybe, but never went with his mom again.

Jason performed another solitary baptism, born again in the halogen. He wasn't a religious person, but he understood that to mean that no one else was going to save his own soul for him. So, he regularly baptized himself—just to feel new again. Maybe it would help him clear his mind. He was tired of his mom floating around in there, clogging shit up.

He swam on the surface for a long time. His muscles were taut as he backstroked. He began slapping the water harder and harder with each stroke until eventually he was standing up, his elbows bent, both hands slapping the water as hard as he could, the claps echoing off the hillside.

"Hey, hey, you! What you got yourself into then?" a voice called out from beside the pool.

Jason stopped his hand, fingers held open wide in midair.

The old man who had been smoking his cigar was now sitting sidesaddle on a chair with taut plastic strips, though he seemed to be balancing in a squat, not fully trusting it to hold him. He puffed his cigar, and blue-tinted smoke swirled above the pool, reflecting off the pallid floodlight that lit the area. The man looked like Billy Dee Williams moonlighting as a middle-class grandpa at a roadside motel.

Jason cleared his throat and leaned into a backstroke as casually as possible.

"Gotten myself into?" Jason asked, looking up at the stars.

"That's right. Must be in some kind of trouble, the way you're carrying on here. Or you're looking to get yourself in trouble—I can't tell."

Jason exhaled loudly and pushed back away from the man, though the pool was small and circular, which made gaining any distance difficult. So, he stood up and rested his palms on the glassy surface of the water as if it might hold the weight of his hands. At first, he only nodded slowly as if he were agreeing. "Just getting some exercise."

"You always do that when you swim, then?" The old man seemed amused, relaxed as he sucked the end of the cigar, only occasionally breathing the smoke into his mouth. He mimicked Jason's slapping for a second. "That's how you stay so skinny?"

"I guess so."

"Okay. Just seemed to me you might want to do some talking. That vein in your neck, I could see it pulsing from the balcony up there." The man removed his hat to scratch his bald head, which glistened under the floodlight. He wore an open cardigan, and Jason noticed how cool it had gotten since the sun went down.

He sunk his chin into the water and blew out air for a few seconds. "Yeah, if you really want to know, I left my place because my girlfriend got pregnant and then I fucked it up. Acted like an asshole and left, *by far*, the best thing that ever happened to me. I mean, *by far*. Got my old job back here in town, so I drove here in my piece-of-shit truck. I probably made a mistake, but she didn't leave me any choice. She asked me to leave. I don't know if my truck will even make it back to Idaho because there are some belt issues happening under the hood. So that's what's going on."

The old man frowned, nodding slowly. He sucked at his cigar and then ran his tongue across his lips once. "I see. Sounds like you know what you need to do, then."

Jason's eyes tightened, and he laughed once to himself. He waited for the man to say something else, but he only lay back in the chair and looked up at the stars.

Eventually, Jason returned to his room because the hot tub next to the pool had been invaded by loudmouthed vacationers.

That night, Jason lay in bed and read the entire paperback novel in one sitting. It was missing its cover, but according to the blurb on the back, it was a "racy, absorbing romance." When he finally set the book down, it was only to press a single tear back into his eye with the knuckle of his pointer finger.

Jason found the voice recorder tangled in the comforter and hit the record button. "You were a good teacher. I never knew it at the time though. Sometimes you were straight-up annoying, to be honest. I'll never forget when you slammed on the steering wheel that day—we were coming into town, passed a cop car. You had been telling me for years, 'If you have a run-in with the cops, the first thing you say is that you're Marcus Peterson's son.' Even as a kid, I rolled my eyes, like, 'My dad thinks he's a big shot.' But that day you hit the wheel and yelled, so you'd get through to me. It wasn't until after you left that it hit me. All those damn pancake breakfasts and fish fries that you made sure to cover for the paper. All the pictures you took for every police department in southern Minnesota—you wanted them to know who you were, know your face. It wasn't for the paper. It was for you—to keep you safe. And it was for me too. Well, I made it out of Minnesota. Can't say that for everybody, though. You'd be hitting that wheel too many times. There was one day looking down at all those papers that mom started stacking on the floor when it just hit me. But guess what, Dad? Didn't do you any good in the end, did it? That judge, that small-time, small-town judge with all that power, how does that make sense? A man who called himself your friend too—he was the one who let your killer loose. She spent *two weeks* in jail and then just walked away. How's that for keeping yourself safe? All that time running around the state making nice with the cops. Got you nowhere." Jason hit the stop button and threw the recorder down on the bed next to him.

"What the hell am I doing here?" he asked himself.

Taking heavy breaths, he psyched himself up to pick up the phone and dial a series of numbers. Into a voice mailbox: "Lex, I read your book. I should have read it sooner. I'm lost—I lost my phone, so I'm up at a hotel in Santa Rosa. I made a mistake. The biggest mistake of my life. All right? My mistake. I'm headed your way."

SANTA ROSA, CALIFORNIA

The next day, Lo and John went back to the farm and spoke to the gatekeeper, who radioed the man in the office, who confirmed that Jason Peterson never returned. It seemed their best chance at finding him rested with the woman in Idaho. John tried calling Blanche with no luck. They figured she let her phone die or else left it on the kitchen counter while she smoked and watched her game shows. But that didn't help them decide whether it was time to go or if they should keep looking.

They'd already checked out of the hotel. It was Thursday morning, and John was expected to be back to work at the garage on Sunday at 7:00 a.m. Lo didn't work until the following Wednesday, since the club was only open four days a week. Initially, she had hoped she would make it back to pick up a Saturday shift, but she knew now that wouldn't happen, not unless they left immediately. The drive home was long, and since neither of them had slept the last several nights, they couldn't do it all in one day.

She didn't want to do the drive all in one day. As much as she was ready to get back to her *real* life, she didn't want to rush it . . . for a variety of reasons.

"What's with you?" John glanced over at her from the driver's seat. She hadn't realized she was grinning like a fool, thinking about the last few late nights. They were parked at a small organic grocery store—a compromise. Lo hoped they could find something with more sustainable practices, though she didn't trust this grocery store to offer anything other than lip service. These types of stores were full of nonrecyclable plastic containers, frozen food shipped from across the world, highly processed laboratory vegan products, and on top of that, they charged exorbitant prices for everything.

"Huh?" she responded, straightening her face. "Me? I was actually thinking about last night, to be honest."

He reached out and grabbed her upper thigh, leaning toward her. She pushed him back playfully, but he didn't budge, so she grabbed his face and held it in both of her hands. He leaned forward and tried to kiss her, but she was too overwhelmed by the moment and instead laughed and turned away from him.

"Hey, Lo?" he asked.

"*Mhm?*"

"Think I could have a kiss? I was really hoping . . . just then." He was still leaning forward over the center console, smiling at her.

There was something about him that she was unable to resist. The kiss turned into a whole affair and carried on until she was worried someone might get the wrong idea and notify the authorities.

"You know, I've never kissed anyone with blue eyes before. You believe that?" she asked, pushing away an uncomfortable feeling rising from the intimacy of the moment.

"Well, I've never dated anyone with brown eyes before."

She glared at him, narrowing her eyes. "We're not dating, and I don't believe you."

He lifted a shoulder innocently. "I was only trying to make you feel better."

Lo rolled her eyes. "Okay, no more distractions, John. Think. Of. A. Plan."

He leaned back in his seat and gripped the bridge of his nose. "You go in, take some of Blanche's cash. I'll wait for a call and see if I can come up with something—some possible way to get that number, and then I'll call the drug farm again to see if he's shown up."

Lo went into the store, which proved all her assumptions correct, though they did have a local section of unwrapped fruit, bakery items and jams in glass jars. When she returned to the car, John was sleeping.

She slammed the door shut hard and he jolted awake. "Good god, Lo, you were the one who kept me up all night." She smirked, watching his chest rise and fall, his eyes drifting back shut. She threw a glass jar of some locally sourced iced tea onto his lap, which caused him to grunt a little and double over.

"Oh, sorry," she mumbled awkwardly, looking out the window. "Anyway, I figured out a plan while you were sleeping. We just need to call someone in town and get them to go over to Blanche's house, tell her to charge her phone and then call the woman in Idaho. If the woman in Twin Falls hasn't heard anything, all we can do is head home. It's not like we didn't try."

John nodded and opened the jar of tea. He took a drink and frowned. "This is interesting." He held the jar in front of his face and read the label, squinting at it as if it were in a language he couldn't interpret.

"It's yerba mate sweetened with stevia." Lo shrugged. "The closest thing they had to sweet tea."

"If you say so." He took another drink and swallowed dramatically, like it was a shot of whiskey and not loose-leaf tea. "Fine, who can you call? Your dad?" He screwed the lid of the tea jar closed and set it down next to Lo in her seat. "You can have that."

"I don't want to get my dad involved. What about Ric or Aldo? They're just down the street, right?" Lo picked up the fresh loaf of bread and inhaled. A group of teenagers stumbled behind their car, laughing and shoving each other.

"Maybe, but, you know, people in town." He lifted his shoulders and looked hesitant. "His English isn't perfect. Neither is Blanche's, if I'm honest. Her accent is leagues beyond yours. Not sure I want to ask him to run over to an old lady's house and knock on the door uninvited."

"Oh, come on, it's Elysian. Everyone knows everyone. He told me once that his English is much better than your Spanish." She laughed, but John just shook his head.

"I don't want to put them in that situation."

Lo sighed, too tired to think clearly. "I mean, I could ask Parker, I guess. Or wait! What about Mike Nelson? Lefty's is literally across the street." A woman in a fur vest pushed a cart with a toddler eating a lollipop and parked it right behind Lo's car. She popped the trunk of her massive SUV and began loading bags of groceries. Lo turned around to watch her. "What if we wanted to back up?" she asked no one in particular.

"Yeah, just call 'em. See who answers. It's noon there. Mike might be across the street already, so he could just run over. And if the stories are true about Blanche's drinkin' days, they know each other pretty well."

Lo tried Parker first, but she didn't answer, so she called the bar, hoping Mike Nelson would pick up. When he did, she explained briefly that she was looking for Blanche Peterson and wondered if he would walk over there. He sounded a little gruff, but Lo didn't imagine he had a full bar at noon on a weekday. Eventually, he agreed to run over and tell Blanche to look at her phone. Lo gave him her number and hung up.

"Before my very short nap, I did make *one* plan while you were in the store," he said and turned the key in the ignition. The woman unloading her groceries had finished but was now standing with one hand on the cart, one hand scrolling on her cell phone. John had to fend Lo off from holding down the horn, both laughing and somewhat delirious after another night of little sleep, when the woman finally wandered off to the cart return.

John drove them to a state park just north of town. He turned off the car and looked at Lo expectantly. She was already in the middle of throwing open the door and running toward a stand of redwoods, leaving John in the driver's seat. She hugged one as hard as she could, her hands not even making it halfway around the trunk. "These trees are so magical," she murmured into its bark.

They ate lunch on a beach overlooking a clear lake flanked by small mountains. The sun was warm, but the breeze over the lake was cold, and Lo tucked her legs into John's sweatshirt. Lo sensed that John was unsure about the meal of fresh bread and fig jam. He didn't eat much, but he scooted as close to her as he could, eventually turning his head and resting it on her shoulder, his face half hidden in her curls. His long back curved to bend down to her level.

Mike hadn't called back yet, which had begun irritating Lo before they had even pulled into the park. Once they finished their meal, the beach was relatively crowded with a group of mothers. It was still too cold to swim, but a dozen toddlers stood ankle-deep in the lake, screaming and splashing, holding small plastic buckets and beach shovels.

"Should I call him back?" she asked John for the third time.

"It's only been an hour. Maybe he got a few customers."

"Even if he did, he could still walk over there for a few minutes. It's not like he's got to keep the place on guard." They watched the kids for a few minutes before John laughed, pointing to a little girl who would demand her mother fill a bucket with sand to make a tower only so she could jump on it, laughing maniacally each time she destroyed it. Lo grunted.

"Let me guess, you hate children?" he asked.

"I don't hate them." She turned her head toward him. He was leaning back on his elbows, and Lo imagined he was desperate to lie down and take a nap, but maybe she was just projecting. "I don't think people should have so many kids. It's the number one rule of ecological sustainability—humans need to stop overproducing."

She dug another piece of sourdough into the jam jar. "I'm not surprised," he said with a strange expression on his face. Then her phone rang. She wanted to ask him what kind of family he envisioned. She imagined that he, like most normies, wanted 2.2 children and already had a junior-size fishing rod stowed away for his future son.

She answered the phone but kept her eyes on John, a stern look that said, *Don't test me on this, buddy.*

Mike Nelson was slightly out of breath, panting into the phone's speaker. She said hello while he caught his breath, then asked if he'd had a chance to walk over to Blanche's yet.

"I knocked and she didn't answer. The door was unlocked, and knowing her my whole life, I just swung it open. I called out to her. When she didn't answer, I thought something was wrong. I found her in a chair in front of the television. I've been getting the emergency vehicle out from Mankato, talking with folks who walked up to see what the ambulance was about. Then I remembered it was you who had told me to check on her. So, I ran back over to call you. Thing is, Blanche is dead."

"Fuck," was all Lo could say. John sat up quickly.

"Yep, you betcha," Mike responded, still breathing heavily.

Lo put her head down and sighed deeply. Her throat burned. One of the toddlers ventured deeper into the lake, and his mom was forced to chase after him into the cold water. "Yeah, she's gone," was all Lo said after she hung up.

He looked out over the lake, tightening his jaw. "Can I have the phone back? I need to ask Mike something."

TWIN FALLS, IDAHO

"All the choices I made—I spent a lot of time wondering what you would have thought about them. Would you have been proud? I mean, I didn't speak it out loud or whatever. For a long time, I just pushed it all away, but when I got my first teaching job I thought, *damn*, that might make a father proud. You always said education was important and that Minnesota had good schools and that was one thing you liked about it besides the catfish and obviously the Vikings but never the snow. And I had a good teacher once. There was one who helped me stay on track, apply to colleges, all that. But I hated teaching in the end because there was too much bullshit, until I felt like I wasn't helping anyone at all—tests and pretests and practice tests and filling out endless forms for politicians to toss in the garbage. I worried that you would have been mad after I quit that 'real job,' but people need food too, you know, and I like being outside, watching things grow. I just wondered what you'd say . . ." Jason paused and turned the wheel without thinking. He knew exactly where he was now.

"Yeah, I'm almost back to Alexis. Hope I didn't mess it up for good. She is the one thing, I swear, that I know you'd be proud of me for. We're good together. And her wanting us to get some land, wanting us to make a life—should I be mad at her for that? That's commitment, right? And I am committed. I just worry, is all. It's a lot. I missed out on watching you do all that. What I do remember, you did it right. Even Mom was all right at it—at doing life—before you left. It was the after where it all went to shit." He hit the stop button and hid the recorder deep in his duffel bag.

There was no gatekeeper near the sun-faded sign that read MARKHAM FARMS as Jason pulled onto a gravel road and then turned down a long driveway. The farm store was closed for the night, lights off and lot empty as he drove by. Small painted signs stuck into the grass read: CBD PRODUCTS, LOCAL JAMS, ORGANIC PRODUCE, GRASS-FED BEEF.

Then the red Jeep was flanked by fields of recently planted hemp seedlings. And then the old white farmhouse on the right, the couple who owned the place inside for the night with their kids, maybe giving them baths or reading to them from picture books or whatever normal parents did with their kids at night.

The gardens were cordoned off on both sides of the gravel road, tilled into perfect squares. One entire portion was allotted for pumpkins and gourds. This field brought in a lot of revenue in the fall. Nothing was ripe now, nothing much even growing yet. After the gardens sat a big red barn. A handful of Black Angus wandered in the pasture behind it, far in the back field.

He took his foot off the pedal. There, to his right, were two log cabins pressed up against a narrow creek. Past the cabins were a couple of cream-colored yurts set back even farther, where two narrow rows of pines offered some privacy.

Jason got out of the car and sniffed his armpit. He made a face, shrugged slightly and unzipped his duffel bag. He applied deodorant, changed into a clean shirt, shrugged again and then took a deep breath that filled his lungs.

As he approached the yurt, he said, "Lex?" There was no response. When he came to the door, he reached for the handle and faltered. Eventually, he kept his right hand on the handle and knocked with his left. "Lex?"

No one answered. He pulled the door open slowly and found Alexis and Giuseppe sitting on the two chairs watching one of her favorite movies. It was the book he had just read—the one he told her he had finished on the voicemail he had left. When was that? Just last night?

"Stop," she said loudly. "Uh-uh."

Giuseppe hopped out of his chair, smiling. "Hey, this is like a movie. He's back, Lexi! All right, well, I suppose you two have a lot to talk about, and we'll see whether she can find it in her heart to forgive you and all that. I'm glad you're back though, either way. Okay, Lexi, can I borrow this DVD? I want to finish this one." Jason thought he might keep rambling all night.

Giuseppe took his time opening the DVD player, smiling at Jason the whole time. Jason stared at him, waiting for him to leave, while he prepared to deliver the speech he had practiced during the drive. Giuseppe finally slipped his shoes on and left, waving to Alexis and squinting kindly at Jason.

Just as he was about to open his mouth, she spoke.

"Jason, I needed you and you left me. You won't even believe what I had *expected* and hoped you were going to do when I told you. I expected you to smile! To be excited! Can you believe that? I thought, okay, this wasn't planned but it's a happy accident! I expected you, at the very least, to be supportive of what I was going through. *And where the hell were you? Whose number did you call me from?* And where is your phone? And, damn it, you stole my favorite book."

"I—" He had forgotten his entire speech. "Lex, I read the book. I read it all in one night. It's the best book I've ever read." He stammered now.

"Okay, well, I thought that book was 'chick-lit garbage.' But that is *really* not the point, is it?" She looked at him, eyes raised, but he just shook his head from side to side, not saying a word.

"I just needed a drive. I didn't want to leave. I never wanted to leave. You told me to. I just"—he made a triangle shape with his hands—"made a weird loop around the country and came right back. My phone is in Utah, I guess, at the bottom of the Great Salt Lake."

She took a deep breath in. "I can't believe you would walk out on me—even if I asked you to! You were supposed to, I don't know"—she waved her hands in circles—"know what to do. I was scared. We needed to talk about this like adults."

"I'm open to anything, Lex. I swear. I'll talk to you about it all night, all day tomorrow, the next day. It was a mistake to leave. I just freaked out. It was a lot to take in, and I wasn't prepared for it. But you asked me to go, and I had to respect that. Right?"

"Jason." She sighed loudly. "I'm not going to do it. I knew all along I wasn't going to, but I wanted to see what choice you would make first. I wasn't going to force you to do anything you didn't want to do. So, if you came back thinking you're off the hook, you can head back out. I'm going to keep the baby."

He stood still for a minute. "Hold on, were you going to have my baby and not tell me?"

"No. I was going to call my parents, sort it out with them and figure it all out. If you had a phone, I would have told you too. Eventually."

He narrowed his eyes but wasn't sure what to say. "Okay, so you're keeping the baby? Our baby?" The room quieted suddenly. The whole world quieted, and they were the only two people in it. That old feeling suddenly returned to him. The internal compass that had always been there to guide him was suddenly back and flickered in the direction of Alexis, it swiveled toward the words she had just said—the true north he'd been heading toward the whole trip. He couldn't stop himself from grinning. He tried to bite his lips together, but it turned into a full smile. "So, we're having a baby?"

"I'm having a baby. I don't know what you're doing."

"I'm just saying, I should have never left. I never want to leave you. Ever again. I want to have this baby with you—"

"I wish you could *have* this baby for me, but I'm pretty sure only I can do that." She tilted her head, and he could tell she was trying to hold back a smile too.

"I swear to you, I would if I could."

"Oh, yeah right. We still got a lot of talking to do about this. A whole lot to figure out. But there's something else I need to tell you.

Maybe I should have told you when you walked in the door. It's just that I don't really know how to say it, and I know you two weren't close, but I talked to your mom a few days ago."

"What? How?"

"She called looking for you and told me she was sick. But then I got another call today. She's gone. I'm sorry, J. I know it was really weird between you, but I think we should go, so you can at least say good-bye. The guy on the phone said her house is full of family stuff, and that someone will need to go through it. I've never seen a baby picture of you. So . . ." She trailed off.

"My mom died?" Jason asked again, confused. It didn't make sense. She wasn't even old. He tried to remember what year she was born but couldn't. Was she even sixty? "Are you sure? How do you know?" It wasn't like he ever wanted to see her again, necessarily. But there was something about knowing she was *there*. A connection to his dad, to his childhood.

"I'm sorry. It's a long story. She called the farm the day you left. From what you've told me, I didn't know if I should believe her. I gave her the number in Santa Rosa but figured it didn't matter because I knew you were coming back here. If I had known she was really going to die, I might have given her your cell number, but—" Alexis's eyes were watering now.

"Yeah, I was coming back. I'm always coming back. Hey, it's all good, Lex. You didn't do anything wrong. I threw my phone in the lake anyway, so she couldn't have called." He blew out a long breath. "I guess we're going to Minnesota."

WEST TO MIDWEST, USA

As soon as John and Lo heard the news about Blanche, they left California. John convinced Mike Nelson to look for Blanche's phone, which he found resting on the kitchen counter, and asked him to scroll through the contacts. There it was, saved under "Twin Peaks"—the number they needed. John called the woman, Alexis, and she told him that she might be in contact with Jason soon. They left the message for him that his mother had passed. It was the best they could do.

Then they drove through northern Nevada where towns were sparse and hidden away in the valleys of dusty, chartreuse hills. They took turns driving through Utah with its strange salt flats that morphed into imposing white-capped mountains and stands of ponderosa pines. They both strained their necks until it was too dark to see.

They decided to head south from Salt Lake, so they could stay outside of Grand Junction for the night. Lo herself had insisted that they couldn't miss the Colorado Rockies. Her feelings about returning to Elysian vacillated between an urgency to be home and a desire to never go back.

Going home meant she could finally get serious about moving to Minneapolis, which was an exciting prospect. But the road trip was, in many ways, an escape from real life, and despite the disappointing ending, it had been an adventure. Either way, she was committed to seeing the Rockies. And of course, a part of her was nervous about the idea of stopping at her mother's house, so *just maybe* she was attempting to put the final decision off as long as she could.

That night, at a rest stop on the border of Utah and Colorado, John kissed Lo after he returned from brushing his teeth, a clean mint flavor. What was most surprising to her was how expected it was, how familiar the touch of his lips were beginning to feel, even there at a rest stop in the middle of nowhere. She knew her feelings toward John had changed in a few short days, but she still couldn't keep track of where they stood. She had promised herself she would find a partner who could appreciate her values, but when she was with John, she *wished* that person could be him.

Just like earlier in the day, one kiss led to more kissing, with only brief moments of pause as they froze, laughing, whenever people drove past their car on the hazy edge of a streetlight. It was easy for Lo to forget all her objections to John once his open palm was cupping her cheek, as soon as his hands found her exposed skin. If he wasn't going to worry about what the future held for the two of them, as they maneuvered together in the tight back seat of the sedan, then why should she? All Lo really knew was that she wanted him right then, wanted him much more than she was worried about what might come later.

The next morning, Lo couldn't find her underwear anywhere.

John drove while Lo strained her neck to take in the tallest peaks of the Rocky Mountains. For so long, Pikes Peak had only been a name on a bumper sticker to her. While she was growing up, someone in town had a green sticker with a white font that read I MADE IT TO THE TOP OF PIKES PEAK. Now she had made it too, even if it meant a significant detour. After their failure with Jason Peterson, she felt the need to redeem the trip however possible. John wouldn't have much sleep before work, but they would make it back in time.

It was at the top of the peak where she concluded resolutely that it was time to stop in Des Moines. They had visited John's sister, perhaps *his* whole reason for agreeing to the trip. So, she wanted to make this trip worth it for her too. John questioned her gently. *Should we drive back down next weekend after some rest? Do you want to talk to your dad about it? Should you write a letter first? Are you sure?*

She tried to explain her urgency while chewing on the side of her thumb and watching the scenery from the passenger seat, which grew increasingly dull and familiar after they passed through the Rockies. The foothills had turned into flat plains and then slowly morphed into empty fields filled with dried, half-broken stalks of corn.

And then Lo found herself standing in front of a pale yellow, two-story house. Each window had a fake candle in the center, faux flickering into the fading twilight. She tried to keep her breath even as she walked from the curb to the front door.

It was time to meet her mother.

She was ready. She hoped she was ready.

Lo pushed the doorbell lit with a dying sepia light and chipped gold rim. The house looked like all the others in the subdivision. Oversized, struggling brown sod, plastic siding and not a garden in sight. No one answered, so she knocked. As she was knocking, the garage door opened, and a sedan pulled into the driveway. She turned and looked. A man and a woman, both midforties, seemed to notice her at the same time. The woman frowned from behind the windshield. The car pulled into the garage. The door closed. The sun lowered behind the horizon line.

Lo looked back to John. He scratched his head and gave her what she imagined was an encouraging half smile under a streetlight that started to hum with electricity. It was possible that the address she had found online wasn't even correct. Maybe this wasn't her mother's house after all.

A minute later the front door opened. It was a man in an orange sweater pilling at the sleeves. She looked up at him and smiled as politely as she could, but she had a feeling it was more of an awkward grimace. The man stood, slightly confused, furrowing his brow as Lo stood on the concrete slab that served as a porch. There was no furniture, no plants, just empty concrete and Lois Gunderson. She started to sweat.

"Can I help you?" he asked, not bothering to hide his irritation. Lo pressed on her abdomen in an attempt to flatten her wrinkled puffy coat, which had been smashed behind the passenger seat under several glass jars filled with water. She took a breath.

"Can I speak to Mandy?"

"Mandy?" the man asked.

"Um—yes. I mean Amanda Monroe." Lo corrected herself.

He stared at her blankly for a second but only nodded. He came back with his wife, who stood in the doorway with a kitchen towel, drying her hands. She looked Lo up and down. "*Mhm?*" she asked.

She wore slacks and a wool jacket, slightly different shades of blue. Underneath she wore a white camisole, the same material as her pants. The touch of that rayon fabric on the racks of the thrift store made Lo's teeth grind together whenever she rubbed it between her fingers. The woman's hair was ashy blonde, thin and straight, cut right below her ears. The woman looked nothing like Lo. She wore a single gold chain with a cross on it. Lo could see a stairway when she glanced inside. A white banister and wooden steps led up to a landing that showcased a framed picture of one set of footprints on a sandy beach.

"Hi, I was wondering if I might have a word with you outside." Who knows what Mandy Monroe had told her husband about her past? Perhaps it was a secret buried away, hidden under layers of years spent together in the suburbs. The woman appeared irritated for a moment but then examined Lo more closely. Her eyes tightened for a few seconds and then went wide, only slightly, with what Lo understood to be recognition. She was attempting to maintain decorum. This felt like a bad sign. Shouldn't her mother be reaching out to hug her? To smooth her wild hair?

She nodded to Lo just once and turned to her husband. "I'll just be a minute." The husband scowled, but the wife shut the door behind her and left him inside.

"Are you Amanda Monroe?" Lo asked. The woman's eyes were blank of any emotion Lo could comprehend. She looked past Lo at the old white sedan on the street and then down at Lo's dirty jacket.

Amanda took a deep breath in and straightened her posture. "Hasn't been Monroe for quite some time. So, you're her then? Jerry's daughter?"

Lo chest was tight. Thick with emotion, she asked, "I'm—am I your daughter? I think you're my mother."

The woman turned her head and seemed to be watching something happening down the street while she shook her head imperceptibly. Lo noticed three moles in sequence on her neck. Finally, the woman turned her head back toward Lo.

"I'm no one's mother." She raised her eyebrows once as if in warning, then turned and walked back to the door. As she opened it, she looked back at Lo and whispered, "Don't ever come back here." She shut the door.

The night was dark now, and Lo imagined the massive, glowing ball of gas falling below the flat, ugly Iowa landscape to start a new day somewhere better. It was suddenly very cold outside.

Lo stood, stunned. An involuntary cough left her throat, and she wanted desperately to sit down somewhere. She heard John open the car door with a loud creak. For a second she reached toward Amanda's front door, imagining herself throwing it open and shouting her secret—their shared secret—into the house. Lo stumbled toward the woman's front door when John came around the car and called to her quietly.

Eventually, she found herself sitting in the passenger seat as John turned the wheel. They left the yellow house and Amanda Monroe behind. "What just happened?" she asked quietly, more to herself than to John.

For thirty minutes, she didn't say anything. Lo sat in a kind of trance, holding her hands on her knees and looking out the window. She stared into the dreary night sky. Her view was constantly interrupted by brightly lit billboards advertising law services and medical care, by cars the size of living rooms playing incandescent and vulgar children's movies, by massive white semitrucks hauling tons of plastic shit from here to there. She sighed heavily.

John tried to ask her a few questions, but all Lo could say was, "It's okay. She's just living her life." John offered sympathy however he could—*What the fuck?*, *That's not cool*, and *I'm really sorry*.

And what had Lo expected? That this woman would invite her in for the night after she just showed up unannounced?

Instead of thinking about Amanda Monroe and all those daydreams from childhood about the moment she would finally meet her mom—the comforting hug she had been waiting for her entire life, the image of her mother as her identical twin with brown curly hair and a green thumb, as someone who could help Lo make sense in the world—she pushed all of it down, and then even further down. Instead of wondering at how quickly all those fragile hopes had disintegrated into a mirage, Lo jumped ahead. She imagined a future with people she didn't have to argue with or explain herself to. Who wouldn't reject her for all her quirks and strange ideas because they shared them with her.

As they neared the border of Minnesota, she said, "John, I'm moving to Minneapolis." She could see him shift in his seat a bit.

"Yeah, you mentioned that was your plan."

"No, I mean, I'm going to pack up and leave as soon as I can. Like next week. We can't see each other anymore."

Again, she saw John move in the driver's seat, but she didn't turn his way. "Okay, I'm just not sure if right now is the best time to make decisions. Like right after your mother—that woman—you know, was unkind to you. I don't want you to leave town. I'll tell you right now. Is it selfish? Maybe. But I like it there. And you have a really good life in Elysian, and we could . . ." He stumbled over his words and then reached over to turn off the radio, which had begun to play static loudly in the car. "From the minute you came into the garage, I didn't want to be away from you for too long. There are people who would never reject you like she did, you know? I would never do that. I just want to be around you all the time . . ." He trailed off.

On another day, Lo might have been touched. But not tonight. "I can't go back to a town where I'm pitied, where I'm seen as a charity case because I don't want to live like they do. I realized on this trip that

I can find *better* people, a better community who understand what I care about and why."

John took a heavy breath. "Hey, no one pities you. Lo, every person in town knows your dad is a lawyer—the only lawyer—the county judge who owns the giant mansion at the end of Main Street. If anything, they admire and even envy—" His tone was imploring like he was trying to convince a child that Santa Claus was indeed real.

"That's not what I mean."

"Then what do you mean? Do you not see they care for you? Jesus, think about the owner of the grocery store—do you think he believes you can't afford groceries? No. He probably appreciates the fact that food isn't being thrown away. You think those ladies save their old blenders and quilts because they pity you? No. I grew up poor. Nobody gave us new shoes or free blenders to juice organic beets or whatever. You're talking about pity? Did charity organizations come to your school offering backpacks full of toys and blankets? Because they drove in from god-knows-where and saw all the trailers and broken-down cars and thought you needed charity?"

He breathed in and out loudly, and she could see him gripping the wheel. Lo had turned the heat up after they left Des Moines— its strange smell, like sweet almonds, filled the car, and at the time the consistent white noise of the air blowing through the vents was a comfort to her. Now she was sweating but couldn't bring herself to move her body to turn it down. She sat like a stone and looked out the window.

"And you know what? Your neighbor doesn't *accidentally* cook twice as much food as he can eat every night. He's probably lonely and likes seeing your face when he brings you leftovers. You're not a charity case. And you don't even see how these people treat you. They treat you like— well—god, they treat you like a mother would."

Lo's mouth opened, then closed, and for a minute she sat speechless while her hands dug into her thighs. "They *aren't* my mother, though, are they? Just because someone saves me an old rug and makes me dinner—that doesn't replace my fucking mother. And it doesn't mean that I haven't *always* felt like an outcast, like the village idiot, the way they all look at me—"

"I shouldn't have said that, about your mom. It's just . . . Lo, you just gotta get over yourself. They look at you because you're interesting, because you're beautiful and you're strong—the most alive thing that town probably ever produced. No one thinks you're an idiot. No one."

She made several dismissive noises while she took in what he said. "No. They look at me because they think I'm strange, like a bug they can't identify and aren't sure whether to be afraid of."

She could see John shake his head. The streetlights near Albert Lea were bright as they exited the interstate and found the highway back to Elysian. Did he look angry?

"What you believe and what's true are two different things."

"Oh, Jesus. You've been here, what? A few years? You don't understand that town or my family or me. We literally just met a few weeks ago. You don't even understand your own family. You got the *choice* to leave your parents, they didn't make the choice to leave you. It doesn't matter anyway. I'm leaving Elysian, to find people who care about the planet, who don't think *I'm* the strange one."

"You know, Lo, you get on me for buying a bottle of tea or a cup of coffee, but you never asked me what I *do* know, because you don't think I could possibly know anything. I'm just some redneck garbage-polluter from the backwoods."

Lo furrowed her brow and almost laughed.

John continued, "You think Deb and I were brought to Walmart to get a new toy every time we felt bad? I played with sticks in the yard, and we threw sweet-gum balls at each other for fun. We hunted deer, we made jerky. We fished, we collected blackberries and wild strawberries, and occasionally, sure, we got a dollar cheeseburger from McDonald's on payday if we were lucky. And you never asked, but I still hunt, and I skin 'em and clean 'em myself. I catch catfish, and I clean them, cook 'em and freeze some too. But you really believe you're the only one who does anything good in the world. And, you know what? Most of what you think you got for free, you actually got because of who your dad is.

No one else who goes around asking for free stuff and expired food is treated like the town darling. I promise you that, and stuff doesn't just fall in their laps like it does yours. Okay?"

"That's not true at all. And, just so you know, people only need to hunt deer in Minnesota because all the wolves died when the land was turned into cornfields. What are you—are we still talking about me moving to Minneapolis?"

He gripped the wheel tighter. "I don't know. I just—I wish you wouldn't make that decision *right now*. Even if you do decide to move, I just don't understand why you can't see how good you've got it. There's a lot of good there. People do the best they can."

"No. They don't. They do what's easy, and they judge people who do better because they feel guilty."

John straightened his posture and began nodding aggressively in a way that made Lo nervous. "Hey, you know why I don't ever want to have kids?" She had no idea where he was going with this and was not interested in discussing children with a man who she was attempting to disentangle herself from. "Because everyone *always* thinks they've got it right. Everyone needs to feel in charge, like they understand how the world works. Even though no one does. So, once they find this 'perfect' way to live, they teach it to their kids, thinking that will help them feel in control too. You know what that's called? It's called *indoctrination*." John was worked up now; he was steering with his left hand and making chopping motions with his right. "I had to leave my parents because of that. And when I hear you, I imagine that *if* you had kids, you would teach them all these rules, all these things that you believe are right— the *only* right way to live. Don't be a vegetarian, don't drink sweet tea, don't accept your neighbors' goodwill as anything but pity. And you know what that will be called? Indoctrination."

She was finding it difficult to form words, her lips contorting as if she had something hot in her mouth and was trying to swallow it without getting burned. Highway 13 was dark, but she knew that a few windmills spun slowly in the distance.

Suddenly, she realized she was angry with John but also with herself.

Why was she having this argument with a man she barely knew? This was *exactly* what she had been trying to avoid. Cold and detached, like she was reciting unenthusiastic lines in a school play, she said, "You're just mad because I don't want to be with you."

Even in the dark, she could see his mouth open wide. "What?"

"I'm moving, and I don't want to be with you. I don't want to be with someone who I have to constantly defend myself against, who doesn't understand how to *actually* be a part of the solution. It was a promise I made to myself after I dated Artie, so it was a mistake to fool around with you on this trip. That's what you're really mad about. That I'm leaving *you*, but that's stupid because we hardly know each other."

She could feel the energy drain from the argument, the momentum slip away. From the corner of her eye, she saw John slump over in the seat, shaking his head gently.

"Okay. I told you already I'd follow your lead," was all he said for the rest of the drive.

She stared out the window toward the dark fields. She saw a tilted red barn, the light post in the gravel driveway blinking a slow amber. Her eyes burned, and she blinked hard. The lakes heading into town looked like oil slicks in the gloom. She lifted her head and could see Orion's Belt out her window through a break in the clouds, distant and cold and unimpressive.

SUBJECTIVE MYTHOLOGIES

Lore surrounding fireflies is legendary and ancient. Perhaps their lights are the souls of the departed, returning to earth, or the glowing eyes of wandering terrestrial ghosts. In some cultures, glowworms indicate a death on the horizon. Fireflies favor graveyards because they are hushed, undisturbed, and yet full of plant life. A grove of pine trees or wall of kudzu might separate the living from the dead, the dark from the light. And who ever saw a brilliantly lit cemetery? No, they're kept in the shadows, where fireflies can glow undisturbed by light's pollution. It makes sense, then, that their coming and going has been tied to our own for centuries.

Lo was surprised to hear that Blanche's funeral was going to be held at
the Lutheran church at the edge of town. She assumed Blanche had been
Catholic because she couldn't remember ever seeing her on Christmases
or Easters—every Protestant in town showed up on those two days.
Those were the only two days a year she and her dad ever went to church.

While she sat in her car in the parking lot, not ready to enter the
building, she rubbed her hands up and down the steering wheel. Only a
few days ago, John sat there, his hands resting on the wheel. She hadn't
talked to him since Sunday. It was Thursday.

She had slept for most of Monday and much of Tuesday. All the
traveling, all the sleep they had missed either driving or fooling around,
finally caught up with her. John called once on Tuesday night, but Lo
couldn't bring herself to listen to his message. She texted Parker on
Wednesday and asked for another day off to recover from the trip. Really,
she just wasn't ready to face anyone or anything. She needed to stay in
her bed under a blanket.

John texted her on Wednesday and asked her to call him back.
He also apologized for the message he left. After that text apology, she
stared at her phone for several moments but still couldn't bring herself
to listen to the voicemail. If anything, she was tempted to delete it. She
had made herself clear, if a bit harshly, and didn't feel the need for res-
olution. It would only make leaving harder.

When the doorbell rang on Wednesday night, she was anxious it would be John, but instead it was her neighbor Mike Bauer offering her a plate of mashed potatoes with Swedish meatballs and sautéed onions. She hadn't expected the crush of disappointment she felt when she first pulled the door open and realized that it wasn't who she thought it would be.

So instead of listening to the message, she spent an incomprehensible amount of time staring at John's name in her missed calls list.

She was afraid he would demand an apology. Just like Artie, maybe John would obsess over their nonrelationship-nonbreakup, and now she would have to avoid the street in front of the garage and anywhere else she might run into him.

She'd been in contact with Parker's friends who worked at the neighborhood co-op in Minneapolis. They had a cheap room for Lo in a massive old house near the university; five other people lived there. She was heading up on Sunday to inspect the room as well as the people. More than anything, she hoped the house had a woodstove. For some reason, this felt like her highest priority.

In the church parking lot, rain spattered on the windshield while Lo began to search for an umbrella. She felt under her seat and scanned the back. How could she have not prepared for this? Tears stung her eyes, and she held her breath while she felt in the pockets behind both seats. She chided herself for being overly emotional, but this only led to more tears. The rain started to fall heavy, and Lo had to suppress a sob that she felt deep in her chest, when she heard a knock on her window. She turned quickly, expecting to see John standing there, but it was only her dad.

He nodded once and held up his umbrella as an offering. They walked into the old church together. The smell of the sanctuary immediately reminded her of childhood, a combination of reheated coffee and rice casserole, the distinct smell of shoe powder and mothballs, as well as wax candles—vanilla and lingering smoke.

As a girl, Lo had been told that buildings like this old Lutheran church were all shaped like an upside-down Viking ship because that's what the immigrant Norwegians knew how to build. She wasn't sure if that was a myth, but as she walked down the aisle next to her father, she admired the arched ceiling, the wooden crossbeams painted white, spaced like curving rib bones. The burning in her chest subsided as she began recognizing faces—everyone offering polite frowns and small waves to Jerry Gunderson and his daughter.

The day outside was gray and the church dimly lit. Red-and-blue hues filtered through the tall stained-glass windows on either side of the nave. She had studied those windows throughout her childhood. Over the years, she came to the conclusion that her favorite was the one where Jesus held a loaf of bread in one hand and a whole fish in the other, preparing to feed the hungry. She hadn't realized until this moment that it was likely a town favorite since Elysian was chock-full of people who loved to fish, and the fish that Jesus held, brownish-green with two spiked fins on top and two small flippers below, looked suspiciously like a massive walleye.

Her dad harrumphed and then sat down at the edge of a pew near the back of the church. Lo had to cross in front of him to sit down. She was going to say something about how they should scoot to the end for people coming in when she noticed John's thick brown hair and curved posture two pews ahead of them. She investigated her lap and didn't say a word.

The church was less than half full. Lo recognized Jason Peterson from Blanche's photos. He was sitting in the front row, his body leaning against a woman who Lo imagined was his girlfriend. She made the connection and wondered vaguely if this was Blanche's contact in Idaho.

Still, she felt strange seeing Jason. She had failed in her task, and now she had possession of a free car from a dead woman she barely knew. And here was this man, her son, finally back in town, just not in time to see his mother alive.

Should she offer him the car? Did she deserve to have it now? Should she apologize for not reaching him in time? Should she say anything to him at all? She realized she hadn't been listening to the funeral service when everyone else stood except for her. She stood quickly and found John's gaze, who had turned back, his eyes searching. She looked at the stained glass, then down at the floor.

As soon as people were excused, she mumbled goodbye to her father and practically ran to her car in the falling rain.

It was the bar that had gotten Blanche through the worst period of her life, so in the end, the reception was held at Lefty's.

Before then, Lo needed to cash her work check. She had car insurance to pay for now and also had to reimburse her dad for the electric bill, which she did every month. He would never have asked her to, but it was motivation to keep the bill as low as possible, a regular reminder that energy cost money and emissions. She was already a few days late and didn't want to give her dad the impression she was slipping, right as she was about to move out on her own.

She parked the car at The Locust and wiped what she told herself was rain from her face while she fanned her cheeks with her hands, trying to regain composure. It had been strange seeing Blanche up there in the casket at the front of the church. Even from a distance, it was a shock to see someone who just a week before had been standing in front of her, handing John an envelope full of cash.

Her check would be in the office in an envelope with her name on it. The rain was only a fine mist as she got out of her car. The field behind the club had turned to mud. Lo hated how uncovered fields were left all winter, even though they were awful for the health of the soil and the risk of runoff, but the massive farming ventures that bought so much of the land around Elysian didn't care about any of that.

She unlocked the big black door to the club, pulled it open and heard quiet music coming from the speakers. Depressing nineties indie rock. She groaned inwardly. That could only mean one thing.

Lo was wearing all black, a skintight bodysuit that had probably belonged to a teenage ballerina and a flowing, tiered skirt. The best plan she could come up with was to sneak around the club like some kind of trained assassin, hiding behind shadows in her dark clothing in order to avoid meeting Artie face-to-face.

The plan fell apart immediately. The lights were bright, and he sat sprawled on the floor over the sound console with a laptop connected to it, a series of gadgets and wires spread around him in a broad circle. He looked up pleasantly, probably expecting Parker, but his face froze when he saw Lo. He scowled and returned to his work. Lo sighed dramatically and walked past him to get her check.

She grabbed her check, then left the office and found herself watching Artie work for a minute. She watched his curved back as he hunched over the console, looking very busy. He sat there like he owned the place, helping Parker by creating some fancy sound console, as if anyone came to The Locust for hi-fi audio. They didn't—they came to get out of the house, for a sense of community, for something to do. Only Artie cared about the frequencies and mixes and reverb or whatever else he went on about.

She walked up to him, her skirt swishing against her legs. The burning in her chest had returned. She looked over toward the table and stools where John had sat the night he came in to watch Magenta Crush.

"Listen, Artie. You can stop giving Parker shit about me because I'm leaving. Talking bad about me to my best friend is low, and I think you need to evolve. If you can't handle a simple breakup, then adult life is going to be very difficult for you." She looked down at him sitting on the floor in his too-tight band t-shirt and studded belt, relics from another time.

Artie lifted his head, a look of disbelief on his face. "Oh, right, Lo. You want to *help me*. I see. Your advice is never completely judgmental or bitchy, looking down from your high horse, it's only to save me from myself."

Her eyes went wide. He'd turned the lights as bright as possible to work on the console, and she suddenly felt exposed where she stood.

"My god, we only dated for a few months. It wasn't that big of a deal. It's like you're trying to ruin my life for no reason. Yes, I think you need advice."

"It wasn't like that, Lo. One day you were completely avoiding me, the next week you're talking about me moving in with you, the next day you're berating me about how I'm destroying the planet by not recycling the fucking wires correctly." He gestured to the mess around him on the floor. "But the very next time you were lonely, you'd text me like everything was normal. It was never normal. You pushed me away, pulled me back, pushed me away. You're the one who needs to 'evolve.'"

Lo laughed dryly, too loud, the sound echoing in the empty club. "So, I'm the one who needs to change so that I don't make you so uncomfortable telling you to not destroy the earth? We were just getting to know each other, Artie—"

"I've known you since you were eight! We've always known each other. You were using me. I don't know what for—to prove that you can't be happy here? Everyone knows you hate it. So, you turned me into some useful idiot. Never good enough, never doing the right things to make you happy. But then I realized you were just trying to control me. 'Do *this* right and maybe we can be together. Change yourself completely, Artie. Learn how to compost and eat cow hooves and then maybe we can be together.' Then I hear you're on a road trip with John Blank, who is *also* dating Shay Rose. What a shit show. I don't care. I just don't want to see you manipulate Parker, and I don't think I should have to work with someone like that either."

Lo opened her mouth and eyes as wide as humanly possible. She stammered for a minute. "Wow," was all she said at first, then made a series of sounds indicating her outrage. "Wow. So because I care about the planet and want to save it—"

"No, Lo. We all care about the planet. We do. Okay? Not everyone reads as many ancient hippie books from the library, but do you really think I don't care about the planet? You just take it upon yourself to 'save' everyone because you think you're the world's ambassador of righteousness or some shit. Just think—you agreed to go find a man who had *purposely* cut himself off from his alcoholic mother, as if you knew what he should be doing with his life. You think people can't see *right through you*. But I do, and I let Parker know because she's my cousin."

"What the fuck, Artie?" She was yelling now. "I was just doing a favor for a dying old woman."

"Think about it, Lo. Really, think. You believe Jason Peterson couldn't make his own decisions? You think he forgot where his mother had lived for his entire life and didn't know how to reach her if he wanted to?" He said the last few words with emphasis, still sitting on the floor awkwardly. "I mean—really? People should make their own choices. He made a choice to get away from his mom. And there you go, driving across the country to tell him that you know what's best. It's the perfect, *perfect* fucking example of what I'm talking about. You can never trust that people will do what's best for themselves or the best they know how."

She saw a vision of her mother standing in her yellow doorway. A bottle of sweet tea in John's hand. Her dad's cheeseburger. She shook her head to clear it. "I was just trying to help Blanche, who, by the way, is dead now. I just want to help. I just want people to know how to help the planet—"

"Yeah, well, if you had said, 'Hey, Artie, here's a good way to help the planet,' then I might have been grateful for your advice. But instead, you judged me constantly, made me feel like shit, and then because I didn't *already* know everything that you did, I was an undatable asshole." He was gripping a tiny screwdriver in his right hand so hard that his knuckles were white under the spotlight.

He stared at her for a minute. If he expected her to respond, he would wait forever. She had nothing else to say to him. She stood there, glaring. After a few moments, he scoffed, pushed himself off the floor and walked toward the back office.

With his back turned, she yelled, "You are an undatable asshole!"

As she headed toward the exit, she heard him yell, "No, I'm not!"

She pulled the heavy door open and ran directly into Parker.

Parker looked happy to see her, but then caught Lo's expression and stopped short. Lo tried to hold her breath, but once she made eye contact with Parker, she lost her composure completely.

They sat at the edge of the open field not saying much. Lo wiped her face with her skirt. Her hair was blowing wildly in the breeze. Though the rain had stopped for the time being, the temperature was dropping quickly. Maybe it would snow tonight. She suddenly longed for her woodstove, the wool rug that lay beside it, a warm blanket.

Parker broke the silence. "I bought this field," she said casually.

"What?"

"Yeah, Teresa and I have been talking about it for a while."

"I don't—why?" Lo hiccuped.

"Remember when you told me about how losing the prairie killed off entire species? And made the bees disappear?"

Lo nodded. She'd probably told her that fifty times. "Well, it got me thinking. There's been a For Sale sign on this plot forever. It's not much acreage, cut off from the bigger fields, which is why I think the corporation that bought up the land is selling it back. Not worth their time, you know? And I was thinking about that stuff you said. So I thought, wouldn't it be cool to restore prairie here? Imagine the club surrounded by grass and flowers instead of this bullshit." She held her hand out to the broken earth. "So, Terry and I fought about it on and off for a few months, and finally we agreed, but she said we have to mow a path to the center to put picnic tables and shit to make a kind of park. She wanted a new boat, so she was kind of mad about agreeing to buy a dirt field instead."

Lo didn't know what to say. She started crying for what felt like the tenth time that day. She looked away uncomfortably. As a rule, Lo understood that Minnesotans were supposed to hold it in—tears, anger, rage, loneliness. She couldn't stop breaking that rule today.

"So, how was the funeral?" Parker asked.

Lo shook her head. "No, I'm okay. I mean, it was sad, I guess. And to think she didn't get to see her son. I feel awful. But also, Artie just yelled at me, and then I yelled at him. So, that was fun. And John and I are done. Well, we weren't ever really together, but we're definitely done now. I was pretty mean to him, actually. And I'm moving to Minneapolis. And you bought a field! And it caused you and Teresa to fight, which I hate. Wasn't the land expensive?" Lo had to simply allow her tears to fall into the wide lap of her skirt as she sat cross-legged on the wet grass.

Parker chuckled and put her arm around Lo. "It sounds like you deserve a nice cry. Don't feel bad about Terry. We fight on the regular. Be weirder if we didn't, right? She's excited about it now, and we really *did not* need a new boat. Yeah, a field costs money. I know you hate money, and I get that, so I didn't ever say anything. But there's actually some good you can do with it too, you know? Shit, we probably could have talked your dad into buying this field, now that I think about it."

They sat together quietly as the humidity turned back into a heavy drizzle. Lo wanted to keep sitting on the edge of the field with Parker, but it was getting colder, and she started to shiver. She was uncomfortable with the suggestion that her dad might have simply bought her a field. Sure, money could help to revitalize this unplowed field back into prairie land, but is that the way the world should work? What if *all* people just decided to take care of the planet, without needing all that money to purchase land of their own? She knew these questions were worth asking, but Parker triggered a sense of her own naivete that left Lo unsure of herself. Still, why should those with money have the power to decide what was worth saving or investing in? It wasn't fair.

"I think it's cool you want to move. But don't go because of Artie. He can be such a little bitch. How many times have I told you that?"

Lo scoffed and then rested her face in her palms, just enough of a crack to speak through. "It's not because of Artie." But she was unsettled after her conversation with him. *Was she the judgmental one? The close-minded one?* She let her cheeks rest in the palms of her hands.

Parker was buying a field. And even Artie, the undatable asshole, volunteered every week at the town's tiny animal shelter. Lo had openly criticized him for that. She maintained that pets were a burden on the environment and its resources, and reminded him as such, repeatedly. Lo felt the wet ground through her skirt, but still, she sat and looked over the field.

She thought about John for just a minute until she noticed her hands stung. When she looked down, they were small and bright red and splotchy from the cold. She blew warm air into them and then stood up. She tried to picture the field as prairie land, and her forehead softened a little.

"All right, it's time to go," she said.

ELYSIAN, MINNESOTA

The sidewalk started before there were any houses. That had always both-ered Jason. It was creepy sitting there doing nothing. An empty plot of weeds fronted by a sidewalk to nowhere welcomed them into town.

Jason, Alexis and her mom, Paige, had all traveled to Minnesota to stay in two hotel rooms side by side in a college town near Elysian. It was kind of Paige to fly in from Modesto and offer to help them go through his mom's house. But Jason knew she had ulterior motives. Alexis's parents had taken the news of their first grandchild in stride but then immediately began sending them real estate ads for land in Califor-nia. Paige had already mentioned a potential move half-a-dozen times.

Jason drove the women through town—that didn't take long—with his hands on the leather steering wheel of a rental sedan. He pointed infrequently, and a small portion of a story unfolded.

"My friend Nate's house. Lives in New England now." Then noth-ing for a minute. "Here's Main Street, most of the stores are closed, as you can see." Then nothing for a minute. "I'll show you where my dad worked on the paper. I used to help him make deliveries sometimes, back when I thought it was fun to wake up at four a.m." They passed Lefty's, the only bar in town except for the members-only VFW, and Jason shook his head. "Guess that's where they decided to have the re-ception. Not surprising, I guess. It was her favorite place in town."

"You could have asked them to do it at the church," Alexis suggested, looking out the window with a concerned expression.

"Doesn't matter," he replied quietly. He pulled in front of the house but didn't move in his seat, staring for a minute. "Looks a lot worse than I remember. Maybe they can burn it down, and we can just sell the lot."

"No, Jason. I want your baby pictures. And we should get the pictures of your parents and your grandparents. You want me and my mom to do it? You could just go back to the hotel?"

"No. It's fine. I should do it. I need to do it."

From the back seat, Paige said, "It's all right, honey. Let's do that later. We can come back tomorrow if you want. We have a few days to get it done."

"Yeah, all right. But maybe we should just head in real quick and see what we're getting into."

The three of them walked through the front porch littered with discarded mittens, wet mail and soda cans. Jason pushed open the front door, which was unlocked at his request, since no one in town had been able to locate a set of keys anywhere.

When he walked in, the dining-room table was stacked full of junk. He nodded at the old newspapers pushed against the walls. "She saved every Sunday paper."

"That's right. Your father was a journalist."

Jason shrugged. "Yeah, I guess. I just remembered I forgot something in the car. You want to scope out the rest of the house?"

"You two, look over there," Paige whispered. She pointed to the forgotten oxygen tank standing alone in the sunroom next to a TV tray with two ashtrays, both overflowing with butts. "Is that safe?" No one knew the answer, so Jason carefully carried the tank outside and set it a safe distance from the house. He would have to call someone about that.

He dug through his duffel bag in the trunk and found what he was looking for. He stuck the voice recorder in his back pocket and walked back into the house, shivering in the wind. It was still full-on winter in Minnesota.

When he pushed open the door, he saw Paige looking at a display of pictures hung from the wall. He couldn't be sure, but he thought that none had been changed since before his dad died, except for one. A picture of him in his high school graduation cap. He didn't even know how she had gotten that picture. Not like she was there for his graduation ceremony. He shrugged. It didn't matter anymore.

Paige turned toward him and said, "You were a cute baby, Jason. That's good. I'm glad to see it. Alexis was a beautiful baby."

He heard Alexis call for him from upstairs, which was more like an attic with a small bathroom, a hallway and a single bedroom—his childhood bedroom.

Alexis stood in the center of his room, which clearly hadn't been touched since he left. "Should you be wearing a face covering or something? This room hasn't been cleaned in fifteen years. Watch out for the dust. Probably not safe for you to be up here, actually."

"Oh, stop. You're as bad as my mom, I swear." She smiled at him. "I had those same plastic stars in my room. Some of yours have fallen. But that's the Big Dipper, yeah? And Orion over there? Did you do these yourself? Little manmade constellations?"

He let out a single laugh. "I got them in a stocking one year, I remember. They were all the rage back then. My parents helped me put them up. They spent a long time trying to figure out the shape of the constellations. I got so bored that I went downstairs and when I came back up, they were done."

She smiled wistfully. "That's what parents are for, I guess. It sounds like a good memory."

He shrugged. "My mom was probably drunk."

"Did she drink a lot? You know—before?"

"I think so. I don't remember much, just certain memories, you know . . ." He looked around the room that felt both familiar and like a stranger's. "I don't really want to be in here."

"Hey, J. It's all right. We just have to get this stuff out so they can sell the house."

"It's too much—"

"I know. But we'll get through it. I want your family pictures, so our baby knows where they come from."

"You want him to know he came from this? Why? Let's just forget all this. Get rid of it all and start over."

"*Him*? So now you know our baby is a boy?" She raised her eyebrows.

"Listen to me, Lex. I don't think I can do this. There's so much shit in here."

"Okay, well, I told you my mom and I would—"

"It's all these memories, you know. I had forgotten all about these stars and this old purple-and-gold bedspread. It's just—hey, listen, you can't leave me—like nothing can ever happen to you."

"Jason, what are you talking about? What's going to happen to me?"

"I don't ever want to find out—I don't ever want to have to learn whether I'm better than my mom was. Because I don't think I am. If I lost the only good thing in my life and was supposed to keep on living, keep going—"

"No, Jason. *You* were good in her life, and she let *you* down. You are stronger than her. Nothing's going to happen to me, but you need to know that about yourself. You hear?"

He nodded and let out a breath. It was too much all at once. He didn't know if he believed what Alexis said, but he trusted her, and that was enough. She pulled open the small-slatted blinds of the room's single window. Even in the dim sunlight, her eyes lit up like gold when she walked toward him and leaned against him. He put his arm around her and rested his chin where her neck met her shoulder. "I always wished I could sneak girls up here back in the day."

Alexis laughed. "Yeah, babe. I'm sure my mom wouldn't wander up here wondering what we were doing."

"We have a little time before we have to go." He played with one of her twists between two fingers. She'd just had it done, and it was inter- laced with thin golden threads. He wanted to bury himself in her hair and forget about everything else.

Alexis pushed him away gently, still laughing. "What happened to being worried about kicking up dust? And don't think for a second I'm about to roll around in sheets that haven't been changed since you were a teenager."

With one arm still around Alexis, Jason reached up to the slanted ceilings. It was so much shorter than he remembered. He started pulling down the stars one by one. "I feel like maybe we should keep these."

Jason had requested that only family be invited to the burial, which meant the three of them stood, hands thrust into pockets, freezing while a pastor he had never seen before read the Apostles' Creed. This wasn't something he wanted to do with the rest of the town, and he doubted anyone would mind. She wasn't one of the city's most beloved citizens, being that she'd spent the last twenty years of her life drunk at Lefty's. At first, freezing rain came down, which eventually let up but continued in a form of perpetual drizzle. The word *miserable* was uttered more than once.

Jason noticed the wrap covering Paige's hair was soaked, and that she was shivering through the service. It was probably forty degrees warmer in Modesto. So, as they were parking for the reception that he didn't want to attend, he decided to head back into his mom's house. "There will be coats in there. I'll find some scarves and maybe old cardigans or coats." Jason shrugged and headed into the bedroom on the main floor. The old Christmas tree stood mute behind him, finally unplugged.

He came out of the bedroom with a couple of colorful cardigans from the early nineties, two flannel scarves and a brown waxed Carhartt jacket, which he slipped on and decided he would keep. He offered the sweaters to the women, who took them hesitantly.

"Well, these are vintage designs." Paige smiled politely. "It's a shame she couldn't give those things up," she said as she turned her back to the overstuffed ashtrays and slipped on a dusty cardigan that had once belonged to his dad.

A knock came from the front door. They all looked at each other for a minute until Alexis said, "Well, you want me to get it?"

It was a woman Jason had never seen before, too young to have been one of his classmates.

"Is this your friend from school, Jason?" Paige asked.

"Uh, don't think so." Jason nodded at the woman. "Who are you?"

"Are you here to ask about the house? We were thinking eighty for the lot." Paige smiled, and Jason couldn't help but shake his head at her industriousness. It was clear that Paige had her eye on a down payment for land in Modesto.

"Uh, hi. Not here for the house. Hoping I could talk to Jason. I know his mom. *Knew her*, I guess."

"We were about to head over to the reception," Jason responded.

"Oh, yeah. It'll just be a minute." She ended the sentence like a question.

Alexis chimed in, "It's all right. We'll warm up in the kitchen and see how it looks in there." He frowned at her. He wasn't sure how much more of this town he could take.

"Sorry, I'll make it fast. My name is Lo. I met your mom a few weeks ago when I followed up on an ad she put in the paper—she was giving away her car for free, which might sound kind of weird. But she did tell me that my dad and your dad were friends. You know, back in the day. So, your mom gave me the car, but then asked me to drive to Santa Rosa to see if I could convince you to visit her before she died. Obviously, we didn't find you, and I'm really sorry about that. We went to the address her contact had given her, but you weren't there. I guess we missed you. Anyway, I was wondering whether you wanted the car back, and also I need to give you this." The woman handed him a white envelope. Reluctantly, he pulled it open and found that it was full of cash.

"What's this about?" Jason asked slowly.

"Your mom gave it to us in case we needed money for food or hotels. We barely used any of it, so you should have it. I mean, we would have given it back to her, but we can't now because—well, you know why."

"I don't really understand what's going on here. My mom gave you a car and a stack of cash to track me down and bring me back home? Is that it? That's shocking, like, huh—you agreed to that?"

The woman suddenly became defensive. "Well, I wasn't going to, but she was desperate to see you, and if I had a mom who was desperate to see me, I would have been happy to know that before she died." Jason was still holding the envelope of cash out awkwardly, unsure of what he should do with it.

"Only desperate for forgiveness."

"She had a hard life."

He laughed now. "Yeah, well, she made my life harder too. She doesn't need your pity. So, I don't know—"

"I'm telling you, Blanche was a good soul. Your mom had heart. I hate my mom because she hates me. And now refuses to see my face after my dad paid her a shitload of money not to abort me. So, at least your mom still cared about you. Blanche was just so sad about her husband . . ." The woman trailed off, then looked like the wind had been knocked out of her. She rubbed her face with both hands. "Wow, that was too much. I'm sorry. It's been a weird day. Do you want the car? It's a '96 Corsica."

"What? No. I do not." He already had an old car, but at least his was cool. It would have cost more to cancel his return flight than his mom's old car was worth. "Look, we have to go—you know—to my mom's funeral reception now. Thanks for this cash, though."

She backed up toward the door, reached for the handle and was gone through the porch.

Jason found Alexis and Paige in the kitchen. "Well, that was strange."

"What'd she say?" Alexis asked, standing in front of the open fridge door with a frown on her face.

"I guess my mom hired her to find me in Santa Rosa."

"To do what now?"

"To convince me to come visit before she died."

"Oh, wow. That's intense. When she contacted me, I just assumed she'd—I don't know—try to leave you a message. What would you have done if they found you?"

Jason looked around the house, the dirty kitchen, the bare cabinets that Paige and Alexis had pulled open. "I made that decision the day I left town. Nothing would have changed my mind. I'm here now, though. We should go to the thing, but I got to do something real quick."

He went upstairs to his bedroom and found the shoebox he was looking for shoved under his bed. Inside was his dad's old tape recorder, the size of a grown man's hand, with a tape still inside. He'd listened to one tape so many times that he practically had it memorized. His dad had mostly just recorded over the same one repeatedly, but there were a few extra tapes Jason had found lying around the house after the accident. None of them contained anything very important—just voice notes of news items to cover around the region, recorded interviews, things like that.

But there was one interview he had replayed countless times. His dad was interviewing Jason's fourth-grade teacher for some science fair up in the Cities. At the end of the session, Marcus asked the teacher how Jason was doing in class. She told him that he was doing great and that his project covered Minnesota's soil layers. Before his dad cut the tape, he had responded, "That's nice. Sounds good. We think he's pretty special, all right."

The teacher agreed. "Jason's a smart boy. He's definitely going places."

"I can promise you that," his dad responded and then cut the tape.

Jason set his voice recorder into the box with his dad's. Compared to the dated technology of the older one, his looked robotic and futuristic. It was unsettling to see how much things had changed since then—the contrast made the passage of time painfully clear. He put the lid back on the box and carried it downstairs. That box was coming with him.

The three of them walked over to Lefty's. It was more crowded now. Jason needed some coaxing to enter the bar that he had only been in once before, age thirteen, looking for his mom. He had found her sitting on a barstool staring mindlessly at a small square TV. Jason told her there was nothing to eat at home and asked her what was for dinner. She handed him a crumpled ten-dollar bill and sent him to the grocery store. Before he left, she scolded him, slurring, "Kids aren't allowed in here. Don't you come looking for me in here." From that day on, there were either a few cans of soup in the cabinet or microwave dinners in the freezer, or else she would leave a few dollars on the kitchen table when she couldn't be bothered to stop at the store.

When they walked into Lefty's, people quieted down. A line formed near the front door. Alexis and Paige quickly removed the ugly sweaters and laid them across the back of barstools near the window. People shook hands, welcomed Jason back into town, brought up his father and the unfortunate decline of the town's newspaper, a few even had a kind word to say about his mom.

Once the line dwindled, they found a tall table against the window and watched heavy snow begin to fall.

"I didn't know it could snow this close to spring," Paige said quietly as she sipped her wine.

After half an hour, Jason stood up to leave, mumbling something about ice after dark, when he heard a shout. The same woman who had stopped at his mom's house was yelling at an old man whose face was hidden from him.

She screamed, "I deserved to know!" and the bar grew dead quiet. All heads turned toward her as she stomped out the front door, stumbling a little and holding a full pint of beer.

Jason looked at Alexis and sighed. "This place sucks."

She nodded back and only said, "*Mmm*," and then moved her hand in front of her belly. She smiled faintly, and he smiled back. He looked up and suddenly recognized the man the woman had been yelling at.

Alexis opened her mouth to say something but before anything came out, Jason moved past her toward the old man walking out the door.

Jerry Gunderson took a few steps down the slick sidewalk, and Jason followed him, clearing his throat. "A lot of nerve showing up here, Gunderson," Jason said. He looked down at him, eyes narrowed.

"Oh. Jason, hello," the old man responded, clearly flustered by the encounter with the woman. "Just paying my respects to your family."

"Couldn't have paid those twenty years ago?"

"What do you mean by that?"

"She served two weeks. The woman driving the car that killed my

dad served two fucking weeks in jail. As a kid, I didn't understand—"
he whispered intensely with a clenched jaw, his hands in fists. "Honestly, as a grown man, I still don't understand how you let that happen."

The old man seemed to slump even further, his back a short arc.
"She'd lost her baby, Jason. Her little infant died in that accident. You
think she hasn't paid for that her entire life? If you were a father yourself,
you'd understand that. It was your mom's choice in the end. She advocated for Betsy—wrote a letter. I'm sure it's on record if you want to—"

Jason stammered out the question, "What are you talking about?"

"Your mom asked me to null her sentence—asked that I give her
the minimum I possibly could. Her baby died in the accident. You remember that? Your mom believed that was enough punishment."

"My mom only asked for her to get off because she felt guilty. You
know how many times that baby *could have been me*? How many times
my mother drove me around the state half-blind by booze?" It came
out with such force that Jason surprised himself. He might have been
shocked by this revelation, but it had only taken him a split second to
make the connection. It must have been her own complicity that led his
mother to advocate for the woman who killed his father.

Jerry Gunderson finally met Jason's glare. He stammered back,
"Well . . . I . . . I don't think she's quite that self-aware, is she? We both
know your mother, or we *knew* her, I guess. I don't believe she was considering herself at the time. As a mother herself, she felt pity for Betsy."

"And what about justice?"

The temperature dropped with sundown. It was snowing heavily
under the streetlights.

Jerry sighed. "You know, nothing could have brought him back,
Jason. Not even justice. But would it have changed your life, do you
think, if Betsy Lowe had spent her own life in prison for a drunken mistake? A big mistake, mind you. She barely blew the limit. She said she
was sleep-deprived, that she was falling asleep on the road that night. It
was the worst thing that ever happened in this town, and I'm sorry you
bore the brunt of it. Heck, I don't know. I'm sorry if I took something
away from you. But nothing I could have done would have brought him

back, and that's what you really needed—your dad. Your mom, too, I suppose, but she never was able to move past it. But you did all right for yourself, didn't you?"

Jason was distracted as Paige and Alexis left the bar and joined him on the sidewalk. Paige pointed up at the streetlight, the snow on full display. She and Alexis watched the snow fall while Jason watched Jerry Gunderson turn and walk down the street.

"You okay?" Alexis asked.

He nodded. "I will be."

A DREAM

She was in her childhood home, the seven-bedroom Victorian with mahogany crown molding and matching wood floors. She knew someone was after her, but their face kept changing. First it was a movie mobster, then it was a ghost, a murderer, her fifth-grade teacher. She ran from room to room, but silent screams made rescue inconceivable. She turned down the hallway toward the bathroom, which only led to another room filled with ornate Tiffany lamps and Persian rugs. Then more rooms through more doors, filled with foreign objects she didn't recognize—Maltese crosses, ancient tomes and Bibles opened on wooden stands, metal swords, insects and butterflies displayed in glass cases, mason jars filled with dying grasshoppers and fading fireflies. She wasn't sure whether anyone was chasing her anymore, but still, she ran. One room led to another, and as fast or as far as she ran, it was never far enough.

Lo slept in a heap on the floor in front of the woodstove that she had been too drunk to light. She lifted her head to look at the thermometer mounted out the front window. The mercury was hovering around thirty-five degrees. She shivered in her blanket and sat upright, reaching for the space between her eyes, which pulsed painfully.

"When you dream of a house, you're the house," she croaked into the empty living room, recalling something she had read in one of the old metaphysical tomes on her bookshelf. She tried to crawl across the living room to find the dream book and figure out what all those rooms were trying to tell her, but her head was too heavy. She was afraid she would throw up.

Lo had been very drunk when she got home but had still proceeded to drink most of a bottle of vodka she found stowed in the freezer, while she stumbled around the living room attempting to avoid her feelings and failing to get the stove lit.

The previous day came back to her but only in fragments. She clicked her phone, which had been half-hidden under the coffee table. Two messages and a missed call from John, a message from Parker and a message from Artie. Perhaps most embarrassing was a voicemail from a local number that her phone dubbed as *Maybe: Lefty's Bar.*

Lo set her phone on the table, stood up cautiously and lumbered to the kitchen to make coffee. She noticed the piece of jasper and the scorpion tchotchke sitting on the coffee table, the small half-circle of glass enshrining the embalmed arachnid. She must have pulled them out late last night but had no recollection. What had she been doing? Staring deeply into its dead scorpion eyes for some clue as to why nothing in her life made sense to her anymore? Or maybe she just wanted to touch something that John had touched. She recalled the woman at the market in Albuquerque. Jasper had nurturing properties, she had mystically instructed them.

She remembered the funeral service, arguing with Artie, talking with Parker, and then the incredibly awkward encounter with Jason Peterson—the day had been a certified roller coaster of emotions. But when she got to Lefty's and immediately began drinking 7-and-7s, her drink of choice when she was trying to get very drunk very quickly, things got hazy. Parker had come and gone, dropping off a peace lily from "The Locust Family," which had rested on the bar with a few other floral arrangements.

Lo had gone to the reception with zero intention of bringing up her stop in Des Moines. Her dad sat on a stool at a high table with her, sipping soda water and having conversation after conversation with townspeople. About an hour—and five drinks—into the reception, Lo vaguely recollected saying something about Amanda Monroe being a *real bitch*. Her dad looked horrified for a moment then very confused. "Who?" he had asked her. "What?"

Lo stood barefoot in her kitchen moving from foot to foot, taking turns pressing the lifted sole of each foot into her sweatpants for warmth. She squinted in the sunshine streaming through the kitchen window. It was still early but already full daylight. Hanging on the wall to her left was a wooden cutout of the state of Minnesota, lacquered and glossy with little golden etches that named several of the state's biggest lakes—Superior, Mille Lacs, Lake of the Woods, Minnetonka. Lakes big enough to imitate oceans. She had stood on all their shores and was never able to see across to the other side.

Her father had looked mortified after she mumbled something about ringing the doorbell of Amanda Monroe's suburban house. Then he proceeded to ask her several questions. "Where did you get her address?

Who told you you could do that?" and then, "You violated the terms of the contract."

This had been the wrong thing for him to say. She didn't remember who was sitting close enough to hear, and she couldn't remember quite how she put it, but she knew a lot had spilled out that she had kept carefully contained for so long. The only things she remembered clearly were her father's slumped shoulders, and in her blurred memory, he kept getting smaller and more hunched until she finally marched away.

As the kettle began to scream, she fumbled around to find a cup and noticed the pint glass she had stolen from Lefty's sitting in the sink. It was coming back now. She had asked Mike for another cocktail, only to be served a beer. She suspected it was the 3.2 brew that the more *self-possessed* elderly farmers favored. Lo covered her face with her elbow and groaned.

After she finished a full cup of coffee and finally lit the woodstove, she sat on the love seat, wrapped in her comforter, and picked up her phone. She clicked on the message from Parker: Heard what happened. Don't feel bad. You deserve to be mad. Call me.

She pushed out a breath.

She opened Artie's message with a preemptive roll of her eyes. I was too harsh. We should all stop judging each other. Me included. Peace.

She raised her eyebrows.

Whatever, Artie.

Lo set her phone down for a minute and pretended to look out the window. She picked it back up impulsively and clicked on John's texts. To her eternal embarrassment, she scanned several that she had sent to John begging him to come over. She winced. He had responded twice. The first one: I tried to call. Sorry about my voicemail. I want to talk. And the second: I heard what happened at Lefty's. Hope you're ok. I can't come over now. Call me back?

She hadn't really wanted him to come over. Or more like, she had but was relieved *now* that he hadn't. Still, the fact that he refused made her nauseous. And why was he so sorry for that voicemail he had left?

Her finger hovered above his message for several seconds before she clicked her phone off and sunk back down into the love seat, asleep within minutes.

She woke up at noon to the sound of her phone vibrating. It was John. She held it in front of her face and watched until it stopped ringing. Lo leaned back on the love seat and looked out the window toward the brown branches of an oak tree. The sky was a pale blue with thin white clouds that stretched low across the horizon.

I'm fine. Sorry I bothered you last night. She texted back, but then he called again as soon as the text went through. She threw the phone down in the blankets and went to get dressed.

She walked down the broad sidewalk with the pint glass in her hand. She had found a massive pair of old sunglasses in a kitchen drawer and was wearing John's oversized sweatshirt she had decided to keep, as well as a pair of shiny yellow leggings with her snow boots. The mercury on the thermometer had only risen slightly since the morning; the wind was glacial.

Lo pushed the door to Lefty's open and found Mike Nelson sitting on a barstool watching *Family Feud* on the ancient box TV. He was eating potato salad out of a Styrofoam takeout container from the Teakettle. Lo tried not to make a disapproving face at his takeout container as she walked up to the bar and set the glass down. "Sorry," she said loudly.

"No problem." Mike shrugged. "You all right, then?" he asked.

"Guess not," she responded.

"Want a drink?"

"Sure."

He mixed her a Bloody Mary and set a couple of pull tabs in front of her, and then moved back around the bar to eat his potato salad. They sat together watching *Family Feud* without speaking. Out the side window, she noticed a car pull up to Blanche's house. If Jason Peterson had even shown up to the reception, she hadn't noticed in her drunken state. She would have been too embarrassed to talk to him again anyway, after the awkwardness of their first encounter.

"Did Blanche's son come yesterday?" she asked Mike as he shoveled a bite of potato salad into his mouth. He wiped his face with the back of his hand and nodded once. She sucked down her drink and looked for some cash in her purse.

Mike grunted. "Drink's on me. Let me find the letter."

"Huh?"

"Like I said on the voicemail. I found a letter with your name on it at Blanche's house."

Lo stared at him. "I didn't listen to the voicemail yet. I only came to apologize for stealing the glass."

Mike stood up and walked slowly back around the bar. He pulled out an envelope that was sitting next to the cash register and handed it to her. It was labeled with her name in shaky cursive. "What is this? What's in it?" she asked.

"Well, I did look inside, out of curiosity. It's just a clipping—a newspaper clipping from your birth. Thought maybe you had asked her to find it for you." He coughed a little and handed her the envelope, his hands cracked and dry.

Lo lifted her eyebrows at Mike for admitting that he had opened a letter addressed to her but didn't say anything. He was treating her kindly, even after she caused such a ruckus in his bar last night.

"I didn't ask Blanche for anything. Why would she have a clipping for me?"

"Marcus worked at the paper, you know. You saw Blanche's house. Saves everything. Want another one?" He nodded to the drink, resting one hand on the wooden bar top. Lo shook her head and sat back down on the stool. She wasn't sure if she wanted to open it right now in front of Mike, or if she should walk over and apologize to Jason Peterson. If he had been at the reception, she had acted out of line and needed to apologize. If he hadn't, she felt like yesterday's impression shouldn't be the one he left town with. She bounced the edge of the envelope against her lips, thinking.

"Gonna open it?" Mike asked.

She side-eyed him as he took another bite of potato salad. A commercial for a law firm played quietly in the background. "I'll wait till I get home. I don't want to miss Jason before he leaves town." She stood up to go. "I won ten bucks." She pointed to the pull tab on top of the stack. "Keep it."

"Right." Jason nodded, his eyes wide. "Okay, well, you don't need to keep apologizing. I would never in this lifetime have gotten into that shitty old car to take a two-day drive with a couple of strangers and no return ticket at the request of my mom. I hope the trip was worth it anyway."

"I just had a weird day yesterday, so I was mostly apologizing for yelling—"

"Screaming."

"Right, sorry. For screaming at your mom's funeral reception."

"Listen, I got a lot to do. If you want any of this stuff, you can just take it. Otherwise, it's all going to the dumpster."

"All of it?" she asked. "Well, surely there are things worth saving. Pots? Pans? The kitchen table?"

"Everything smells like smoke, but if you want it, you can have it. The faster we get it out, the sooner we can sell the place." He scratched his head and was looking anxiously at the house.

"I'll ask my dad about getting a truck as soon as we can. He knew your dad. We'll take some of it, for sure." Her first impulse had been to ask John for help and that unsettled her.

"All right. Who's your dad, then? Even after fifteen damn years, I'm sure I still know everyone in town."

"Jerry Gunderson. Yes, I was yelling at my own dad in the bar. Pretty much everyone knows him—he's the judge."

Lo couldn't read Jason's expression at first, but he said, "I thought maybe you were screaming at him because of something he did to you or—I don't know. Forget it. We'll take care of it today. I actually need to get out of town as soon as I can."

She just stood there, confused by his change in tone. "Are you sure? I don't mind grabbing it and helping clear it out. Yeah, our dads were friends, right? Something he did to me? I don't understand."

"I got to go help them inside."

"I'm sorry. What do you mean?"

He started walking toward the house while Lo stood in the street shivering.

"Is everything okay? I get it. I used to think Elysian was the worst place in the world, but it's actually not so bad. The people are nice. A lot of good we could do with all that stuff too," she was rambling, bewildered by the turn in the conversation.

Jason turned around and faced her. "You know what—I bet you do love it here. A lot of good here for you—no doubt. But for me, there's nothing good. I thought you were yelling at him because of a court decision he made or something like that."

"I don't know what you mean."

"Yeah, well, your dad let my dad's killer loose. She walked right out of jail after two weeks."

"But I thought it was a car accident?" Lo stammered. "His killer?"

"She was a drunk driver, right? She killed him, right?"

"Yeah, I guess. I'm sorry. I think her baby—"

"I know. But what about me? What about my dad's baby? What about my baby, who won't ever meet him?"

Lo stood near the curb, awkwardly leaning over the edge, wishing she wasn't having this conversation that she wasn't mentally equipped for. "Listen. I'm really hungover. I am really sorry about everything. Your mom, your dad—"

"Please stop." He held his hand up. "That's not what I'm here for. I have to go now." Jason Peterson walked inside the house without looking back.

She walked home slowly, the envelope in one hand. The sun was bright but not warm, and she lifted her face under the striped light shining through bare maple branches. She tried to make sense of the conversation with Jason but was too overwhelmed. Why had her dad let that woman go? Did he regret that decision? According to what Blanche had told her, Marcus and her dad were friends. Blanche had never mentioned any of this.

She hugged herself in John's oversized sweatshirt, sniffing the collar. It smelled mostly like her car, dusty fabric mixed with the sweet smell the heater expelled, but when she covertly sniffed the armpit it still smelled like his deodorant—cologne and pinewood.

A block ahead she noticed her neighbor bent in front of her flower beds, digging up weeds and old roots before spring planting. She walked past and waved. "Hello, Mrs. Carlisle."

"Oh, Lois," the woman's voice croaked just a bit, "how are you, dear? I ran into your father this afternoon at the café. He said he was waiting to meet you."

Lo's leaned back on her heels and cringed. "I totally forgot we rescheduled for today." She was surprised to hear her dad had shown up at all, after last night.

Melinda only smiled and took off her gardening gloves. Her windbreaker reminded Lo of what she had worn in middle school—bright pink-and-yellow parachute material. Melinda's wardrobe was always very colorful; she liked that about her. "I have to say, I thought of you this year when planning my box out front. Think I'll add a little rosemary and some thyme for ground cover—like those edible gardens you were telling me about!"

"That's great, Mrs. Carlisle."

Melinda smiled. "Oh, hold on! I got you something." She moved slowly around the side of the house to the garage and returned carrying a garden pad identical to the one she had been kneeling on. "Look at this! They make them out of recycled flip-flops, can you believe that?" She handed Lo the gardening pad, a seafoam green mottled with pink flecks.

"Thank you so much. I've needed one of these." Lo felt horrible. Suddenly and inexplicably horrible.

Melinda scooted back to her garden. "I'm excited to see what you do with your boxes this year, Lois!" she said as she carefully bent down to her knees and began looking for weeds that needed pulling.

Lo crossed the street to her duplex. She set the gardening pad in a small coat closet and added more wood chips to the red embers that still glowed from earlier that day. She scooted as close as she could to the stove, resisting the urge to hug it. Lo held the white envelope in her hand, traced Blanche's cursive with her pointer finger and then opened it.

A yellow Post-it Note fell onto the floor. She left it where it lay and held the newspaper clipping in two hands. It was a black-and-white picture of her dad holding a tiny baby in his arms, smiling. She knew exactly how old he was in the picture because he had been fifty when she was born. Amanda Monroe had been nineteen, and the thought pulled her chest down toward the floor, her heart suddenly granite. *Poor girl*, she murmured aloud, but she wasn't sure if she was talking about her mother or herself. She touched the faces, a blurred gray, and noticed a fat teardrop had fallen and smeared the text a bit. She rubbed it in with her thumb and began to read.

Jerry Gunderson welcomes baby girl, Lois Elizabeth Gunderson, born healthy and happy in Minneapolis on May 1. We asked Jerry how he felt about being a first-time father. "It's the greatest joy of my life. Everything's better now that Lois is here with me. My biggest blessing."

There was a note below in italics:

Note from the Editor: Let's remember the famous adage that it takes a village to raise a child and let Jerry and Lois know we are here to support them as part of our community.

She held the clipping close to her face and scrutinized her father's smile, her own small round baby face pixelated in shades of gray. She marveled at the fact that he had made a birth announcement at all. At age fifty, what had he given up by raising her, a tiny baby? How had he altered his life, his home, his schedule? Then she ran her finger over the editor's note. Had it been Blanche's husband who wrote that? More teardrops began to fall heavy on the clipping, which she didn't want to see ruined.

She set it down and noticed the Post-it on the floor. It had a greasy thumbprint that Lo realized with an intake of breath must be Blanche's.

It read: *Found this in an old paper. I saved all of them that Marcus worked on. I miss him.*

She shivered again and wished she could crawl on top of the wood-stove and curl up in a blanket the way she used to lie on top of the radiator at her dad's house on the coldest winter days.

She would play in the snow after school, kicking a circular path in the front lawn, the moat for a snow castle. Their big white Samoyed, whom she had ingeniously named Snowy, would bark and kick up snow, ruining her perfect circle. She remembered hollering at him over and over, *Sit, Snowy!* until he finally lay down, rolling back and forth and whining softly, watching her have all the fun. Eventually, her dad would get home from work and meticulously put his snow clothes on while she waited impatiently—the long underwear, the snowsuit, the wool socks, boots. By then she would have the moat ready and all the excavated snow heaped high in the center. They would carve out a hole, pack in the sides of the walls and make a space wide enough for a door that her dad's shoulders could fit through. In the moonlight, they would tramp into the house, leaving their wet snow clothes dripping by the front door. She would gather up her warmest blanket, sit on the radiator covered like a nun, and wait for her father to bring her a cup of hot chocolate.

This memory was a composite since the same routine had occurred many times in her youth. Once, the castle had collapsed on top of her, and Lo had cried until her dad carried her inside and set the cup of hot cocoa in her hands. Another time it was full daylight, maybe a Saturday, and the neighborhood kids and their parents helped to create an elaborate kingdom on the Gunderson's massive front lawn. They had found a frozen brown oak branch and placed it on the top of the biggest snow castle like a flag. The memories seemed to choke her now.

She understood it then. Her father had saved her life. She wouldn't have been born if he hadn't done what he did. Lo knew almost nothing of his affair with Amanda Monroe, but she finally realized that she didn't have to hate them for it.

She felt a flood of sympathy for Mandy, a teenager, who Lo guessed had gotten wrapped up in some daddy-issues affair. Or maybe she had been lonely, or scared living in a new city, or bored. Maybe Mandy had actually believed they were in love, or maybe her dad really had been a creep. She had never witnessed this creepiness herself, but she knew it was possible. She felt sad for Amanda Monroe *and* for Jerry Gunderson. Despite what his sins may or may not have been, in the end, he had decided to bring Lo home.

Lo fervently supported a woman's right to choose, and she believed that having children was irresponsible considering the current ecological state of the world, but even given all that, she was grateful to be alive and to have a father who had worked tirelessly to carve her castles in the snow. To have all those old women who saved her oil paintings, wool blankets, gardening tools. Mike Bauer with his "leftovers." Were they all part of the village that had raised her under the instruction of Marcus Peterson? And had her dad made a huge mistake in letting Marcus's killer go?

Everything became too heavy, thoughts became jumbled. She lay down for a minute, holding the newspaper clipping to her chest.

As she began to breathe more evenly, John floated into her consciousness. Dark brown hair and pale blue eyes, the sweatshirt that smelled
like both of them, the nights they spent together, the refinery lights in
Texas, the hours reading to him from her firefly book, his hand gripping the steering wheel of her car.

She reached for her phone and without thinking, clicked on his
voicemail and listened. When she heard his voice, she let out a small
moan.

"Lo," he said in his southern accent, "Lo, I'm sorry things got messed
up. I shouldn't have said what I did about indoctrination and all that.
Not after what happened with your mom. I know you're only trying to
save the world. Sorry, I'm kinda drunk. Parker got me out here at Lefty's.
Wish you were here, but you won't answer. Anyway, just wanted to say
that you're right, and you're always right. I mean that, not just sayin' it.
You should go to Minneapolis and be happy, find people who like to
compost tomatoes and even their own shit or whatever. And you know
what, I'm saying this because I like you, and I want you to be happy.
So, I just wanted to say good luck in Minneapolis, and I hope maybe
we can be friends, and if you want—" And then the voicemail cut out
with a long beep.

"Oh, Jesus Christ," Lo murmured into her hand, flat against her face.

She hadn't been right about anything. Or maybe she had only been
right about half of the things she thought she knew and wrong about
the rest.

Maybe she didn't know anything at all.

Lying flat on the floor, one hand stretched out clinging her phone,
the other holding the newspaper clipping, Lo realized that her father
had loved her all along. Apparently, she had suppressed a dozen beautiful
memories and had chosen to cling most tightly to all those little—well,
some big—things that bothered her about him.

What came next surprised her. She hid her face under a blanket as
she was flooded with waves of embarrassment. This was intensified by
a pop in the stove and the pungent scent of sizzling red oak—a putrid,
vomity smell. She had previously felt ambivalent about it because even

though it stunk, it burned well. In that moment, she decided then that she would never burn it again.

Lo had dismissed her father as a lost cause to consumerism, as someone who would never understand her or what she stood for. Of course, she had been the one forcing dozens—*okay, hundreds*—of unsolicited opinions and rules on how he had to live.

She'd given her own father advice on how to live—something he had been doing for fifty years before she got there. He was more gracious than she had ever been when others made choices she didn't understand. But Lo had judged him nearly every day. Her dad wasn't perfect. He criticized her generation broadly, grumbled and groaned, and sometimes slammed cupboards. He would use sarcasm and a petulant, childlike voice to mock overly emotional people. And, of course, there was the love affair with a teenager that had resulted in Lo's life. Yes, he had his flaws, but . . .

Sunlight dappled her body as cirrus clouds, low and thin, halfheartedly shaded the sun. Her head rested on the thick wool carpet, and she noticed the clouds were moving impossibly fast.

The memories from her childhood came in a torrent then, and not just the snow castles and hot cocoa, but the pads and tampons that had shown up under her bathroom sink long before she needed them. Lingering, hot summer Saturdays at the lake. And arguments, too, like when she was angry he had forgotten about Muffins with Mom or Grandparent's Day. She wondered now, for the first time, how difficult losing his parents had been for him, both gone before she had any memories of them. Arguments about her radio blaring or her messy bedroom in middle school. He was there for her through them all. Yes, Jerry Gunderson and Amanda Monroe both could have made better choices, but many of those choices would have likely led to Lo never being born. And despite it all, she was glad she was here. And she was grateful for them both.

"He was a good dad," she said aloud.

She pictured Amanda Monroe again—a stranger with thin blonde hair and rayon pants, her gold cross dangling from her creased neck, warning Lo never to come back.

It was hard to admit, but Lo was beginning to understand that perhaps she had no right to make demands on this woman who had known precisely where she had been for decades but had never chosen to contact her. And what had Lo expected? That a hug from a woman she had only met once, as she was pulled from her womb, would erase all her fears and insecurities?

She lifted a hand to massage the pulsing pain between her eyes. The hair-of-the-dog drink at Lefty's had not improved her hangover one bit.

All her rationality didn't matter, though. Maybe one hug from her mother really would have worked wonders. She would never know now. Lo had always held onto hope that when she put herself in front of Amanda Monroe, something would click into place, and the world would suddenly make more sense. She imagined that the woman would be dressed like an old hippie, that she would be manicuring her winter garden while listening to the Dead, and Lo would finally see a reflection of herself in the world. But getting to know John had taught her a few things, and one of those things was that children recognizing their own reflection in their parents wasn't necessarily as common as she had daydreamed.

If she had never gone to see Amanda, then those questions would still be floating around in a space of possibilities. Instead, all her oldest questions and fears surrounding the identity of her mother had been answered. Where she had hoped for a moment of unconditional healing, she had only found more heartache.

On the cold floor, only her toes warmed by the woodstove, she realized that probably wasn't how wounds healed—miraculously and within moments. Maybe it would take as long to heal those wounds as it had taken to create them. It was going to be more difficult than she had expected, different than she had hoped, but at least now she knew the truth.

OBJECTIVE SCIENTIFIC FACTS

The glowing orbs of fireflies would never be visible to the human eye if they did not open their elytra, the hard, protective wings that encase their bodies. While these outer wings protect their vulnerable parts, no lightning bug would achieve flight without opening their elytra wings and trusting the world. These hard shells protect the beetles when grounded. They also offer a sense of balance during flight, some gravity, a bit of weight. They serve their purposes. But within the elytra are softer, more delicate parts. These are the vulnerable wings that allow for flight. Even deeper inside is the light.

ELYSIAN, MINNESOTA

Lo pulled herself together enough to walk over to her dad's house. When he opened the door, she couldn't bring herself to say what she had planned, so she started with a few gentle apologies. At first it was an apology for yelling—screaming—at him the night before.

Then the floodgates opened. She told him she was sorry for the times she had judged him or held him to higher standards, as if he should have been her mother and grandparents, as well as her father. She told him he had been a good dad and that she remembered all the snow castles he had built for her when she was young.

Eventually, she asked about Marcus Peterson, but her dad told her he couldn't talk about case decisions with her. Lo might have tried pushing harder for answers, but he looked like he'd shrunk a few inches through the night. He suddenly looked older, frailer.

Most of the conversation occurred with Lo looking down at the dark ocher color of the Persian rug, or over at the mahogany half-columns that separated the living room from the other, bigger living room. Her father had mostly responded with, "All right, okay, thank you, Lois." Until finally she asked about Amanda Monroe.

He cleared his throat. "Honestly, Lois, it didn't even last long. I never expected—" he stammered and looked toward the opposite wall. Then he began the story of her parents' affair.

LONG STORY SHORT

I went up to the Cities a lot after I became a judge. Conferences, meetings, networking, you know. She worked at a steakhouse I loved—great seafood, cold beer. I was newly single, since my wife decided she wasn't happy anymore and ran off with a coworker—the principal at the school where she taught. You know that part already. But you might not know that it was a great embarrassment to me, and I suppose very painful at the time. We never had kids, as you know. She was unable. He had three from his first marriage. I hear she embraced the family life.

Anyway, Mandy worked at the steakhouse. And I would talk to her, just harmless flirting. I felt pretty good winning the judgeship. I eventually asked her out one night, just to talk after her shift ended, but she said no. Not that I expected any different.

We were still cordial after that, and I still stopped in when I worked in the Cities. After a few months, she comes up to me and asks if my offer still stands. I tell her of course it does. So, we go out one night, and she told me how she'd been through a breakup with the manager where she worked. She was struggling in school, you know. She grew up in this small town in northern Iowa, wasn't doing well in the Cities. We go out and have a good time, just listening to each other. The next time I went up, we did the same thing. It was just like that, a few times, you know. And I had some money to get nice hotel rooms, nice meals, which she had never had. A total of five dates, maybe six. I went every few weeks, nothing serious. It made me feel good, feel young again after the divorce. She was so young, and I was too foolish to care. When you were around that age—I never told you this—but I couldn't imagine that, a man in his fifties, you know. It's why I couldn't let you go up to the Cities right after high school. I just couldn't imagine . . .

Well, I went up one Friday for no particular reason, just left a message on her answering machine and told her I was coming up and that she should meet me at the hotel. That was the night she told me she was pregnant, was going to have an abortion and was going to move back home to go to some small Christian college that a bunch of her high school friends went to.

I didn't argue, at first. I was stunned and kind of confused. But that night I thought about it, lying in the hotel room all alone, and kind of figured out this way to ask her if she would keep the baby—keep you—just through the pregnancy. Then she could go home and go to that other school, back to the life she wanted. I didn't know if it was crazy, but I thought, what do I have to show for myself? I felt that even with the house and the job, I didn't really have much to be proud of, but I was feeling low about her age and how her parents might take it. It occurred to me that they were probably younger than I was. It was a long night.

So anyway, after some discussion and phone calls and whatnot, she agreed. I don't think she wanted an abortion. You know, growing up like she did, religious and all that. I've told you many times before that I don't think women ought to be governed in that way—it was about the baby to me. I mean, it was about you, and what I wanted for my life. You were something meaningful and a way for me to do good in the world, a legacy or, you know, these fanciful ideas people have.

I wrote up some contract, and in the contract, it said that I would never contact her. I guess it never said you couldn't, so no need to apologize for that. It's my fault for not telling you all this, for not being more open about where you came from, but I had always hoped that I was enough, but I see now that maybe I wasn't.

ELYSIAN, MINNESOTA

Lo stood behind the bar, fully stocked and cleaned, waiting for Artie. Finally, sunlight cut into the club and then disappeared, the swish of the massive black door audible in the quiet. He was carrying a gallon-sized plastic bag bulging with cords and wires wrapped neatly. She cleared her throat, and he jumped a little, squinting his eyes in the dim light. It was always impossible to see anything in the club for a few seconds after coming in from full daylight.

"Jesus, Lo. You scared me."

"Sorry. Listen, Artie. I need to apologize for, well, my general treatment of you the last few months. I thought about what you said, and I think in the end, we just weren't right for each other. And instead of admitting it, I turned you into a bad guy, maybe to feel justified in breaking up with you. And maybe you were right. I was trying to make Elysian seem worse than it is, so I could finally talk myself into leaving, and you got tangled up in that. I'm sorry."

"Oh," was all he said, widening his eyes and then blinking them repeatedly. "Wow, Lo. I appreciate you saying that." He didn't say anything else, nor did he apologize for trying to get her fired.

She only shrugged and pretended to clean the freezer top.

He started to walk toward the soundboard in the back. Impulsively, Lo asked, "Hey Artie, did you really like me? I mean, why?"

She realized immediately that this is what she had wanted to ask John when instead she asked him what he liked about Shay Rose. For the most part, Lo already knew that people found her *strange*, but she was coming to realize that she had never been curious enough about her more positive traits, or at least how other people interpreted them. Surely, there were a few . . .

He scoffed quietly. "Okay, Lo, sure. But you first."

"Oh—no." She mumbled, caught off guard by the reversal. What had she liked about Artie? After their first night together, she dreaded being alone with him. Whenever they hung out, she experienced low-key anxiety when he would try to come on to her. Of course, this wasn't necessarily his fault. He hadn't done anything wrong, except be the wrong person for her, and she had been too lonely or too dishonest to tell him as soon as she realized it.

"There's a lot to like, Artie." She sighed, realizing with some surprise that she meant it. "I liked watching those foreign movies with you. I would never have seen them if you hadn't shown me. And you're neat and careful with your work, the console and how you care so much about the acoustics and all that. And how much you love cats and dogs, even if we disagreed about that. You're a decent cook."

"I know you miss those wings." He smirked and turned halfway around, awkwardly swinging the top part of his body toward the door to the backroom as if part of him wanted to leave, but he kept his feet planted. "Well, Lo, I've liked you since we were little, so, what can I say? You stand up for what you believe in. You're interested in so many things, so that conversations with you are different from conversations with other people—better, I guess. I mean, you're pretty, and your hair . . ." He shrugged. Artie was in the shadows, but Lo thought maybe he was blushing. She nodded once, suppressing a smile.

"Thanks, Artie."

"Yeah, you too, Lo."

"But, Artie," she said, looking up at him.

"Yeah?"

"We're definitely broken up now," she said. "Just to be clear."

She spent the whole night distracted, messing up orders and forgetting to refill the empties in the cooler. In the space of a few hours, she realized that her feelings for John hadn't changed since that second drink in Albuquerque. She wanted him. Maybe she had wanted him since the first time they walked down the icy street together that night he got her car started, but the whole time she had been attempting to control the situation and protect herself from potential pain, instead of just seeing what might unfold between them. Her conversation with Artie only made her miss him more. *What did I like about John?* she asked herself. She came up with a running bullet list in her head that distracted her from counting correct change to customers.

The way he never gave in when she pushed him away. He just sat up straight and strong, like he wouldn't crumble under all her shoving. How he gripped the steering wheel when he was upset or anxious, and how he also gripped the steering wheel whenever she flirted with him. Just him gripping things, in general. How he had flirted with her relentlessly, and then stopped when she asked him to. He listened to her read about fireflies for several hours without complaining. The accent—let's be honest. God, in bed (she laughed out loud—so dumb), so good in bed. They certainly had chemistry like she had never experienced before.

Then someone would ask for something—a beer, a pop, a bag of pickle chips—and she would look at them as if they had interrupted something important.

The sweatshirt that was now hers. Deb and Raul were a plus. Willing to find a dumpster for her to dive into. Underneath, he was vulnerable and probably traumatized from childhood, but he was still willing to be kind.

She was beginning to open up to the possibility that maybe she didn't need someone who thought just like her or cared about the exact same things—maybe that had been too extreme. It didn't necessarily mean that *she* had to change. It only meant that she didn't need to change *him*.

Eventually, Parker took her by her narrow shoulders and asked her what was wrong. She responded, straightforward, "I think I'm in love."

Parker's smiled for a second and then asked, "Well, what are you going to do about it?"

After work she called John. He picked up after a few rings and it sounded like he had been sleeping. "Lo, hey," he murmured.

"Hey, sorry it's so late, and sorry I didn't call back after the funeral. I was trying to figure some things out. Um, do you think we could talk for a bit?"

"Sure, yeah, do you want to come over right now?"

She grinned and realized by his surprised tone that this must sound like *that* kind of call.

"Maybe tomorrow sometime?"

"I really do want to talk to you, but I work at seven, and you probably work at four, so I don't know. I could come by The Locust, if you want."

"No, it's so loud here. I'll come by the shop earlier in the day."

Lo hung up and held the phone to her chest. The truth was she did want to go over to his house now and had to force herself not to call him back. He had to work early, and it was already past midnight. Besides, she knew she had to tread carefully, lay out her plan and find a way to sort through the future in an attempt to keep John in it.

The speech began like this: John, I want to be with you. We haven't known each other that long, but please move to Minneapolis with me and find a new job, new friends and live with me in a commune.

From there, it morphed into more intricate sentences like: John, I hope we can continue dating after I move to the Cities. I know that I told you I don't want to be with you, but I was lying. I'll come visit on the weekends. I know that hasn't worked out well for you with Shay Rose, but . . .

Then it was simply: I want to be with you, but I have to go.

In the end, nothing made sense. When she finally pulled open the heavy metal door to the lobby of Jefe's, she abandoned her speeches completely.

John stood behind the old computer. The screen did something otherworldly to his eyes, causing the irises to glow iridescent. "Hey," she said.

He clicked the mouse once more and glanced up at her. His eyes were smiling, but his lips were pressed together tight. She coughed into her elbow and realized she was wearing his sweatshirt. It fell nearly to her knees.

She figured it would be like ripping off a bandage. "Hey. I found you a mouse pad at the thrift store since you don't have one. Anyway, sorry about how intense I was in the car after we left Des Moines. The whole thing with my mom . . ." She meant to set the mouse pad down coolly but instead threw it down on the counter in an awkward spasm.

"It's fine, Lo. I shouldn't have said all that. Jesus, and right after what happened at your mom's. It wasn't even true, what I said. I was really tired, and when you said you were moving so soon, I couldn't deal with it."

"I know, I sprung it on you."

"No, you didn't. You told me that was your plan on the drive down. I just hoped—I don't know. Anyway, it doesn't matter. You should move, I think. It'd be good for you."

She was frowning and nodding frantically. "Okay," she said, finally exhaling. "Well, can we be friends?"

John cleared his throat. She tried to read his expression but couldn't. Did he look pleased with that suggestion? She thought maybe he did and then immediately wanted to take it back. *Can we be lovers?* would have sounded ridiculous, but it was what she wanted. The words of all her failed speeches swirled in her head. She was going; he was staying.

"Can I ask you a favor?" she asked.

"*Mhm*," he said, a look of mock worry on his face.

"Would you drive to Minneapolis with me tomorrow if they don't need you here? To check out this house? Make sure I don't get murdered?"

"Did you find this place on Craigslist?" He looked serious, his eyes narrowing.

She assured him the person she was meeting at the house was Parker's friend, someone from Elysian. John looked suspicious but agreed to drive with her under one condition—they were going to take his truck. When he asked what time she wanted to be picked up, she found herself saying, "I'll meet you at your place."

"All right." He lifted a shoulder. "You might like the view, actually."

As soon as she left the garage, she called Parker.

That night, Lo stood behind the bar while a high school band screamed into staticky microphones. More than once she looked at Artie only to see a barely disguised look of disgust on his face as he watched them tune their instruments midsong. She would catch his eye and make an alarmed face, and they would both laugh and cringe simultaneously. Work felt fun again.

A few lonely parents, looking out of place, ordered beers. Otherwise, Lo just refilled the water pitcher and tried to look like she was enjoying herself. Or at least tried *not* to look like she was bored out of her mind.

Near closing time, Parker sat down on a barstool, and they talked through Lo's revelation that she wanted to be with John Blank. They discussed the facts of the case: she was going to Minneapolis and he was not. They disagreed on how to approach the problem.

Parker told Lo that all she had to do was tell John to pack up his shit and move to Minneapolis with her. She insisted the solution was really that simple.

It wasn't though. They weren't even dating. She couldn't ask someone to move in with her who wasn't even her boyfriend. Also, while Lo hoped John's relationship with Shay Rose was over, she had no reason to believe it was. Especially after the impression she had given him on the drive back into town. Would Lo just turn into another of his when-I'm-around-town flings? The thought tormented her.

Parker and Lo decided that she had to check out the house in Minneapolis first. Maybe it would be nasty, and she would then need to rethink the whole plan. But if the house was suitable, then after moving, she could just regularly show up around town. If this happened often enough, maybe she would feel comfortable asking about a *real* long-distance relationship.

That was the plan that made the most sense, but it still didn't feel like enough.

MINNEAPOLIS-SAINT PAUL INTERNATIONAL AIRPORT

A massive stuffed moose stood seven feet tall on a rolling platform. Its black marble eyes were staring directly at a grizzly bear on a similar platform across the hallway. Paige was getting ready to walk to her gate, straightening her legs a bit, flexing her knees. "Alexis knows the area well enough to figure out how far each property is from our house. The closer you are, the more we can babysit." It wasn't the first time she had said it. The plan had materialized into more of a reality with each day that Jason and Alexis spent with Paige. She was tenacious, sure, but he could already tell she was going to make an amazing grandmother.

They ended up calling a company to come pick everything up. Jason authorized them to do whatever they saw fit with what was left. He wasn't about to leave it all to Gunderson's daughter. Though all the furniture was so coated in a thick layer of cigarette smoke, he probably did her a favor in the end. A local cleaning crew was going to give it the old college try, but he still worried the house wouldn't be worth much to anybody.

Before they left Elysian, they sorted through a hundred boxes of photo albums from when Jason's parents were children, from when he was a kid. He had been a chubby baby and, according to Alexis, very cute. She would hold up a baby picture and then rub her own belly while Jason grinned or grimaced, depending on how embarrassing the picture was.

The pictures didn't tell the full story. For better or worse, Jason didn't know the context of his parents' childhoods. If they had told him when he was young, whether they had been happy and well-cared for or not, those memories were lost. There weren't many people left to ask—an errant aunt he'd barely known, a distant cousin somewhere up the family tree. He decided it didn't matter now. He was planting new seeds.

Pictures only showed single moments, so Jason questioned their worth as memorabilia. What would they have shown if Jason had been the one holding the camera when he was growing up? His own brown eyes in the viewfinder, his finger choosing what to capture. Eventually, a missing father and a drunk mother. Of course, no one remembers how their parents cared for them as infants, those memories are buried too deep. Regardless, he had looked happy then, as a baby in the photos. He just couldn't remember that feeling anymore.

Paige had pocketed a handful of Jason's baby pictures, and he could only imagine the collage she would create out of his and Alexis's together, along with the photoshoots she was already mentally arranging for the new baby. It made sense to him now why Alexis was pushing for Modesto from the moment she realized she was pregnant.

Outwardly, he joked with Alexis about how obsessed her mom was with their unborn child, but below the surface, he was grateful for Paige's enthusiasm, her willingness to step in. He got the feeling that she was preparing to take on the role of two grandmothers in one, as if her attending his mother's funeral were part of a promise Paige was making to his own mom. Maybe he was only imagining it, but her single-minded determination to get them back to Modesto quickly led Jason to believe that living near her was the only sensible thing to do.

They both stood to hug Paige goodbye. Once she had turned the corner of a long corridor, Jason said, "I get the feeling she wants us to live in Modesto."

Alexis scoffed. "Yeah, ya think? Well, I want that too. We could do what we're doing now but *better*. White and purple asparagus, hemp, gourds and pumpkins in the fall." She raised her eyes a little. "And she's right. We wouldn't have to borrow for a down payment if your mom's lot sells on the high end. And then my parents can watch this kid so we can go out once in a while."

"Oh, fun—dates in Modesto. At Sizzler?" In truth, it didn't matter to him where they ate meals, as long as they ate them together.

"It's gotten cuter since I left," Alexis protested, then turned and looked at him, and the busyness of the airport hushed around them. "This kid will change everything. We need a plan."

"Here's my plan. You know how I told you Pokémon raised me? Just, hear me out, what about naming the baby Pikachu?"

"Ha! No, that's a hard no." She glared at him.

"Hey, Lex, I think before we make life plans, we need to talk about what happened after you told me you were pregnant. I wasn't myself after that, and I was thinking about it. You know when people say 'fight or flight'?"

She frowned, nodding slightly. "You chose flight?"

"There's another one, actually," he said. "Fight, flight or freeze. And I froze. I don't normally do that, but I did then. I froze until you asked me to leave. But I should have stayed to fight. To figure out what I really wanted—I know now that was you, had been all along. I should have stayed and made that clear to you."

"Yeah, you should have. But you were caught off guard. It was un-expected."

Jason drummed his fingers on the table, looking out at the throng of travelers. "Life is full of unexpected shit." He lifted a shoulder. "I just need to be ready for it."

"I hear you. But I knew you were coming back. I really did." She smiled slightly. "But I'm still not naming our baby after a Pokémon. Hey, what do you think of Marcus, if he's a boy?"

Jason grinned, leaning back on the hard metal chair. "It's a good name. Let's put it on the list. I've also been thinking I could check out some schools in the valley, get credentialed in California. There are probably a few schools that are getting away from all that bureaucracy. It'd be nice to have insurance, 401(K), all those things that 'real adults' need to think about."

Alexis reached across the table with one hand and rested it on his cheek for just a second. "If you want to teach, then you should, but I've been doing my *own* research. We could do that all that ourselves, you know. We can make the money work. I looked into a bunch of funds we can apply for." She was listing these off with her fingers. "I can't promise anything, but I'm looking into stuff. Not saying it will be easy, not saying it'll fall into place right away. But we can figure it out."

Jason watched her take a sip of her drink. She was wearing one of his dad's old wool cardigans that had cycled back into style. He wasn't sure what to do with all the stuff he had taken from his parents' house or what to do with his new voice recorder that was packed in a suitcase next to his dad's old tape recorder. Would he save them for his own kid? Let them collect dust in an attic for someone else to sort through one day? All he knew was that when he was with Alexis, he felt like he was doing the right thing. Like he was where he was supposed to be—whatever that meant. "I think California is a good plan . . . at least for now. And you're right, we can make this work."

SOUTHERN MINNESOTA

A cabin sat near the edge of the smallest lake in town, which Lo thought of as more of a pond than an actual lake—every Minnesotan was well equipped to decide which was which. She wondered idly whether it allowed motorboats, but it had never mattered to her before because her dad had a dock on Lake Elysian, which spanned several counties, almost the entire length between Highway 60 to Highway 14, near Janesville. Still, the cabin was beautiful with dark brown lacquered wood and red trim on the windows. All this contemplation on the size and shape of lakes was only a stalling tactic. Lo was pulling into John's driveway.

It was her first time seeing John's car. A shiny black four-door truck sat in the cul-de-sac of his driveway. She laughed out loud when she realized that they drove her ancient and ugly sedan across the country when they could have taken John's brand-new truck, but in the end, it had been an adventure.

She drove slowly to avoid kicking up gravel. She was also taking her time examining where John lived, all alone, out on the lake. A lone pine stood by the shoreline in front of her, and she could see a beach chair leaning against it, rusting through the winter. A small silver metal dock held a military-green canoe resting upside down. Otherwise, there were no other visible clues about John's home life.

He stepped out the front door, locked it and then waved awkwardly with one hand. As he walked to his truck, she pushed her car door open and yelled, "Hold on, mister! I want a tour!" John stopped short and made an about-face back toward the house without saying a word, so she didn't get to see his expression after she invited herself in.

"It's a bachelor pad," he warned her as he unlocked the front door. His hair was still wet from the shower. He was wearing a nice pair of jeans that she had never seen before, along with an open flannel over a Locust t-shirt. "The couple who own the house moved for work or something, so they're renting it for now. Someone Randy knew from high school."

"Where'd you get that t-shirt?" she asked.

"Oh, Parker and Teresa stopped by to use the canoe a few days ago and left it for me as a thank-you, I guess." He smirked. "They're something, huh?"

Lo felt a tinge of jealousy that her friends were interacting without her and would continue to do so after she moved, but she only smiled.

John's house smelled like cedarwood. The air was cool inside. Lo laughed when she saw his orange-and-brown floral sofa. "Oh wow, did you get that couch in town? Pretty sure that was my grandparents'. There's a picture of me on it when I was an infant."

"It was in my uncle's basement; they let me take it when I moved out. Who knows? That'd be cool if it was your grandparents'. It's ugly but very comfortable."

The downstairs was mostly open, a large living room sparsely decorated—the old velvet floral couch, a scratched-up leather chair and matching ottoman. The kitchen had square pine-colored tiles, somewhat dated but almost back in vogue. A cream-colored vintage fridge stood about five feet high on the far-left wall. "Neat fridge."

"Yeah, found it at the junkyard and fixed it up. Think it's from the sixties."

She ran her hand over the back of the couch then pointed to a closed door. "That the bedroom?"

He shook his head, grinning. "Nope, it's kind of scary in there."

She raised her eyebrows. "Why, is it the sex dungeon?"

Inside the room sat a collapsible card table, a rolling desk chair pushed against it. The room had a couple of old appliances on the floor in a circle around the table. The table itself was covered with pieces of machinery Lo couldn't identify, maybe car parts.

She looked back at him. "Okay, not the sex dungeon. Just the office. No TV, I see."

"What would I watch?" he asked. She noted that he didn't riff off her sex dungeon joke and wondered what that meant.

She nodded. "I don't have one either."

"I figured," he said, a smile on his face. "I'm lyin', though. I got one upstairs in the bedroom. I just wanted you to think I was analog like you."

She laughed. "Oh, that's what I am? Analog?"

"Well, you're something."

Lo gave him an exaggerated eye roll and put one foot on the first step that led upstairs to the loft. "This must be the bedroom then."

"*Mhm*," he nodded.

"Can I go up?"

"You can," he said, and it felt like a dare.

His bedroom was exactly what she had expected. A box spring and a mattress on the floor with an old blue comforter. One pillow, the pillowcase half slipped off. At the foot of the bed was a wooden coffee table that held a small flat-screen TV. She was going to ask him about the table, which looked handmade, when she heard him coming up the stairs. Her eyes widened in the dim bedroom light. She rushed over to the window on the opposite side of the room and pulled open the blinds. "You gotta let some light in here."

"Told you it wasn't much. Definitely living like a bachelor in here."

"I would've been more surprised to find a perfectly decorated cabin decked out with a bearskin rug and designer furniture," she said politely as he walked closer.

"You know, Lo, I've thought about you a lot since last week."

She cleared her throat. "You have?"

"Yeah, and I realized I should have come by or—you know—I went over to The Locust Wednesday night but you weren't there." He kept walking closer.

"What? Parker didn't tell me."

"I didn't see her. Just the lady who works the bar with you some-times. She said you called in sick. I was going to stop by your place, but it seemed like you didn't want to talk." He stood near the foot of the bed and shoved his hands in his pockets but didn't take his eyes off her. Lo realized she should have asked *why* he had been looking for her and what he had planned to do with her when he found her, but the moment had passed.

"Ready to go?" he asked, turning toward the stairs.

Lo leaned back against the window blinds, wishing John had kept walking toward her. "I don't know," she answered.

"What?"

All she could do was shake her head.

"You're not ready to go?" he asked.

Lo pressed her lips together. She felt planted where she stood, unable to move just yet. John was standing still, awkwardly situated with one foot on the step leading downstairs and one still on the loft floor. Nei-ther of them moved for a minute.

"It's just . . ." Lo trailed off. She wished she could tell him what she wanted without saying it. She wasn't even sure she'd be able to get the words out coherently. None of the speeches she had planned ear-lier that week made sense anyway. Regardless of how their future plans might eventually separate them, Lo knew exactly what she wanted in the moment they were in right now. So, she stood mute, watching him there, half-twisted, waiting for her to give him the go-ahead. If he was waiting for the go-ahead to walk down those steps and out the door, he could wait forever. That wasn't what she wanted. Whatever look she gave him, her best attempt at conveying what it was she was ready to do, he seemed perfectly capable of interpreting.

John didn't say anything either. He slowly lifted his foot from the step and turned toward her. Still, she didn't move as he crossed his room and was within an inch of her body in what felt like a single second, maybe two. Lo looked up at him, biting her lower lip.

"You're not ready to go just yet?" he asked her.

She shook her head. "No, not yet."

He bent his knees, reached both arms around her and picked her up, his forearms crossing along the backside of her upper thighs.

"Is this what you want?" he asked.

"It is," was her only response.

Then he carried her to the bed without another word.

They pulled in front of a huge Victorian house with a long driveway that led to a side entrance. Lo knocked on the metal storm door, and it rattled in its frame. The plastic window was smudged with finger-prints, and a bucket filled with wet sand and cigarette butts sat on the concrete in the driveway.

A man came to the door wearing a black bicycle hat, the kind that fit tight with a short brim. He introduced himself as Dane, Parker's friend from high school. Once inside, they found themselves in the kitchen, a broad wooden farm table was covered in permanent marker writing and doodles. A few dirty dishes sat on the linoleum counter. Under the window was a tall silver radiator that hummed a little, glistening with perspiration.

"Cute," Lo said. John looked around but didn't say anything. When they entered the living room, four people perked up. Two were lying next to each other on the mattress of a pull-out couch reading a copy of *National Geographic*. One woman was drinking a cup of coffee and scrolling on her phone and someone sat across from her reading a paperback novel. When they entered the room, everyone looked ex-pectantly at Lo.

Introductions were made, and Lo surmised that the couple on the mattress shared one room and then Dane and the other two each had their own rooms. She noticed a Japanese screen that closed off a make-shift bedroom and remembered Dane had told her that part of the living room was used as a bedroom to keep rent low—thankfully that wasn't the one they were offering her.

The woman holding the cup of coffee asked Lo if she had any questions for them.

"Do you all work at the co-op?" Lo asked. She was embarrassed standing while they all sat staring at her. She felt the urge to grab John's hand.

The man lying on the bed with a *National Geographic* resting on his chest responded, "I work at a local coffee shop and roaster, but we sell to the co-op. Dane just started at a bike shop. These three still work at the co-op. It's a good place to meet people, but the pay isn't great and the hours are worse—not enough to go around, too many members. Perks are nice though—food, discounts and a lot of local bartering connections." He shrugged, and they all smiled at each other awkwardly.

She nodded. "Cool."

"Bedroom's upstairs," Dane chimed in. It was a small corner room with a door that led to the attic. Dane told her the attic was scary and full of bats and didn't offer to show her. The bedroom had dark-stained wooden floorboards and a big rectangular window that overlooked the driveway. Lo immediately began to wonder what she would pack and what she would donate, as she had somehow managed to tastefully fill her home with free furniture over the past eight years.

"I do have to say, everyone is totally welcome to have partners spend the night, but we might eventually vote on whether that person needs to be charged rent. Abdi's girlfriend just moved in, which is totally cool. We decided to charge an extra one-fifty for the room to pay for utilities and food, which we share."

"Okay, cool. No, I mean, we—"

"I'm not moving in," John said flatly. Lo smiled at Dane politely and looked out the window. If she leaned against the far edge, she could see the lake across the street.

"A lake view," she said to no one in particular.

The sun was shining, and the temperature was above fifty degrees for the first time that year. Lo leaned against John's truck and tilted her head toward the sky. She could hear the faint lap of water coming from the lake across the street, the spring breeze creating minuscule

waves. She heard the click of the remote unlock and then John opening the driver's side door. She stood still for a minute longer until he
started the truck.

They sat in the quiet for a few minutes. She glanced over at him.
They made eye contact and then frowned awkwardly at each other. Lo
made a repeated clicking noise with the tip of her tongue against the
roof of her mouth and thought about mentioning the weather.

Yesterday, in her daydreams, she imagined John coming up and
visiting her in the Cities. They would do what they had just done earlier that day in his bedroom, then they might have breakfast with her
roommates, maybe visit the Falls. Picnics by the river. She could surprise
him with a Twins game. But John's current mood dimmed her future
plans into a haze, and she wasn't sure how to approach him now. She
ventured, "That was cool, right?"

"*Hmm*," was all he said.

"Cute house. They all seemed nice."

He nodded and pressed his lips together as if he were trying to smile
in response but couldn't bring himself to do it. They passed several large
Victorian houses that framed the lake on the way out of town, a few
fast-food restaurants interspersed with local coffee shops.

"I need to figure out what I can fit in that room and what I'll need
to donate."

"So, you're going to take the room?"

"Yeah, I mean, the kitchen was messy, and the room was small. And
I'm worried about the hours at the co-op. Dane promised the job was
mine, but a few hours a week probably won't be enough. Still, the house
was pretty much what I expected."

John drew in a deep breath. "Just seems like a step backward, you
know. You've already got a job you like, a place of your own, family
and friends. That's where the word commune comes from, right? From
the word *community*? Seems like you have all of that in Elysian, like
better versions of what they offered at that house, what with one tiny
bedroom and a part-time job they all agreed wasn't that great. I mean,
if anywhere in the world is set up to offer you free rent, free stuff and

a useful community—it's where you're livin' now. But, sure," he conceded, "they seemed nice."

Only recently, Lo herself had come to these realizations about Elysian, so instead of getting defensive, she took a deep breath. "I don't know. Who says it's a step backward? A society that wants us to have bigger houses and more shit? Yes, my job at The Locust is great. I'm *definitely* going to cry when I hug my woodstove goodbye. It's just—I need a change. I've lived in Elysian my whole life. I thought about what you said. I want to take some space from my dad. To see whether you were right when you said that he *funds* my 'free' lifestyle. Don't worry, I'm not arguing with you. I'm serious. It's time to spread my wings and fly or some crap like that."

"Is change for the sake of change really flying?" he asked.

"Maybe. Change for the sake of growth. Change for a change in scenery, I don't want to live in the same town of eight hundred people and a handful of tourists for the rest of my life."

He was quiet for a minute, and she could see his Adam's apple move as he clenched his jaw. "I get it," he said quietly. "Actually, Deb and Raul have been pushing me to move to Albuquerque."

Lo's hands, which had been resting on her lap, squeezed tight on her thighs. "Oh?" she asked, not hiding her surprise. "I know they mentioned that when we visited, but you said you were happy in Elysian."

"Well, Raul's been texting me applications for garages and thinks it'd be easy for me to find a job since I speak a little Spanish. Deb's always been there for me. It was good to see her again, and she acted like no time had passed since we were kids. And if they ever have kids of their own, I'd be an uncle." Lo had a foreboding feeling that the idea was becoming more concrete as he spoke it out loud. "And I miss the mountains."

"Huh?" was all she could manage.

"Yeah, I miss the mountains, you know. Some change in scenery." He moved his right hand in a wavelike pattern. "Topography is the right word, I guess. It's nothing like North Carolina, brown and rugged instead of green and humid. But I miss the mountains. Deb has been sending me pictures of campgrounds down there. More like back home where the campsites are hidden in forests and on top of mountains." He laughed a little. "Randy and my uncle took me camping here once, just an open field staring into other people's tents. It was weird."

"You can camp like that up north in the Boundary Waters or over in the Black Hills. There's plenty of places like that here." She didn't know what else to say; she felt the need to defend the campgrounds of the upper Midwest.

"It's like you said, maybe I'm ready to spread my wings and fly."

Lo's chest was tight. The scenery outside had morphed from city into suburb. They passed the exit for the Mall of America, which made Lo feel worse than ever before. Eventually, they passed the smaller mall at the southern tip of the suburbs where she had shopped with her dad for school clothes. That one was near the manmade ski resort where she had attempted to downhill ski a few times—a regular winter field trip for every school in the state.

She knew each exit from there to Elysian. The exit with the diner and giant movie theater, the one with the cute but overpriced woolen mill with hand-dyed blankets and scarves, scratchy and warm, that her dad gifted her every year. And eventually came the exit that led to Elysian. It skirted a dozen lakes and rivers, and while the reflection of the sun off the water never failed to charm her, she knew exactly what was coming and exactly what to expect.

John fiddled with the radio until he found country classics. She recognized Dolly Parton's voice as she wailed about a man she couldn't stand to lose. Lo looked out at the lakes that came and went like mirages.

She imagined herself packing up her belongings, arranging her small room, cleaning up after her roommates, drinking tea in the mornings while they read magazines and scrolled on their phones and complained about work. Would her dad have to manage the landscaping at her duplex? Would he hire someone else to do it for him? Would that person care for her garden boxes the right way, rotating the crops and using cow manure and animal meal, not cheap store-bought nitrogen fertilizers?

She imagined driving back to Elysian, passing the same malls, three different Perkins, the perpetually falling fake snow pumped out by the ski resort, and pulling into town knowing John wasn't there. A knot in her chest rose slowly, inch by inch, until her throat felt strangled like she was slowly suffocating.

Eventually, John pulled into his driveway and turned the truck off. They both sat still for a long time.

Finally, he asked, "Do you want to fish?"

"What?"

"The lake thawed. Do you want to go fishing with me?" he repeated.

"Sure." She managed a weak smile.

She sat alone in the single lawn chair on the end of the dock while John prepared their poles and tied on the lures.

Lo knew that spring was coming.

The heat of the sun was finally warming her after offering nothing through the long winter months. It was past lunch, and she hadn't eaten, so she was relieved when John came out with a plate of sandwiches. "I know you like tomatoes, so I added extra. Want a bobber?" he asked with a smirk.

"As a matter of fact, I do—to both of those things."

"I brought one down just in case." He was laughing to himself now. He tied the red-and-white ball onto the end of her fishing line and handed her the rod.

"It's like the bumpers in bowling. Why not make it easy on yourself? Are you laughing at my bobber?" she asked.

"No, Lo. I'm just glad you're here with me." He looked serious now, and she felt that same knot in her chest, the same slow nausea rising up into her throat.

"John?"

"Lo?"

"Can I spend the night?"

He stopped and looked up from the lure he was tying to his line. "Yeah, please do. You don't even need to ask me that. You have an open invitation from here on out."

She expected the knot to loosen, but it didn't. She did want to spend the night, but that wasn't what she'd wanted to ask him.

Sitting in the chair, she held her arms out to John. He grinned at her for a minute and then carefully sat down in her lap. The chair creaked under their weight and the dock wobbled slightly. She exhaled dramatically. "Jesus. You're heavy." Lo wrapped her arms around him and held tightly, her cheek pressed against his back. He tried to turn around to look at her, but he was too tall, and Lo and the chair were too small. She worried they would tip over into the freezing lake, which didn't yet know that spring had returned. They both started laughing, but she didn't let go.

"John? I think I want to go to New Mexico with you. I mean, can I? Could I go with you?"

With her cheek against John's back, she could look over the small lake and watch the shoreline with its reedy cattails and lonely pines. What would she miss about Minnesota if she left? Parker and her dream of a prairie. Rows of endless cornfields, tall and orderly by late summer. Freshly painted red barns decorated with perfectly symmetrical Norwegian hexes and overflowing with scrappy farm cats. She would miss flaking white birchbark, snow falling in the streetlights, generous neighbors, the single Main Street in the town where she'd grown up, the friendly diner with her dad eating a burger. In July, she'd miss constellations of fireflies glowing on the shorelines of ten thousand lakes.

John's body tensed under her arms. "Lo," was his only response.

ACKNOWLEDGMENTS

Thanks to my husband, Adam, and my kids, Keaton, Asa and Sylvie. To my parents, my siblings and their families, the Sullivan cousins and my extended family up in Minnesota. I love you all. Thanks to my NCSU cohort—Jesse Wang, Jendayi Brooks-Flemister, Paul Watts-Offret and Isaac Hughes Green. To the second years when I came in and the first years (even on Zoom, we connected) when I left. I wouldn't be here without all your support, feedback and friendships. I love you all too. To Belle Boggs for your time and mentorship, as well as Cadwell, Wilton, Elaine, Cat, Jill, Eduardo and Dorianne—I learned so much from all of you. Special thanks to Aaron Gwyn. I wouldn't have gotten here without your support. To UNCC English and Bryn Chancellor—thanks for your guidance. To Liz Vaagen and Allison Darcy for the critiques and to Sarah Grunder Ruiz for all your help through the process. As a mother of three, the privilege to attend graduate school fell on stipends, fellowships, assistantships and tuition remission. Collegiate funding of the arts is more important now than ever, and it's my hope that funding grows and becomes more accessible to artists interested in further education. Thanks to Mark Gottlieb at Trident Media Group for believing in earlier drafts of this manuscript, everyone at Blackstone Publishing and the ingenious editorial work of William Boggess. And finally, thanks to the

TBS fam, our NoDa community and the NoDa Super Girls. You guide me through.

Much of the firefly wisdom in this novel was garnered from *Fireflies, Glow-worms and Lighting Bugs: Identification and Natural History of the Fireflies of the Eastern and Central United States and Canada* by Lynn Frierson Faust. Much like Lo, I've cherished this entomological text from the very first day it found its way into my life.